Hero Wanted

HERO WANTED

BETINA KRAHN

THORNDIKE PRESS
A part of Gale, a Cengage Company

GALE
A Cengage Company

LIBRARY OF CONGRESS CIP DATA ON FILE.
CATALOGUING IN PUBLICATION FOR THIS BOOK
IS AVAILABLE FROM THE LIBRARY OF CONGRESS.

ISBN-13: 979-8-8857-8025-4 (hardcover alk. paper)

Published in 2022 by arrangement with Zebra Books, an imprint of Kensington Publishing Corp.

Printed in Mexico
Print Number : 1   Print Year : 2022

For two wonderful young women I love
and admire:
Kristine Lord Krahn
and
Dorlinda Stone Carlson
You light the way for the rest of us.

ONE

Lauren Alcott and her fiancé hadn't been on the river long when their rowboat struck something along a bend in the river. She was forced to grab the sides with both hands to remain upright.

"We've struck something," she said.

"Obviously." Her fiance's face reddened as he tried to free an oar to push them free of the obstruction only to find the oars were pinned in place by iron pegs on either side of the oarlock. Apparently, the rental agency was determined not to lose another oar.

Lauren bit her lip and averted her gaze, tamping down her own irritation and pretending not to notice his.

A woman's voice — a cry — came from across the way and she turned to see what was happening.

A boat had just overturned in the channel of the river, spilling its two female oc-

7

cupants into the spring-swollen current. She gasped as the women struggled to hold onto their overturned boat.

She turned to her fiancé with fresh urgency.

"We have to do something."

"I am doing something," Rafe Townsend growled. "I'm getting us free so we can row over to them." He pulled mightily on the oars, his straining muscles visible through his shirt.

She looked back at the women, whose skirts initially billowed around them, providing some buoyancy. Now one had lost her grip on the boat and her skirts would soon be waterlogged and dragging her down.

Rowing closer to tow them to shore was clearly out of the question. She scoured the banks of the river for other assistance. There was no one else close enough to render aid in time. She stared at him in dismay.

What was the matter with the man?

How could he sit there, fiddling with the oars, and not jump in to save them? She had seen him only a few times since their engagement, but she would never have thought him so callous as to watch people drown without doing everything possible to save them.

Tall, fair, and elegant . . . he had seemed

most admirable husband material at the start. He was the scion of a wealthy family whose fortune began with the founding of a trading company nearly two hundred years ago. The Townsends were never titled, but had a number of knighthoods in their lineage and were known as one of the first families of commerce.

He had attended university and read widely — often in the original Latin, Greek, or French. He was all too aware of his superior pedigree and it was clear he only agreed to the betrothal because he considered her an "acceptable" match. But there were other qualities, Lauren was learning, that the handsome and superior Mr. Townsend lacked.

The cries from the water became more desperate.

She stood up in their boat, unbuttoned her blouse, and yanked the starched cotton from her shoulders. Her belt was next; it hit the gaping Oxford man, who was too stunned by what she was doing to duck. The commotion of the women flailing in the water fifty yards away drowned out most of his protest.

"What the devil do you think you're — you cannot possibly —"

"The devil I can't." She shoved her skirt

down her hips in one fierce movement. Tamping it underfoot, she shot him a blistering look. "*Someone* has to."

"Hold on! I'm coming!" she called urgently to the women being carried downstream with their overturned boat. Her petticoat joined her skirt in the bottom of the boat. Thank heaven she'd left off her stays.

"Miss Alcott! Really!" He yanked his gaze from her combinations and trained it on the forms flowing downstream. "Silly women have no business taking out a boat if they don't know how to manage it properly!"

"Silly women." Words guaranteed to push her over the edge. Literally.

Her scantily clad form made a graceful arc in the sunlight before slicing into the cool, dark water. A second later she surfaced and began to swim. Her stroke was so sure and her form so clean that she barely churned a wake.

Sputters and protests faded behind her as she focused on rescuing the women, calling to them to kick their feet and keep their faces above the surface. She reached them in time to ferry the girl back to the overturned boat and then snag the older lady just as the woman's strength gave out.

Warmth drained from her at an alarming rate. It took all her concentration and strength to swim for the closest bank while holding the waterlogged woman's head above water. She felt like she was towing a leaky barge full of cotton bales! When they finally reached the opposite bank she dragged the woman out of the water and rolled her onto her side to cough up water. Satisfied that the woman was breathing, she dove back into the water to rescue the one hanging on to the receding boat.

The chilled water took a toll on her reserves and the girl, while younger, was larger and seemed to weigh twice as much. It was a desperate struggle to get her to the bank and haul her out of the water. As they collapsed together on the bank, it became clear why she'd had such difficulty getting the pair to shore — they were both wearing sizable bustles, a full complement of petticoats, and complete sets of stays. Whatever possessed them to go out on the river in such garments?

The women struggled under the weight of their waterlogged clothes to reach each other and sat embracing, sobbing. It came out that they were mother and daughter and had tried to re-create one of their favorite times with their recently deceased husband and father. They had rented a boat to float down the river . . . too caught up in memory and emotion to recall that it was always Papa who had done the rowing and steering on their Sunday river outings.

"You'll be all right." Lauren accepted a blanket from someone who had finally come running to render aid. She wrapped it around the women and rubbed their shoulders to warm them. "Anyone have a spot of brandy?" she called to those hurrying down the bank toward them. One man halted in his tracks, nodded, and then went running back up the bank.

"Thank you so much, young woman." The anguished mother looked up as Lauren knelt beside them. "We never meant to — my arms got so tired and numb that I dropped the oar. When I tried to reach it . . ."

"It's all right, really. You're safe now, and there was no harm done." Lauren gently stroked the woman's icy cheek.

Moments later she looked up to find the boat and the man she had abandoned inching through the nearby weeds at the edge of the bank. She turned to see him standing in the bow, scowling as he searched for a dry patch on which to set his elegant Italian shoes.

"Really, Miss Alcott!" He rushed up the soggy bank holding out his silk-lined coat in front of him. "Have you no modesty?"

She followed his gaze to the cause of his outrage. The lawn of her combinations was wet and clinging to her, revealing as much of her anatomy as they concealed. She looked up to find him staring at her, red-faced with indignation. Never mind that she had just hazarded her own life and limb to save two lives. Clearly, he found the exposure of her body more disturbing than the thought of two women drowning!

The lives belonged to "silly women," after all.

She pushed aside the coat he tried to fling around her and stalked down the bank to the boat and the clothes she had discarded earlier.

"I've never witnessed such a *spectacle* in my life," he declared, stalking after her. "Unthinkable."

Wordless with anger, she grabbed her clothes out of the boat and carried them back up the bank, where she dumped most of them into a pile and began to dry herself with her petticoat. She paused, clutching the lace-rimmed cotton to her, and met his censuring gaze.

"I'll tell you what is unthinkable, Mr. Townsend." Each step she advanced sent him back an equal distance. "It is you sit-

13

ting on your pampered arse in a boat watching two women *die* because you refuse to get your precious trousers wet. *That* is what is 'unthinkable.'"

"You honestly expected me to abandon a perfectly good boat to — ? I–I had tried all reasonable options. I had you to think about, Miss Alcott." He pulled down his vest and raised his chin. "A man has priorities."

She stiffened. "How dare you use me as an excuse for your cowardice!"

"Cowardice?" His gaze flicked to the people collecting on the bank nearby, and he lowered his voice to a growl. "Really, Miss Alcott, you go too far."

"Too far?" Her eyes narrowed as she realized they had reached the edge of the water, and she glanced down to find him teetering on his toes to keep from getting his precious shoes wet. "Not by half."

She gave him a shove that set him flailing. After a brief but wickedly entertaining imitation of a windmill, he went over . . . flat on his back. The splash caused cries of dismay and hoots of laughter from the people gawking at them. He managed to sit up, gasping.

She took the diamond-and-ruby ring from her hand and tossed it onto the wet linen on his lap.

"We're through, Mr. Townsend." Her eyes narrowed and her chin rose. "After today I wouldn't marry you if you were the last man on earth."

One of the massive front doors of Alcott House swung open to admit her, and Lauren stormed inside with her petticoat balled up under one arm and a sizable wicker hamper in the other hand. The hamper hit the polished checkerboard marble of the entry hall with an unmistakable shatter and tinkle that caused the butler to halt in his tracks. He looked in dismay from the hamper to her wet hair and damp, disheveled garments.

"Miss?"

"Where are they, Weathersby?" she demanded, tossing the bundled petticoat onto the floor beside the hamper.

He didn't have to ask to whom she referred.

"Your father and aunt are in the salon, Miss."

She sailed into the grand salon to find her father, Lawrence Alcott, and his plump, rosy-cheeked sister, Amanda Perrix, absorbed in their usual Sunday afternoon pursuits . . . . reading and needlework,

15

respectively. She had to deliver the news before she had time to think better of it. Rafe Townsend was the heir and rising star of Townsend Imports. News of her decision to disrupt the impending union of two empires of commerce was potentially cataclysmic.

"Just so you know — it's off," she declared.

"What's off, dear?" her aunt said without looking up.

"The engagement. With that Townsend man. It's off."

"What?" Her father looked up from his book, blinked, then scowled.

"Oh, dear." Her aunt lowered her embroidery hoop.

She stared at the pair as the news penetrated their Sunday lethargy. A moment later her father was on his feet, his book tossed aside.

"What happened to you?" He looked her over, horror dawning as he took in her wet hair, wilted blouse, and damp skirt.

Clearly she had to explain.

"I have learned that Mr. Townsend, in addition to thinking himself vastly superior to myself and the rest of humanity, has even worse qualities. Arrogance, lack of charity, and a shocking excess of self-interest . . .

16

just a few among them. I cannot imagine marriage to him without suffocating from dread."

"What has he done?" Her father crossed the salon in a few long strides and seized her cold hands. "What's happened between you?"

"I have always had reservations about him. His demeanor is so cold and superior. His every pronouncement is a judgment on someone or something — always expressing displeasure or outright contempt."

"This is Rafe Townsend you're talking about? I know him to be an educated, well-mannered fellow. A bit ambitious, like his father, but young Townsend is widely reputed to be of upstanding character. His reputation for honesty and integrity in business is unparalleled."

"There is more to a man than his business acumen and — though it pains me to say it — than even his education. There are finer sensibilities to be considered; personal qualities of compassion and caring for others, a willingness to act to ensure the welfare of others." She decided to come right out with it. "The man lacks both courage and the most basic urge to assist others in distress."

"He failed to —" He gasped. "Your boat

17

overturned!"

"Not ours." She straightened under her father's penetrating glare and pulled her hands from his. "Our river outing came to an end when we came upon two women whose boat had overturned. They were in desperate straits and when I suggested he help, he behaved as if I had asked him to harness the moon. He just sat there, appalled by the thought of putting himself at risk to save two women's lives."

"And how did that make you wet, dear?" Aunt Amanda asked.

"I took it upon myself to help them to shore. They were close to succumbing to the water's current and chill."

"You jumped into the river to save them?" Her father looked astounded, then horrified.

"I did."

"You risked life and limb to help complete strangers?" His horror deepened.

"I did. They were both saved. After I towed them to shore all he could do was express outrage that I had shed a few garments in order to help them." She pulled out the sides of her gored skirt, which had absorbed water from her drenched underclothes. "He was more embarrassed by my lack of skirts than grateful that the women

18

were alive. I cannot look at him with respect after such a selfish display."

She backed away a step, then another.

"If you don't mind, I'd like to have a warm bath and change into dry clothes. I am chilled to the bone." She turned on her heel and headed quickly for the stairs, leaving her father in turmoil and her aunt grappling for a response.

She ran the last few yards to her room and quickly closed the door behind her and turned the key in the lock. She swallowed hard, remembering the anger rising in her father's face. He was going to be flaming furious. Normally he was a steady and even-tempered sort, but when pushed he could rattle the windows with his roars.

And there it came. The knob rattled furiously, then his fist banged against the door.

"Lauren Elena Alcott, open this door! You will answer for this headstrong behavior, young lady, right now!" More pounding. He was really angry.

"Bathing, Papa — ch-ch-chilled through and through. I'll be d-down when I'm done, I promise!"

She rushed into her newly installed bathing room and lit the gas heater for her bathwater. She hadn't lied — she was cold and shivering. Her mouth dried as she was

19

beginning to feel the full impact of what she had done. In one tempestuous moment she had wiped blank the slate of her future and upended a long-awaited merger of her father's East Anglia Trading and Horace Townsend's import company. She knew her father had crafted this tricky bit of commerce like a royal diplomat. Every term of the contracts was polished to perfection.

She stripped off her damp clothes, wrapped herself in toweling from the cupboard, and perched on the edge of the clawfooted tub, waiting for the water to heat. The sight of Rafe Townsend's outrage came back to her.

He'd just sat there watching two women flounder and succumb to the water. What happened to chivalry, nobility? Christian charity toward others? Why couldn't he have done something more to help them?

She was right to jump in and help them. Wasn't she?

"I feared all that time swimming at the country house and on those seashore holidays would bring her to no good," Lawrence Alcott said, tromping back and forth in the salon. His face was like red granite.

"Her *swimming* saved two lives today, Lawrence. If anything has brought her to

20

no good it was having no say in her engagement," Amanda said calmly. "Young women these days don't generally care to be bartered and traded like commodities. I did say that, you know."

"I've been negotiating this merger for two years. She knew about it early on and never objected."

"If she had, would you have listened?"

Alcott paced before the long, sunlit windows with his hands clamped firmly behind his back. Clearly he wasn't listening now.

"And those books," he continued. "She's always reading something. Not good for a young girl's eyes, posture, or mental stability. Puts all sorts of notions into their heads." He paused and looked to his sister. "What is that wretched tome she's always going on about?"

"*Ivanhoe*. Sir Walter Scott," Amanda provided with a small smile that contained just enough sympathy to cover her pleasure at being proved right. If there was anything she loved, it was saying *I told you so.* Especially to her older brother Lawrence.

"Reading did not bring her to this, Brother. It was your ignorance of your daughter's heart and your incessant maneuvering to get the best of Horace Townsend." She took a deep breath. "That, and the

21

younger Townsend's regrettable deficits. I must say, I would find it intolerable to be yoked to a man with no chivalry or charity in him." She shivered noticeably. "My husbands were all men rich in spirit and sensitivity."

"That was all they were rich in," Lawrence grumbled.

"True." She sighed quietly. "They were not adept in finance and worldly matters, but we bumped along quite nicely together. Each was happy to breathe their last in my arms."

"No doubt," Lawrence said tartly. His opinion of his sister's marriages was well-known.

"I have to set her straight and then send a message to Townsend. We shall have to meet." He groaned. "No doubt he'll want concessions — if not reparations for this attempted default. Pray to God the marriage and the merger can both be salvaged."

Amanda rolled her eyes, thinking surely God had better things to do than to rescue Lawrence Alcott from a mess of his own making. In her experience the Almighty made it a policy to leave headstrong fools to the results of their own follies. She removed her spectacles and set her needlework aside.

"I'll see if she's all right." When Lawrence

spun on his heel to glare at her, she added, "And I'll see she comes straight down as soon as she is presentable."

Two

Lauren steeped in warm, rose-scented water, trying to think of a way to make her father understand how desperately she did not want to marry Rafe Townsend. Some kind of punishment was probably in order for her impulsive behavior, but surely her father wouldn't try to force her to recant her rejection. Even if she tried, she doubted the outraged Mr. Townsend would have anything further to do with her. She had all but called him — devil take it, she *had* called him a coward. Her eyes widened. That was not something a man of such pride would soon forget.

The rattling of a key in a lock barely registered as she sank into a quagmire of unpleasant possibilities . . . disinheritance, spinsterhood . . . banishment to a *nunnery. . . .*

"You've done it this time." Aunt Amanda's voice coming from the bathroom doorway startled her.

She covered herself with her arms and sat up sharply, sloshing water from the tub onto the tiled floor.

"How did you . . ." She looked past her aunt and was relieved to see that Amanda was alone.

"The household keys, dear." Amanda jingled a ring of keys, then dropped them back into her pocket. "I want details." She settled on a nearby stool and clasped her hands in her lap. "Don't skip a thing."

Lauren recounted the outing in full: the barely tolerable picnic, the float on the river, and Rafe Townsend's unfeeling reaction to the women in trouble. The "silly" women.

Amanda's eyes narrowed. "I always thought he was superior and standoffish. Not especially good husband material. But you seemed to accept him, so I thought it wrong to interfere."

"Well, you were right. He is cold and utterly self-interested. Every time he looked at me I felt I was being judged against some exalted standard and found barely passable."

"Ridiculous men — concentrating on a woman's face and figure and forgetting that there's a world of other qualities inside that fleshly shell. They crave physical pleasure from women, of course, but their truest desires are for control and status in the eyes of other men." She tsked. "Such limited creatures — sometimes I wonder how they manage. Your father included."

They were silent for a time, and Lauren sank down into the tub.

"What do you think Papa will do?" She stared off into a future as cloudy as her bathwater.

"Hard to say. I think he's confused as much as angry," Amanda mused. "He can't imagine why you would reject such a paragon of masculinity."

"But I just told him. The man's arrogance. Lack of charity. No concern for others. Do you know — in the weeks we have been together, Rafe Townsend has never asked me a single question about my interests, experiences, or opinions? He's never asked if I had learned to ride or traveled abroad or liked to dance. But at the drop of a hat, he would launch into lectures on *his* opinions, as if delivering some bit of wisdom from the halls of Mount Olympus."

Amanda shook her head. "I told Lawrence it was a mistake to announce the engagement before you'd had a chance to get to know the man. He thought I was being silly. You were levelheaded and sensible, he said.

You'd know quality when you saw it and count yourself fortunate to have such a handsome husband."

"Handsome?" Lauren pounced on that. "He truly thought I'd be grateful to have a husband with a pretty face? Surely he knows me better than that. I want someone with verve and daring . . . someone with a noble spirit . . . someone who will fight for goodness and right and decency. Someone like —"

"Ivanhoe." Amanda stared pointedly at her.

They had had this discussion before, she and Aunt Amanda.

"What is wrong with wanting a man to admire and respect? A man of high ideals and the strength to make the world a better place?"

"Nothing, dear." Amanda leaned forward with a patient smile. "It's just that it sounds like what you want is perfection. And perfect men are rather hard to come by in the real world."

"You think I'm too idealistic." Lauren crossed her arms on the side of the tub and planted her chin on them.

"All young women are idealistic. It's part of being young. But with experience comes wisdom and a better understanding of those

27

ideals. Do you think Ivanhoe was a hero to everyone who knew him? Some people, including his own father, thought he was wrong . . . outright treasonous."

"Well, he wasn't. He was noble. And brave. And compassionate. Willing to risk his life for others. He never would have sat in a boat and watched two women drown without lifting a finger to help."

"He was a hero," Amanda said, summing it up.

"Exactly." Lauren felt a welcome certainty expanding through her. "A hero. Courageous, selfless, gallant . . . everything Rafe Townsend is not."

"Well," Amanda said with a sigh of resignation, "one thing is certain. Townsend wouldn't have made much of a lover."

Lauren looked up with surprise. "What makes you say such a thing?"

"Selfish men make dismal lovers, dear. And if he's as arrogant and self-centered as you say, he wouldn't care a whit for your pleasure. Just on and done and on to more important matters." Amanda waved a hand in dismissal. "I had to teach my second husband to slow down and learn some creativity. There are so many lovely ways to make pleasure in the marriage bed, but only one way to make misery. *Selfishness.*" She

28

fixed Lauren with a look that said it was a lesson she must remember. "Loving means sharing and considering the other person in all things. Clearly Mr. Townsend has never learned that."

Amanda rose and straightened under Lauren's widened eyes.

"Stick to your guns, dear. You deserve better."

Lauren watched her go, thoughts racing.

She wasn't sure what she deserved, but thanks to Aunt Amanda's observations on marital relations, she had just discovered what she wanted.

An Ivanhoe.

She wanted a *hero*.

By the time she entered her father's book-lined study later, Lauren was well-warmed and braced to confront the result of her impetuous action. He sat behind his heavy walnut desk, looking somber. His fingers were templed, his brow was furrowed, and he had clearly mastered his anger . . . which Lauren knew made him all the more formidable. It wasn't for naught that the Townsends considered him a worthy rival and maneuvered to make him an ally and partner.

"I want details," he said, nodding her into the lone chair placed strategically in front of his desk.

She took the seat, keeping her back straight and her chin up. At his demand she recounted the incident, leaving nothing out . . . at least nothing of importance. No reason to recount that she was in her smalls and wet to the skin while breaking her engagement.

"And it was solely this incident that made Townsend unacceptable to you? Nothing untoward had happened before?"

"If you call ignoring me and blathering on about himself 'nothing,' I suppose you could say nothing inappropriate happened."

"In other words you took a dislike to him because he wasn't attentive enough to you."

"That is not at all what I meant." Her face reddened. "I dislike him because he is arrogant, condescending, and too full of his own opinions to give credence to anyone else's. You should hear how he disdains mandatory schooling, improving medical care and providing help for the working poor."

She realized that last part was a mistake the moment it left her mouth. Her father stiffened visibly and his eyes narrowed. She knew too well that he believed her personal

30

involvement in progressive causes and charities was not suitable for a young woman of refinement.

"I see." He leaned forward, his face taut with determination. "I believe you need to reconsider some of your notions, missy. You need to start thinking of the future."

"I do think of the future, Papa. Every day." In for a penny, in for a pound; she may as well breach the subject underlying her objection to the man and the marriage. "The future of thousands of children who need books and teachers and decent food and proper shoes — do you have any idea how much children's shoes cost these days?"

"Enough!" Lawrence smacked the arm of his great leather chair.

"It is high time you quit thinking about the nameless, faceless children of the masses and give some thought to producing children of your own."

"They are not nameless and faceless. I see them every day in the streets, in our workers' homes, in the workhouse and St Ambrose's parish school. I know them by name, by their hopeful smiles, and by the stories they love."

"There it is again — you and your blasted books. Reading to those children, filling their heads with daydreams and desires above their station. . . . What can that do besides breed discontent? And I'm not talking about the world's future, missy, I'm talking about *yours*!"

He shot to his feet and glared down at her.

"You are hereby confined to this house . . . forbidden to consort with those rabble-rousing, free-thinking cohorts of yours. There will be no reading to child—" He halted abruptly, giving her a look that said he'd hit upon a perfect punishment. "I shall have your chamber and the solarium cleared of reading material. Going forward, you will read nothing but the Bible and *Mrs. Beeton's Book of Household Management*."

She gasped, truly astounded. Her father was banning her from books, from *reading*? For a moment she was speechless.

"You're not getting any younger, Lauren Elena. Your mother, God rest her soul, was nineteen when we married, and you are . . . are . . ."

"Twenty-two," she supplied, her throat tight and her mouth dry. She was still reeling from his command that she read nothing but scripture and household advice. Did he prize his precious merger so much that he would sell her — body and soul — to acquire it?

32

"At such an age you are old enough to comport yourself rationally. It's not a woman's place to go about saving people. That is a man's job!"

"And if no 'man' is doing the saving —" she came to the edge of her seat, her face heating — "am I to just sit there and watch people drown when I am perfectly capable of rescuing them?"

Her father paused, taken aback by her vehement response.

"Enough! You will obey my orders. You will keep to this house and assist your Aunt Amanda in running it."

"For how long?" She wanted to stand but found her legs too weak.

"Until you come to your senses," he said sharply.

"And what must I do to show I've come to my senses?" She was determined to quickly meet his conditions and regain her independence.

"Marry Rafe Townsend."

THREE

A hellish bright sunbeam sliced through the dark bedchamber and across Rafe Townsend's eyes the next morning. He awakened with a pounding head and an unreasoning resentment that the sun should be so bright in the morning. He rolled over in his richly draped bed, buried his face between the pillows, and groaned.

This was a penance for last night. He and his best friend had drained the cellar bar at his club, and someone — probably the night porter — called cabs for them and sent them home to repent their wicked ways in private. Good God, was he repenting! His mouth tasted like the bottom of a barnmucker's boot, his stomach burned, and he was as parched as if he'd been staked out to dry in a desert.

The wages of sin. Which was why he never indulged in such pointless and punishing pursuits.

Almost never.

Charging out of bed, he yanked the drapes more tightly together to banish that demon sunbeam. He swayed and then braced against a bedpost to stop the world from spinning. As his senses settled, a different turmoil took vertigo's place. Memory flooded back.

Her. More correctly, it was her demand that he jump out of a perfectly good boat into a raging river and save two feckless women from their self-inflicted fate.

Very well . . . the river wasn't quite raging, and the women were, well, probably in a bit of danger. But he'd tried to free their boat to row to the women and he looked for help on the shores. Someone else could have jumped in to rescue them. But noooo; she'd ripped off her clothes, dove into the water, and towed them to shore. Then — good God — she stood there dripping wet, exposed bits-and-brass to the whole bloody world, and accused him of lacking the courage to do it himself.

Him. Lacking courage.

It was a piercing thought.

Lauren Alcott had to be the most unreasonable female he had ever encountered. And his father had all but lashed him to her for the sake of a merger between companies

35

that had been rivals for decades. Horace Townsend was a planner, a plotter, and a schemer par excellence. How could he have missed the Alcott female's disastrous nature? Or did his father just figure she would be *his* problem after the wedding?

How would saddling his son and heir with a half-mad wife ensure the future of Townsend Imports or help his mother acquire the grandchildren she so desperately desired? And speaking of desire . . .

He rubbed his eyes, hoping to dispel the delectable image of Lauren Alcott as she stood on the riverbank dripping wet, her underclothes — lace-infested combinations — clinging lasciviously to every mound and curve she possessed. Shameless female. She'd spurned his jacket and strode to the boat in her altogether like the bloody Queen of the Nile. He squeezed his eyes shut, but that only made the memory more vivid.

He quickly opened them and sucked a deep breath.

Then she threw the damned ring at him, called him a coward, and stalked off to find her own way home.

A coward. How dare the chit?

What did she know about him . . . his naval experience, his successes at Oxford, and the number of times he'd been entreated to stand for Parliament? She hadn't bothered to ask a single question about his plans for the future — ostensibly *her* future as well. In fact, she hardly spoke when they were together. He had to carry the burden of conversation entirely by himself. At Lady Edgerton's dinner party she'd yawned — *yawned!* — in the middle of his rationale for reviving the Board of Trade.

Wretched female — she should be required to wear a sign warning others to beware her erratic nature. Dull as ditchwater one minute and hot-eyed with fury the next. Both wrapped in an oddly fascinating little body that kept filling his mental vision at unexpected moments. Like now.

Again.

Worse yet, he'd have to face his father with the news.

He groaned as the scantily clad vixen riding his memory vanished. The thought of his father's reaction was enough to send a chill through the most stalwart of men. Best to go downstairs and get it over with.

Half an hour later he appeared in the grand, oak-paneled dining room of his parents' house, where his mother and father had just finished a late breakfast and were engaging in their morning ritual of perusing correspondence and *The Times,* respectively.

He seldom joined them for breakfast these days; he spent most nights at his club or at his friend Barclay Howard's fashionable town house. They looked up as he entered and greeted him as they always had — as if he were the sun itself, risen to shine just for them.

"There you are." His mother lowered the engraved note she was inspecting and gave him a beatific smile. Caroline Townsend was a plump, pretty woman with a calm disposition that contrasted markedly with her spouse's bombastic nature. Her gray-blue eyes sparkled with life and her dark hair showed threads of silver that hinted at wisdom paired with the warmth she radiated.

"Made a night of it, eh?" his ruddy, barrel-chested father said with a sly half grin. "Get it out of your system, boy. Can't be out carousing all night when you're a married man."

Rafe paused for a tick in the midst of taking his usual seat at the elegant table. He hadn't expected the topic to be raised so helpfully by his granite-jawed father. It felt like a nudge from the Fates.

"Marriage, I believe, requires a bride as well as a groom," he said, nodding for the servant to begin serving the eggs, bacon, and scones that filled the dining room with delicious aromas. "As of this morning, I am no longer in possession of one of those requirements."

The Times was folded and the invitation lowered.

"Whatever do you mean?" Caroline looked genuinely puzzled.

Rafe leaned to allow the servant to pour him coffee.

"You have a lovely bride-to-be," his mother said with growing concern. "In three months' time you will be —"

"Still a bachelor," he said, biting into one of Cook's delectable scones to stall. "I am no longer betrothed."

A brief silence fell as his parents looked to each other in dismay and then turned to him. Under their scrutiny, his face heated like a guilty sixteen-year-old's.

"What the devil are you blathering on about, boy?" his father demanded, with special emphasis on the last word. It was a tactic that his father had used to intimidate him in his younger years. It hadn't worked to engender fear and obedience in him for years, but was still useful for demonstrating an escalating lack of paternal patience.

"What's happened, dear?" Caroline leaned toward him with an outstretched hand on the tabletop, and suddenly there was a look about her that he had dreaded more than anything else in breaking this news, a look that spoke of tender emotions inside the shell of strength she wore.

He straightened. Best to come straight out with it.

"It's off. The engagement. I have the ring back and it's off. Not a moment too soon." He fortified himself with a gulp of coffee, scrambling to recall the sensible arguments against the match he'd thought of while shaving. "The girl was wholly unsuitable. Unstable. Given to glum silences one moment and alarming, impulsive actions the next. Disastrous wife material. Thank the Trinity I found out the truth of her nature in time."

He stuffed half a scone in his mouth, trying not to look at his parents as he chewed doggedly. Lack of cream and jam and a dry mouth made it almost impossible to swallow.

"Do you have any idea what you have done?" His father rose, shoving his chair back and slapping his newspaper on the table with enough force to rattle the silver resting on his plate. "Who gave you permission to call off a wedding that's been years in the making?"

"*I* didn't call it off. It was more a mutual thing. I found her unacceptable and she — seemed perfectly satisfied to part futures and go on her erratic way alone." He felt he was on firmer ground now and reached for his coffee to rinse down the mass in his mouth. "Good riddance, I say."

He made himself look at his mother. She had a wilted look, and he felt the weight of her disappointment settle on his shoulders like a yoke.

"She seemed like such a pretty and agreeable young woman," she said, leaning back in her chair, sinking visibly into the reality of having lost a longed-for daughter-in-law. His mother had always wanted more children and now counted on him to provide them.

"This is outrageous," his father bellowed. "You cannot, *will not* ruin two empires of commerce because of some lily-livered objection to your bride's silences." He flung out his arms in a gesture that seemed to be asking the cosmos to bear witness to his son's folly. "Good God, boy! Two years down the marriage road you would be thanking the Almighty for some peace and quiet!"

"Horace, really." Caroline straightened with a fierce look at her husband that was

41

shortly transferred to her son. "You went for a picnic and a boat ride? Then something went wrong. Young couples do sometimes disagree. Did you argue?"

Rafe felt color creeping up out of his collar and raised his chin to overcome it.

"Not as such. The chit vaulted out of the boat to swim to some other women floundering in the water. Stripped off her skirts, jumped in the water, and swam them to shore. What kind of woman does such a thing? In front of God and everyone. Then she had the nerve to confront me afterward. She hadn't spoken more than a dozen words to me all afternoon, but after her 'swim' she was babbling like a madwoman."

He gave a visible shudder.

"She gave me back the ring, there and then."

"So —" his father's eyes narrowed to search him "— you didn't ask for it back. You didn't initiate the breakup." Rafe knew that look. Calculation at its best. And worst. Horace Townsend was already determining who was at fault in this breach of contract, already positioning Townsend Imports to benefit somehow from this fracture of his son's nuptial fortunes.

"Given her behavior, I certainly agreed with it. I will not, cannot marry that female."

He stuffed his mouth full of sausage and egg and chewed, surprised by their utter lack of taste, before adding for his mother's benefit, "However, I am willing to look elsewhere for a bride."

His father scowled at him, then at his mother.

"Lawrence — damn his hide — he's behind this," Horace declared. "At the very least he's allowed his daughter free rein for too long. If he thinks —" He straightened, as if stung by a thought. "After all we've invested in this merger, if he thinks to get a better deal elsewhere —"

Rafe watched his father steam out of the dining room like a Bulldog Class engine and felt his stomach sink. The old man was on his way to confront Lawrence Alcott. Blame would be tossed back and forth like a white-hot rivet, and Rafe suspected the explosion of pride would be heard all the way to Windsor Castle.

He also expected they would find a way to patch up their meticulously crafted merger — they had to if they wanted to survive in the current business climate. But they would have to find a way to do it without embroiling their children in the mix. Ridiculous idea, inveigling their offspring into an arranged marriage in this day and age.

■ ■ ■ ■

Indeed, there were fireworks in the office of Lawrence Alcott's East Anglia Trading Company later that day. Blustering and charges of bad faith and poor parenting on both sides brought the clerks and typewriters in the outer office to a standstill — had them staring slack-jawed at the half-open door to their employer's inner sanctum. Clearly the pair's children were not the paragons of virtue and desirability each believed.

"If you had put your foot down with that girl — taught her to obey — she would know better than to throw away a promising future on a whim!" Horace brandished the head of his walking stick under Lawrence's nose.

"You should have put *your* foot down with that boy." Lawrence smacked aside that walking stick, glowering at his would-be partner. "If you had taught him some consideration for others, he might not think he's the blasted center of creation," he blustered, shaking a fist as they met nose-to-nose across his desk. "So impressed with himself that he has no regard for others!"

"What others?" Horace straightened as if

struck. "My son is universally respected. Our business acquaintances clamor to have him handle their accounts . . . while your daughter is considered to be headstrong, impulsive, and even irrational."

"Where did you hear such nonsense?" It was Lawrence's turn to sputter. "You know better, you old bulldog! You've talked with my Lauren and seen her at socials. She charms one and all. Your own wife was taken with her . . . called her a lovely young woman with a nimble mind and a cheerful spirit."

"I know her about as well as you know my son," Horace snarled. "Rafe is strong, educated, and scrupulously honest. He's had his share of admiration from the ladies, I can tell you. I've had a time of it, steering him past undesirable liaisons. And your daughter wrecks all our futures over some ridiculous impulse —"

Lawrence had spent a sleepless night going over and over their predicament. A marriage was the only way to quietly access the plentiful funds in Lauren's inheritance to fund the merger and see them through the present troubles. Once she was married and the entailment was met, her husband would control the funds. He had never imagined she would find the Townsend boy so distasteful. It still confounded him that a fellow so accomplished and good-looking could have made such a foul impression.

He thought on that for a moment, studying his quarrelsome rival.

"Who says it is wrecked?" If there was any hope of setting their much-needed merger back on track, they would need to work together. "I have taken steps to see that she recants her objection to the marriage, and I believe I can promise you that she will come around."

"She had better, Alcott." Some of the tension drained from Townsend, and Lawrence realized that behind the bluster lay genuine anxiety. They both had a great deal riding on this merger. "Otherwise my lawyers will be contacting that pack of hounds you call solicitors."

FOUR

Lawrence followed Townsend into the outer office, where his clerks turned to watch his rival-turned-partner exit in a huff.

As soon as Townsend was out of sight, Lawrence straightened and took a deep breath. He prayed his heavy-handed plan worked quickly to make Lauren recant her rejection of Townsend's son.

"And her mother thought teaching her to walk was exhausting," he muttered, then spotted his staff drawing stealthily together and scowled. The papery rustle, a thump, and the quick sideways step of his head clerk, Higgins, made it clear they were hiding something.

"What is that?" He tilted his head this way and that, trying to make out what was behind Higgins. "What have you got there?"

As he approached, the rest of his office staff scurried back to their desks, leaving Higgins alone to explain.

A newspaper lay on the floor behind his head clerk, who took a step back onto it as if unaware it was there. Lawrence stalked closer, scowling at the man's feet. Fifteen years of loyal service had revealed Higgins to be a diligent and considerate fellow, if sometimes transparent.

"You are standing on a newspaper, Higgins."

"Am I, sir?" The fellow turned scarlet and looked down. "Oh. That."

Lawrence expelled a long-suffering breath and held out his hand.

After a long moment Higgins stepped off the paper, picked it up, and reluctantly handed it to Lawrence. "Don't know how that came to be here, sir. Must have been one of the tradesmen brought it in."

"A tradesman," Lawrence said as he righted the paper and took in the name. "Who cares about *The Morning Post*?"

"Really, sir, it is nothing of consequence. A scandal sheet. An embarrassment to literacy —"

A very popular scandal sheet, Lawrence knew, read by upstairs and downstairs with equal eagerness. Lawrence gave Higgins a censuring look and then perused the page they had folded the paper to reveal. His attention landed on an article appearing on the fold and his mouth dried.

"Daring River Rescue," it said. He froze except for the widening of his eyes as he read. There, in print, was an account of his daughter's impulsive rescue of two drowning women. Even if he hadn't recognized the description of the event, the writer had the temerity to name the young woman responsible: "Miss Lauren Alcott, daughter of wealthy baron of commerce Lawrence Alcott." A "baron of commerce" was he, now? He grinned at the sound of that. Horace would be green with envy.

Then he read further.

"Miss Alcott" was "a rare example of feminine fortitude." His chest swelled as he read that she "should be decorated by the queen for her selflessness and valor." After a general swipe at others present who did not bother to assist in the rescue, the writer singled out the "wealthy and prominent Rafe Townsend" as one of those who merely watched her heroism . . . all of which squared with Lauren's account of the incident.

Then came the bit that set his innards sinking. The writer said that Townsend was betrothed to Miss Alcott until the incident, after which she ended the engagement. However, Miss Alcott's selflessness was accompanied by a brazen exhibition of naked-ness that her fiancé seemed to find as ap-palling as she found his cowardice. It was clearly *not* a match made in Heaven.

Lawrence's face paled as he reread that damning word.

Nakedness. They were saying his impetu-ous daughter was naked when she canceled her betrothal to — dear God — his daughter had called Townsend a *coward*! And a muckraking reporter had been there and had written it all down in a scurrilous report for *The Morning Post.*

He read it through again, then turned and rushed back into his office, recalling Hor-ace's angry face and pugnacious stance.

Nakedness. Cowardice. Horace already was talking lawyers and breach of contract. Good Gods he was going to explode when he saw this!

Horace Townsend was quietly simmering when he arrived at the Townsend Imports offices in the City later that day and found his clerks clustered around a newspaper ly-ing on one of the desks. The way they stepped in front of it and greeted him with furtive looks stopped him in his tracks. He stalked over to see what they found so unsettling and discovered a copy of *The*

Examiner open to a page containing sundry adverts and articles.

His gaze landed on an illustration of a boat, a riverbank, and a prissy, long-nosed fellow drenched and dripping as he sat waist-deep in water beside the boat. He blinked as the situation registered.

"What the bloody hell?" He snatched it up for a closer look and realized the artist had included a shapely female figure arrayed in angelic white — with what could only be called a laurel wreath on her head. His jaw dropped open. "How could the bastards know about this?"

The caption read "The Angel of the River," and the article detailed the very situation Rafe had recounted at breakfast: two women in a boat had overturned and Alcott's daughter shed her skirts and dove into the drink to save them. In the article Lauren Alcott was named a heroine and lauded for her quick thinking and utter selflessness. A chorus of praise from those who witnessed the rescue was presented in florid detail. Then came the words that pierced his pride like a blade.

The writer claimed to have seen with his own eyes the Alcott female's disgust as she accused her fiancé of cowardice and ended the engagement. The water-shy fiancé was

51

named as none other than Rafe Townsend, the scion of Townsend Imports.

Cowardice? The chit called his son a coward? And they had the nerve to print it in one of the most popular penny papers in the nation? *The Examiner* was widely read by their upper-class circle, despite its championing of the lower classes. The story of a wealthy heir being shamed by the woman he was supposed to wed — it was like tossing meat to caged tigers. The rabble would eat it up!

Horace turned on his heel, jammed his hat back on his head, and called immediately for his carriage.

Lawrence Alcott was going to pay for this!

"What are those scruffy-looking men doing slouching around our gate?" Aunt Amanda asked as she peered over Lauren's shoulder at the small front garden and pavement in front of Alcott House.

Moments before, Weathersby had brought word that there were three men in front of their house, watching the front doors as if waiting for someone to exit. Lauren had rushed to the upstairs sitting room to peer down at them and make sense of what she saw. She sank onto a knee on the window seat and pressed her head against the glass to inspect the interlopers.

Three men wearing cheaply made jackets and trousers that could have used a good pressing were lounging about the retaining wall and lamp pillars that framed the entrance to Alcott House. Two of the men wore bowler hats and the third wore a flat woolen cap. They didn't interact, just shifted feet and stared with expectation at the street and the house.

"I have no idea," Lauren said, clearly just as puzzled as her aunt. "I don't believe I've ever seen any of them before."

"Have Weathersby tell them to go roost on someone else's doorstep." Amanda retreated to her lady chair and needlework.

"I believe he's already tried," Lauren said with a scowl. "They moved across the street to the park but then sneaked back. When he demanded to know what they wanted, they peppered him with questions about whether I was home and what time Papa was expected to return."

It wasn't long before Lawrence arrived home in a cab, and the threesome below sprang into action. Pads and pencils came out.

"Is it true?" one of the men yelled at him. "Is the marriage off?"

53

"Were you worried that she might drown when rescuing those women?" another demanded, pressing close enough to grab Lawrence's arm. "What do you have to say about the Naked Angel of the River?"

Then came the crowning question.

"Do you believe Rafe Townsend is a coward?"

Above the street, Lauren couldn't make out much more than her name and Rafe Townsend's but realized it probably had to do with that incident at the river. She grew alarmed by the way they jostled and tried to block her father's entrance to his own house.

But Lawrence Alcott was no easy mark. He demanded they get off his property or he would sic the law on them, and he strong-armed his way to the safety of the door Weathersby quickly opened for him.

Lauren rushed down the stairs and arrived in the main hall just as her choleric father was handing off his hat and walking stick to their butler.

"Papa! Are you all right? What did those men want?" She rushed toward him but stopped short because he brought up the rolled newspaper in his hand and pointed it at her.

"They're news hacks — reporters." His eyes narrowed and nostrils flared. He was genuinely angry. "And they're here about *you.*"

He slapped the newspaper into her hands and strode off to his study with orders to Weathersby to show Horace Townsend into his study the minute he arrived.

Lauren stared after him with an uneasy feeling and unrolled the newspaper. *The Morning Post.* She looked over the front page — entirely adverts — then opened it and inside spotted an article that had been circled. "Daring River Rescue."

"What is it, dear?" Aunt Amanda arrived downstairs and hurried to her side in time to see her face redden.

"They're calling me a heroine," she said with a blink. "Saying I 'saved' those women. Apparently there was a newswriter nearby who saw what happened." She smiled. But by the time she finished reading the article, her sense of vindication had evaporated. That sinking feeling was back as she stared at what followed her journalistic anointing as a heroine.

"Naked . . . they say I was *naked* when I broke it off with Rafe Townsend."

Horace Townsend blew through the front door like a typhoon run aground, and shortly after there were bellows and curses coming from her father's study. It was a battle royal and the choice of weapons seemed to be the names Lauren and Rafe.

Against Amanda's advice, Lauren crept down to the hall outside her father's study. But she didn't have to press her ear against the door to hear the argument.

". . . disgraced my son in front of all of London!" Horace Townsend was spitting angry, demanding something be done. "Not just one gossip rag — now *two*! God knows how many more will pick up the story and spread it all over creation. You have to do something, Alcott. That daughter of yours — you have to make her take it back somehow."

"Take it back? You mean talk to those vultures hanging around my door and plead excuses for your son?" Her father gave a snort. She could imagine his rigid stance and narrowed eyes, the same expression he'd used with her last evening. "A denial from her would only make him look worse — like she felt she had to defend him because he can't defend himself."

There was a tense silence as that thought settled between them.

"She cannot treat my son, my family, with such contempt. Do something about it, Alcott, or the merger is off."

"The merger can't be off, Townsend. You know better. We have to go through with it if we intend to survive the next few years. Ships beating ours through that damnable Suez . . . tariffs gobbling up profits everywhere . . . investors and capital drying up . . ."

Another prickly silence, which meant Horace Townsend either wouldn't or couldn't counter that argument. Lauren was shocked.

"How long do you think it will take for Ledbetter to seize on this debacle?' " Horace changed focus. "If he does, it will take my boy years — *years* to live this down. Ledbetter has arms that reach from here to Bombay!"

Lauren frowned. Ledbetter. The name was familiar — oh, the Undersecretary of Commerce. She had met him once, at the Earl of Margrave's birthday celebration. He was a fusty sort . . . beady, ferretlike eyes and an ever-pursed mouth that made him look as if he'd sucked on a lemon. What on earth did he have to do with — it struck her that there was more going on with her father's business than she imagined. Did that mean there was more to her betrothal to Rafe Townsend than just settling her in a suitable match while giving East Anglia access to Townsend's fleet of ships?

The voices in the study lowered so that it was hard to hear what was said next, and she would never stoop to pressing her ear against the door. She would learn soon enough what price her father and Horace Townsend would exact from her.

She made her way upstairs and sat for some time staring at her only printed companions, the Bible and *Mrs. Beeton's.* She refused to pick up either of them. She'd gotten as far as Exodus, and the scriptures seemed to be chock-full of rules and people breaking them thither and yon, and she simply couldn't bear another revisit to the virtues of turpentine and beeswax as floor-polishing agents. If only she had a copy of her beloved *Ivanhoe.*

The agreed upon solution, she learned later, when called to her father's study, was every bit as dreadful as she feared. Her father handed her a copy of *The Examiner,* open to an article that called her "the Angel of the River" and reported that she'd called her fiancé a coward.

Sweet Heaven Above. A second one?

"You will appear in public with Rafe Townsend, *fully clothed* and behaving pleasantly, and thus declare to all and sundry that the betrothal is still on and that you greatly admire your husband-to-be," her father ordered. "You will demure, if asked outright, and say that the nonsense at the river was misinterpreted. You are to be, in every way, a modest and devoted bride-to-be."

"But — but — I cannot marry that man," she protested, gripping the arms of her chair such that her fingers turned white. "After this business in the papers, he will hate me in earnest. How could you condemn me to marry a man who hates my very liver?"

"I doubt it is your liver he takes issue with," her father declared, leveling a steely gaze on her. "No one has set a date for the wedding. If things go well —" he swallowed hard and forced the words out — "there may not have to be one."

That took a moment to register.

"What are you saying?" A flicker of hope ignited in the gloom settling over her. She held her tongue after that.

"Just that you are to appear with him frequently and congenially . . . to lay to rest all question of his reputation and yours . . . to salvage the merger. The more convincing you are, the shorter this betrothal will be."

"You mean I don't have to actually marry him? Just put up a good front in public until everyone forgets about the 'cowardly fiancé'?"

"That, I believe, would be the most favorable outcome for all concerned . . . since you are being a stubborn twit and he is being a complete horse's arse. The pair of you have gotten us into this mess, and the pair of you will have to get us out of it. The sooner the better."

She teetered between hope and horror, imagining her erstwhile groom's reaction to that same ultimatum. She couldn't imagine how Horace Townsend would frame such orders so they would be acceptable to his arrogant offspring. She remembered her vengeful pleasure at his shock as he sat in the water, his dignity in tatters. Just as she had to deal with the consequences of her action, he would have to weigh the consequences of his. No man of pride could bear being thought a coward. No matter how distasteful, he would eventually have to accept his father's ultimatum.

Good Lord. What had she done?

FIVE

The next afternoon Horace Townsend appeared in their grand entry hall with his irritable-looking son. Lauren's father had ushered her into the grand parlor, after looking her over like a heifer at a country fair and deeming her fit for slaught — er, company. If it were up to her, she would have greeted her erstwhile fiancé in barn boots and a bathrobe.

Aunt Amanda stood by the door, watching, as the Townsends were shown into the parlor. There was a moment of silence, an awkward greeting, and then the fathers retreated to the hall, closing the great doors behind them.

"Are you sure that's wise?" Amanda touched Lawrence's arm, looking concerned. "Leaving them alone together?"

"They are stuck together for who-knows-how-long. They have to work out their differences in private before they confront the world together."

Lauren watched Rafe cross the room toward her and she took a nervous breath. He was tall, broad-shouldered, and moved with an assurance undimmed by his current infamy. She didn't offer her hand, reasoning that he probably wouldn't take it.

They stood facing, assessing each other. She could feel his gaze roaming her blue woolen day dress and had the fleeting thought that she should have worn something better . . . to emphasize the measure of what he had lost by his arrogance, of course. When his gaze rose to rest on her face, she felt her cheeks begin to flush. It was as if he was examining her, truly searching and *seeing* her for the first time.

Best to get it over with, she thought, and when he straightened, she realized she had said it aloud and may as well continue. "I am here to fulfill my father's promise and to undo whatever damage was done to the merger of our families' enterprises." She clasped her hands at her waist and hoped he didn't notice how white and bloodless they were.

"I am here," he said, clamping his hands behind his back, "because my father insists my reputation can only be repaired by the very agent who damaged it."

"Me." She squared her shoulders. "You should know, then: My opinion of your behavior on the river has not changed. Though I am willing to credit that my words may have had a more detrimental effect than intended."

"If that is an apology, it's a pitiful one." He gave her an arch look.

"It's the only one you'll get." She raised her chin a notch, with only glancing eye contact. "Your behavior was at the very least — ungallant."

"*Ungallant?* That is what you expect of a man? Gallantry?"

"A true gentleman bears chivalry in the very core of his being," she responded. It was clear the result of the river incident had given him no pause for self-examination. She realized she expected it would have, and once again was pitifully optimistic concerning him.

"Then, by deduction, I am not your notion of a gentleman at all." He lifted his chin and looked down his nose at her.

"I am glad you see it so clearly," she answered in a frosty tone.

He scowled at her blunt appraisal and fired back. "Then you should know that you are not what I consider a proper lady. You are without a doubt the most impulsive and irrational female I have ever encountered. Shedding your clothes and diving headfirst into unknown waters to haul complete strangers to —"

"I was not *naked.* And I believe strongly in doing what is helpful to those in difficulty, even if it means shocking those with excessively tender sensibilities." She hurled those last words like javelins. When they struck he pushed back the sides of his coat to plant his fists at his waist.

"Oh, so, expecting one's betrothed to remain fully clothed and in the safety of a boat makes my sensibilities prudish?"

"When juxtaposed to two women's lives, yes. Fair warning: I would strip off my garments and dive in again if no one else saw fit to act."

He looked as if he was collecting himself for a flaming condemnation of her unladylike determination. A moment later, as she searched his hazel eyes and ridiculously handsome jaw, she saw him exhale heavily and sensed he had come to a decision.

"Fine." He relaxed his stance and allowed his coat to fall together again. "If that is the way you wish to proceed, we will bear each other's company in public. Just, please, do me the courtesy of letting me know in advance that you're likely to strip off your clothes so I can be prepared with a horse blanket."

She stared at him for a moment as that image bloomed vividly in her mind . . . him chasing her half-naked form around with a horse blanket. She pursed her lips to contain a laugh.

"Again the Townsend charm rears its scaly head," she said tartly. "Perhaps it's best if you don't show much of that when we are in public."

"As long as you don't revert to your penchant for exhibitionism, I believe I can rein in my devastating charm."

She narrowed her eyes and he smiled in a way that was intolerably smug. He'd scored in their duel of wits and he knew it.

"Very well. We're stuck with each other for a time," she said, moving to the sofa and sitting down with emphatic grace. "I think it best we plan an outing or two . . . to be seen together . . . devoted bride and doting groom." She made a gagging expression that widened his eyes.

"Is there anything about you that is normal?" he asked, coming to stand before her with feet apart and arms crossed . . . a colossus of decorum and rectitude.

"If by 'normal' you mean 'ordinary,' I am

afraid not."

"Did you have a strange or alarming childhood? Were you repeatedly dropped on your head or locked in a dark wardrobe?"

"Absolutely not. I recall it as a rather pleasant time."

"Remarkable." He took a deep breath and said, as if to himself, "Delusions that strong are rare."

Her cheeks burned and she clamped her lips tighter. Remaining civil was going to take more effort than she thought.

"Do be seated." She waved a hand at the chairs facing the settee. "Your hovering is most unpleasant."

To her surprise, he sank onto the settee beside her. She drew back, hoping her dismay wasn't too obvious. Did he have to sit beside her?

"I shall need some information in order to plan our public *romance.*" He said the last word with excessive emphasis. "I don't suppose you ride."

"I am good with horses. I learned to ride when I was four."

He seemed oddly disappointed.

"Are you fond of music? The opera? Do you dance?"

"Yes, no, and yes, happily."

He nodded as he sorted those answers.

"Are you frightened of heights?"

"Heights?" She frowned. "I have no idea. But I suggest we avoid finding out the hard way."

His mouth quirked up on one side, and she began to think that planning their itinerary was something she should have a hand in.

"Do you read, Mr. Townsend? Other than racing forms and scandal sheets, I mean."

"I do read. Quite a bit, actually." He ignored her barb.

"I don't suppose you have ever read Sir Walter Scott's *Ivanhoe*?"

"No." He looked pensive. "Isn't that a novel? I avoid novels."

"Not surprising," she said, ranging ahead in her thoughts. "Do you support a charity? Have a favorite foundling home or hospital to help?"

"I leave such things to wild-eyed reformers."

"Do you attend Sunday services?"

"Rarely." At least he was honest about that.

"It shows," she said, finding herself gazing at his face — elegantly cut features and full lips — and feeling an alarming, twiddly sensation in her middle. She resettled herself on her seat. "In the interest of fairness, I believe we should take turns planning outings to demonstrate our renewed betrothal. You take one day, I'll take the next."

"We have to see each other every day?" His voice was strangled, as if those words were a sentence handed down under black silk.

"The sooner we convince society and those wretched gossip papers that we have mended our differences, the sooner they will lose interest and leave us alone," she reasoned aloud. "After a week or two we can reduce to two or three days a week and the occasional dinner party . . . then once a week. . . ."

"I see where this is going," he said flatly. "And we can't reach that destination too quickly, as far as I am concerned."

"Tomorrow is Sunday. I attend services at eleven o'clock at the Church of St Ambrose, so you could —"

"Not be there," he broke in, moving to the edge of his seat.

"I'll be too busy sleeping off a bugger of a hangover that will last until Monday morning. Hopefully, that will be enough time to prepare myself for another encounter with you."

He rose and strode for the doors, where

he paused while opening them. "There is an exhibition of Machinery for Innovation at Upwell Hall. I've been meaning to take it in. There are recent improvements in power mechanics and machinery that could help a project I am working on."

She rose, wondering what sort of project would interest a man who was so thoroughly self-absorbed. The fact that she was curious about that should have given her pause, but she reminded herself she had to spend time with him in public, and knowing more about him might be useful.

"I shall call for you at ten on Monday," he said, tugging on his vest.

And he was gone.

She hurried to the door in time to see him accept his hat, gloves, and walking stick from Weathersby, then stride out the door. Long, graceful strides of long, powerful legs. She had to pull her gaze away. Why were women's legs always "limbs," when men got to use the more anatomical "legs"? Men's and women's appendages weren't all that different, were they?

She raised her skirts to stare at her stocking-clad calves and feet.

To imply that women were more delicate? Weaker?

Little did they know.

Barnaby Pinkum jammed the last glorious bite of beefsteak in his mouth and closed his eyes as he chewed, savoring the taste of his celebratory meal. He sat in a far corner of Ye Olde Cheshire Cheese just off Fleet Street, ignoring the rude camaraderie of his fellow hacks. He had just devoured most of his payment for the "River Rescue" story, which he managed to sell to two scandal rags in quick succession. He was feeling rather satisfied as he drained the last of his pint of stout and gave a belch that would have done a duke proud.

He was on the verge of ordering another pint when he looked up and spotted the second page editor of *The Examiner* ducking through the low entrance door. Barnaby's eyes widened and he looked around for an escape route, but his habit of squirreling away in the corner nook had him trapped. Cigar-chewing Angus Harrell headed straight for him and arrived before he could bolt.

"There you are," Harrell declared with enough volume to draw attention in the pub. Most of the regulars had sold him stories at one time or another and knew he seldom came out of his editorial den to visit the newswriters' favorite haunt. He stopped in front of the corner table, blocking any exit and chewing the stubby end of his unlit cigar. His voice lowered to a growl. "Got a proposition for you, Pinkum."

Barnaby sank warily back onto his seat when Harrell gestured to him to sit. He figured he was in for a trashing, owing to the fact that he'd sold the river story to Harrell and *The Examiner* only after selling it to *The Morning Post.*

"I–I meant to s-say —"

"Yeah, yeah," Harrell said around his clamped cigar. "We got it second — some damnable arse got it to *The Post* ahead of us. But we did it better. Pictures, that's what sells papers. And they bought ours in droves, my boy. Best sales we've seen in weeks. People want to read more about this 'heroine' of yours. Too much bad news lately — bankruptcies, tariffs, no jobs. Have to give 'em a change, and your girl is just the ticket."

"Don't know what more I can get. Old Man Alcott threatened me with the law when I tried to question him," Barnaby said, quickly recalculating the odds of turning this bit of luck into a more substantial boon. Harrell clearly didn't know he'd sold

71

the story twice and now wanted him to write more for *The Examiner*. With a little ingenuity, he might get three or four more stories out of it.

"What else has she done?" Harrell paused for a moment. "A twitch like that, she's got history — I'd lay money on it. See what people know about her. And if you can't find anything, keep an eye out and make whatever does happen sound 'heroic.' "

"And if I do —" Barnaby produced a cagey look "— will it go on the front page?"

The second page editor laughed. "News on the front page? Who the hell would buy that?" Then he thought for a moment and met Barnaby's gaze. "If it's good enough, it could lead the second page . . . above the fold, with illustrations and . . . maybe . . . a signature."

A signature piece! Something seldom granted to even the most respected reporters. Barnaby grinned, and Harrell stepped back to wave him out of the corner. "What are you waitin' for? Go get me a story for Wednesday's edition."

Rafe entered the bar at his club that evening to find a boisterous group of young scions gathered there. He sighed quietly, thinking he perhaps should seek liquid solace elsewhere, when he spotted his friend and sometime housemate, Barclay Howard, tucked into a corner table nursing a drink. Barr's shoulders were rounded — if those broad planks of muscle and sinew could ever be considered round — and he wore a scowl on his sharply chiseled face. At the sight of Rafe, Barclay's expression lightened, then drifted to the pack of well-dressed imbibers.

With a deep breath, Rafe sank to a seat beside Barclay. His friend raised a glass.

"Here's to the bravest bastard in the room," he said before tossing back the liquor.

"I take it you've heard about my misadventure," Rafe said, signaling the barman to bring him a drink and another for his friend.

Barclay made a motion to the group at the bar. "We all have. It's spread like wildfire." He paused to search Rafe visually. "The girl really dumped you? You, the prince of propriety? The disciple of duty?"

"She tried. Apparently I'm harder to jilt than the average son of privilege. Family and business mixed. I fear we're stuck with each other."

Barclay studied him for a moment, glimpsing the gloom beneath his polished surface.

"Maybe we should go somewhere else to —"

"Well, well. Look who's here!" came the strident voice of a fellow swerving his way from the bar to their table with a handful of similarly inebriated fellows trailing behind. "The lily-livered bridegroom!"

"You're pissing drunk, Fitzroy," Rafe said, his jaw tightening, "as well as rude and annoying. I suggest you go home and sleep it off."

"Ooooh," Fitzroy crowed with a well-lubricated sneer. "That takes bollocks, tellin' me to go home — when it's your presence that fouls the company." He tossed a glance over his shoulder at his followers. "Hear that, my good fellows? The *coward* thinks you an' me should go home."

Rafe rose, ignoring Barclay's insistent grip on his arm. He knew where this was headed, and some part of him welcomed it. Counting the odds — five to one — he scarcely noticed Barclay pushing up with a muttered oath to stand beside him. He took a deep breath and started around Fitzroy, who laughed harshly and gave him a shove. Rafe caught his balance. A second later he straightened and turned back . . . his fist aimed dead-center for Fitzroy's face.

Six

Monday morning came sooner than Lauren wished. She rose early, breakfasted in her room, then set about selecting something suitable to wear for ogling machinery. Nothing too frilly or too plain. She must look as if she was trying to please her groom-to-be. Though God knew what sort of female apparel would suit Mr. Tall, Fair, and Arrogant.

She emptied her wardrobe, holding garment after garment to her and examining their potential in the cheval mirror. Dresses, skirts, and blouses were strewn all around her bedroom when Aunt Amanda appeared.

"What on earth?" She looked around at the chaos.

"What do you think? I have to look nice but not overly stylish, feminine but not flirtatious." She scowled and rubbed her forehead. "Machinery." She paused. "Anything with ruffles or lace is definitely out."

When Amanda didn't say anything Lauren turned to look at her.

"I'm so sorry you have to go through this," Amanda said with a rueful expression. "Stuck with that man for days . . . having to put a good face on it. I tried to talk to Lawrence, but . . ."

Lauren felt a tug of something uncomfortably like guilt.

"It's my fault for spouting off when I should have been more discreet. I don't give a fig about Rafe Townsend's pride, but I know now how much Papa is counting on this merger. The other night, when I heard them talking, he and Mr. Townsend both seemed to believe it is critical." She halted and gazed at the garments strewn around.

"At least these outings get me out of prison." With a flash of inspiration, she picked up a royal-blue woolen jacket with a tailored peplum and paired it with a pale golden skirt trimmed in matching blue cording. "There." She held the items to her for Amanda's inspection. "What do you think?"

"If you're not careful, you'll charm Rafe Townsend into second thoughts."

"It's not him I need to charm," she said wryly. "It's whoever might be watching us."

■ ■ ■ ■

Rafe braced as he stood in the entry hall at Alcott House and forced himself to focus on the grace of the marble floor, the smoothly carved banisters, and the pedestal table in the center, set with an arrangement of pink and white flowers. What he recalled of their parlor was equally pleasant. The Alcotts didn't go in for gaudy, Louis XIV gilding or the dark faux Tudor interiors in vogue with the just-monied class. It was a relief to find himself surrounded by clean, Hepplewhite-style furnishings, and to realize that someone here favored damask drapes that actually admitted light through the house's large windows.

Though, at the moment, he could have used a bit less light. His head was pounding and his eyes — caught on a figure at the top of the stairs.

Her hair was up and capped by a blue, swallow-shaped hat. He forced his eyes wider to take in the stylish, two-piece ensemble that was tailored closely to her noteworthy figure. The color of her jacket brought out the blue of her eyes and the gold of the skirt seemed to echo the highlights of her chestnut hair. Every perfectly

77

groomed strand of her appearance was braided into an air of confidence.

His swollen eye throbbed from the effort of concentrating . . . or her impact. Whatever the cause, he couldn't take his aching gaze from her.

"I hope this machinery of yours won't be dirty," she said, floating down the last few steps, readying her gloves. "This is my favorite skirt."

"Good morning to you, too." He tried to shake off that fascination.

"Whether it is a good morning or not is yet to be —" She halted a few feet away to don her gloves and looked up. Her eyes widened. "Your eye." She edged closer, inspecting his face. "And your lip. What happened to you?"

She seemed genuinely concerned, but he remained silent.

"You have a black eye, a swollen cheek, and a cut lip." She stepped closer, examining him and coming to the all-too-accurate conclusion: "You were in a fight."

He summoned the explanation he had planned.

"I ran into some old boys from school."

She searched his injured face and after a moment landed her gaze on his. He could see her arranging facts into questions.

"I take it spirits were involved. Were you injured elsewhere? Ribs? Hands?" She reached for his hand and studied the bruising on his knuckles.

"I am perfectly fine. We should be going. This exhibit —"

"Can wait," she declared, removing the one glove she had donned. Before he could react she was touching his face, testing the bruising. He winced but didn't draw back. Her fingers felt cool and oddly welcome.

"We have to do something about this," she said, taking him by the arm and pulling him toward the parlor.

"I've already done beefsteak," he grumbled, surprised by the force she could summon. "It will be fine in a couple of days."

"We don't have a couple of days. If reporters see you like this" — she hesitated for a moment — "they'll probably write that I did it."

He had to credit that. His face hurt when he smiled.

She led him to the settee and ordered him to sit — which he surprised himself by doing — before she left the room. He heard her talking to someone, and she returned minutes later with a tray containing a bowl of hot water, what smelled like brewing tea, and some linen.

"What the devil is that?" He peered into the bowl.

"It will reduce the swelling." She dumped the soaked tea leaves onto the thin cloth, then gathered the folds around it to form a poultice of sorts.

"Tea? You're putting tea leaves on my eye?"

"*You're* going to put it on your eye. I'm just preparing it." She put the bag into his hand and then bent his arm to bring the poultice to his eye.

It was hot at first, but he quickly got used to it, and when she tucked a pillow behind his head he let her urge his head back onto it. There was a rustle of skirts and then all was quiet. He opened his good eye and found himself alone. What brought about this sudden surge of compassion toward him? He had half-expected, half-hoped she would refuse to be seen with him in such a condition in public. He closed both eyes and relaxed.

Sometime later he started awake with the cooled poultice on his face and sat up abruptly. The poultice dropped and scattered damp tea leaves all over. He looked up to find her seated nearby.

"I . . . must have dozed off. It fell . . ."

"I doubt it will stain." She knelt on the

rug beside him to collect the linen and as many of the damp leaves as she could. "How is your eye feeling?"

He sat forward, dusting stray tea leaves from his coat, and had to admit it seemed less swollen. It certainly was easier to open.

"I believe your remedy may have some merit," he said.

She paused on her knees beside him and looked up. Her eyes seemed bigger and softer than he had ever seen them. He was drawn into her gaze and felt a strange, warming sensation, akin to the effects of a draught of strong whiskey spreading through him.

Lauren sank back onto her heels, looking up at him, unsettled by his gaze. Those beautiful hazel eyes . . . just now seemed less guarded.

She had spent the last quarter of an hour watching him, trying to make sense of his battered condition. Someone had given him a good trouncing. She had found her hands curling into fists and her protective instincts rising. Then she looked to his damaged knuckles and realized he must have dealt a few blows himself. Imagine him *fighting*.

Now she was staring into his eyes in a way she had never done with a man before.

Searching and being searched. It was alarmingly intimate.

She pulled back, and her knees trembled as she rose and emptied her hands onto the tray. As she wiped her hands with a damp cloth, she looked up to find him standing close and staring at her.

"We should be going. That machinery won't admire itself." Something — embarrassment, or a new sense of vulnerability — made her add, "It's not a Townsend after all."

She caught a quick glimpse of his frown as she turned to head for the hall. When Weathersby opened the front door for them moments later, she felt more in control . . . until she saw their conveyance: an enclosed, two-person cab. She would have to sit cheek-by-jowl with him.

"Just where is this Upwell Hall?" she asked.

"Near the shipyards."

She paused for a moment. "Unlikely to be reporters there. We shall have to go someplace more public afterward. I assume you have made reservations for luncheon."

It was all Rafe could do to contain a groan. Was she going to be like this all day? Terse. Focused. Vaguely dismissive. But the moment she started down the front walk, he found himself staring fixedly at the small bustle swaying with each step she took. Not extravagant, it was just enough to seize his gaze and raise a memory of that very derrière outlined by clinging wet linen.

He stood, transfixed, until she reached the door of the cab.

"From now on we shall take our carriage and make certain the top is down," she said.

As he settled in the cab beside her, she produced a book from under her arm and thrust it into his hands.

"What's this?" He turned the book over in his hands with a frown.

"A book you should read," she answered with an emphatic look.

The smooth leather cover and the disturbed edges of the pages said it had been read before . . . repeatedly . . . probably by her. He looked at the spine. Sir Walter Scott. *Ivanhoe.*

"I'm not interested in fairy tales." He tried to hand it back.

"There is not a single *fairy* in it." She pushed the book back to him. "You may find it enlightening."

Still frowning, he opened the cover, and on the third page was a color plate of a handsome knight on a fine destrier, charging off into battle. A knight. He gave a quiet huff of sufferance and wedged the book on the seat between them, sensing that whatever it contained was probably the opposite of what she considered him to be. Was this a taunt?

Damned cheeky female.

Barnaby Pinkum waited until they were settled in the cab and crept around the brick-and-ironwork fence to spring for the rear of the cab. His favorite form of travel . . . hitching rides on the rear of cabs paid for by unsuspecting swells. It was times like this that he was grateful for his small stature. Neither the cabbie nor his quarry realized he was there.

The exhibition Townsend intended to subject her to was held at Upwell, an old shipwrights' guild hall in the Docklands. It was a large, dreary brick building set with few windows but a number of doors, some clearly made for the passage of large freight or wagons bearing equipment. As they exited the cab she noticed he had left the book behind on the seat. With a huff of annoyance she picked it up.

As he helped her down from the cab she spotted a man in a dusty bowler and checkered coat watching them and had the feeling she had seen him before. Was he one of the men in front of their house three nights ago? How on earth would a reporter find them here? As a precaution, she took Rafe's arm and made sure to smile at her intended.

Inside the hall, machinery of various kinds had been set up on platforms, identified by placards and attended by men wearing suits or coveralls. Some of the machines were scaled models of engines, others were motors or components of equipment used in manufacturing. Numerous spectators, all male, strolled the alleys between exhibits and stopped to question the representatives about their wares. It was busier than it had appeared outside.

Over the noise and bustle had settled a miasma of machine oil, hot rubber, and traces of smoke from coal burning in nearby boilers. The tang in the air pricked her nose and made her eyes water. It was a clattering, chugging, smelly display unlike anything she had ever witnessed. She was on the way to being ripely annoyed until she read the banner strung across the exhibit floor. These machines, it said with pride, drove English military and industrial might. They had built and were continuing to build an empire for the ages.

Why on earth would he bring her to such a place?

Rafe's arm under her hand tightened and his eyes brightened as he spoke with one exhibitor after another until he found the one he was most interested in.

Along one whole side of the hall was a grand display illustrating what the signs called "high-powered steam engines." Touted as the latest thing in sea-going propulsion, they were the very engines carrying the British Navy to supremacy on the world's seven seas. Only recently had the company producing them begun fitting them into commercial ships.

Rafe engaged two men who identified themselves as the engineers responsible for the manufacture of the metal monstrosities. Soon he was climbing all over the platform with them to investigate the engine's construction.

Lauren stood outside the rope railing, feeling conspicuous as the only woman in the hall and annoyed that Rafe had abandoned her on an outing meant to repair his reputation. When a young man in a suit approached her to see if she needed help, she asked what about the engines made them so special. He helped her under the rope and began to show her the separate components and explain the innovations that made them the most powerful engines afloat.

She was surprised to understand the concept behind them as he explained it . . . steam pressure turning a paddle wheel was old stuff . . . inboard engines driving propellers were the current thing. It made sense. The young man answered her questions and smiled back when she smiled. After a time she looked up to find Rafe was standing with his arms crossed, wearing a scowl that looked downright painful on his injured face.

"I hope you've seen enough," he declared. "I certainly have." He held out a hand that insisted she place hers in it.

She was on the verge of a retort when she spotted a bowler hat above a pair of squinty eyes staring at them from behind a nearby display. Their voices weren't raised. No one else was watching. Instinctively, she gave him her hand and smiled as if their lives depended on it. She stepped off the platform and ducked under the rope he held up for her.

She paused in the walkway between exhibits to brush her jacket and skirt. "I seem to have escaped the oil. Fascinating things, engines. Who would have guessed it?" She glanced at the bowler man's location and found him gone. With a deep breath, she took Rafe's arm and smiled up at him in a way she hoped was convincing.

"Now where is this delightful place you've chosen for luncheon?"

Delightful, she recalled too late, was in the eye of the beholder.

They disembarked from the cab in front of a respectable but hardly stylish restaurant minutes later. He helped her down the cab's steps as she looked the place over. The Seven Sisters was announced by a hanging sign bearing seven white stars in a circle. The place had a black-painted front with numerous windows hung with half curtains. A sign in the window nearest the door advertised "The Best Pork Pie in London."

As her shoes touched the pavement, a scuffle a few yards away drew her attention. A man in a shopkeeper's apron had a young boy by the shirt, shaking him and calling him a "filthy little thief." She stopped to stare at them, jolted by the terror in the boy's face.

"Give it back or I'll have th' law on you!" the shopkeeper snarled.

"Warn't me, sarr," the boy cried, struggling wildly to free himself. "I swear, I didn' take nothin'!"

"Bound for Newgate, you are!" the man shouted in the boy's face, and then struck him.

Lauren gasped. A backhand blow followed quickly on and she was in motion before Rafe could prevent it.

"Stop!" She rushed to them. The shopkeeper was startled into pausing but didn't loosen his grip on the boy. "What's happened here?"

"None o' your concern." The shopkeeper turned and, seeing her fine clothes, amended his tone. "Stole a watch chain right off my counter. Him an' his pack of gutter rats scrambled into my shop." He nodded to the small storefront next to the pub. "When I threw 'em out he grabbed a watch chain — an Albert."

"Did you see him do it?" she asked.

"It was one o' the bunch. One's the same as all."

She stooped to look into the boy's face. His chin quivered.

"I didn' take it, miz — on Jesus's bones, it warn't me."

Lauren examined the scrawny boy. Big eyes. Dirty face. A shirt two sizes too big and breeches tied up with string. His shoes were full of holes and too big for his feet.

"Turn out your pockets." She held the

boy's gaze, searching it.

He tried to swallow a lump in his throat and finally managed to confess, "Ain't got no pock-ets."

Rafe had followed her, uncertain whether or not to try hauling her away from meddling in the workings of justice. She was stubborn enough to resist and cause a scene, and — he looked around at the people stopping to watch — he couldn't afford another ghastly report in the papers.

"Miss Alcott, we really must be going," he managed as she stooped and felt the boy's clothes for evidence. Whatever she found, it wasn't a watch chain. She rose and faced the shopkeeper with determination.

"Did you actually see him steal the chain?" she demanded.

The fellow insisted it had to be either him or another of his band of guttersnipes. "They roam the streets in gangs, lookin' for open doors, and push in to make confusion an' take whatever they can."

"Well, there is no evidence that this boy took anything," she said.

"Miss Alcott, this is no concern of ours." Rafe hoped he didn't sound as if he was pleading.

Ignoring him, she asked, "What was the

value of the watch chain?"

"Miss Alcott?" The shopkeeper's eyes widened. "Miss Alcott — th' Angel of the River?"

Surprised, she glanced up into Rafe's pained expression. "The same." At least she had the decency to look dismayed.

The shopkeeper took a half step back and smoothed his apron.

"I know yer a merciful woman, miss, but I got a fam'ly to feed."

After a transfer of two sovereigns the shopkeeper thanked her profusely for restoring his loss and nodded repeatedly. "It were an honor to meet the angel what saved them poor women."

With her face aflame, she nodded and then took the boy's hand to pull him away.

Rafe groaned as she headed for the Seven Sisters with the guttersnipe in tow. It wasn't over yet.

Seven

"What are you going to *do* with him?" he demanded in a loud whisper when they reached the door of the Seven Sisters.

His supposed betrothed looked down at the boy.

"I'm going to — *we're* going to feed him."

Oh no. Not in his favorite Dockland eatery. Before he could protest she had the door open and was dragging the urchin inside.

An indignant owner rushed to meet them.

"No, no, miss." Then he recognized Rafe and lowered his voice. "Mr. Townsend, sir, we cannot have that dirty creature in here."

"He won't be dirty for long," she said. "Where is your washroom?"

"I . . . but . . . the other patrons . . ."

One of the waiters had heard her and motioned to a hall at the back. She sailed off with child in hand, leaving Rafe to deal with the owner.

"Mr. Townsend, I simply cannot accommodate —"

"Just put us at a table in the back," he growled. "He won't be any trouble, I promise. And I'll be *grateful.*"

He felt every eye in the place on him as the unhappy owner led him to a table that was wedged into a corner beside the farthest window. As soon as Rafe seated himself, he heard muffled voices and looked around. There were people outside the nearby window with noses pressed against the glass, peering at him. He made irritable motions to scatter them and then turned to glare at the door through which she had disappeared.

Incorrigible female. He'd have a thing or two to say to her when they were out of the public eye. She had a pure talent for causing scenes. He felt a nasty throb returning to his eye and gently explored the ache with his fingers. Thank God he wasn't shackled to her 'til death did them part.

She reappeared sometime later with a much-improved urchin whose face was red from washing, hands were mostly clean, and hair was wetted back. He rose as she seated the child and plopped the book he had abandoned again on the plate in front of him.

"Mr. Townsend, meet Jims Gardiner. He lives with his mother and sisters in a place called Three Pig. His father died, his mother has to work a lot, and he has two sisters who work, too." She turned to the boy. "Jims, meet Mr. Townsend. He is in the import-export business and is my —" she glanced around to see if anyone was listening — "intended."

"Yer a tall feller," Jims said, clearly awed. "An' dress real fancy."

"Whereas you are short, impertinent, and in drastic need of a good scrubbing." Rafe quirked his nose as if smelling something distasteful.

Lauren gasped, but Jims responded rather matter-of-factly.

"Ma says no need wastin' water — I'd just git dirty a'gin." He looked up at Lauren with hopeful eyes. "You really gonna give me some food?"

They were and they did. She asked Rafe to order and he soon had a full glass of milk sitting in front of the boy with a number of dishes on the way. Jims looked hungrily at the milk, but when he was urged to drink it, he said it tasted . . . sweetlike. He soon got used to it and gulped until Lauren suggested he slow down and save room for some food.

"No worry, miz. I kin eat a whale. Ma says so." He looked thoughtful. "But I never had a whale."

Lauren bit her lip and glanced at Rafe, who shook his head in disbelief. The boy's eyes nearly popped out of his head when they brought out soft rolls and butter, handsome pork pies, potatoes baked with cheese, and fresh green peas. He stuffed a bit of everything in his mouth, as if afraid it would be whisked away any moment. She leaned close to his ear.

"If you're going to eat with a gentleman, you must learn to eat *like* a gentleman. Use the fork, not your fingers. And take a breath now and then. This food isn't going anywhere without you."

The boy's bony shoulders relaxed and he looked up at her, grinning and chewing enthusiastically. He held the fork awkwardly and had trouble with the knife. She showed him how and watched patiently as he struggled to master the cutlery. Moments later he looked up with chagrin.

"All we gots is spoons."

Rafe pulled his gaze from the boy's big, brown eyes, determined to enjoy the hearty food set before him. He covertly studied the concern on Lauren's face as she picked at her food. He saw her features soften. There was genuine tenderness in her touch as she pushed the boy's damp hair back from his face. It struck him forcefully that this was more than an exhibition of charity. She honestly cared about the boy. When Jims looked up at her with a greasy grin, the smile she returned was so full of warmth that his own pie got stuck in his throat.

After a while she leaned back in her chair and focused on him.

"You forgot your book again. One might think you weren't keen to read it."

"I believe I have expressed my opinion of novels."

"Wot's a nozzle?" Jims asked, staring at the volume on the table.

"Novel," she corrected. "It's a book that tells a story that isn't real, but is still enjoyable. Do you know any stories told just for fun?"

The boy thought a moment and then brightened. *"Free Li'l Pigs."*

Rafe made a noise somewhere between a laugh and a snort, then reached for his cup. She frowned at him, then turned back to Jims.

"That's a good story. The one in Mr. Townsend's book is longer and much more detailed. It takes hours to read, but it's a really good story."

"Wot's it about?" Jims paused with food dangling from his fork.

"It's about a knight." When he looked puzzled, she explained, "The men who wore armor and rode huge horses into battle to fight for the king. They were brave and noble and did great deeds."

The boy still seemed puzzled. Did he not even know about knights?

She picked up the book and opened it to the color plate in the front.

"Like this fellow." She showed him the picture, and his eyes widened.

" 'E wearin' metal duds?"

"Strictly speaking, his clothing is under the metal suit. The metal armor keeps his enemies from hurting him in a battle." She looked to Rafe. "Doesn't it, Mr. Townsend?"

"That is generally the idea."

Jims canted his head, staring at him. "You one o' them knights?"

Rafe nearly choked on the coffee in his mouth. It annoyed him that his gaze went straight to Lauren.

"Why would you think that?" Rafe cleared his throat a second time.

"You been fightin'." The boy tapped his own eye, referring to Rafe's blinker. "Ye copped a mouse." He brightened. "Was the king there?"

Lauren's eyes were as big as the boy's when she looked at him, and he could have sworn there was a twinkle of amusement in them.

"I am not a knight," he said succinctly. "Knights in shining armor don't exist anymore. And we have a queen, not a king."

"Oh. Yeah," Jims said, clearly disappointed, before stuffing his mouth with a roll. The bread didn't stop his words from coming through. "Bet if you'da had them metal duds, you wouldn'ta got yer mug beat up."

Lauren was trying to hide a smile behind her napkin. Annoying female. Damned annoying. He scowled at the book, and an idea struck.

"Have you ever had a book before?" he asked the boy.

Jims shook his head, looking between Rafe and the mesmerizing image in the bookplate.

"So you probably can't read."

The boy shook his head again.

"Do you know your letters?"

"Some," the boy said. "P an' T an' J — that's fer my name. An' A. That's for my ma's name. Alice."

"Tell you what," Rafe said, taking the book from her and handing it to the boy. "That is your book now. And when you learn to read some of it, come and find me and I'll give you a position in my company."

Jims glowed with excitement, looking between him and Lauren.

"Wot's a 'po-sit-shun'?"

Lauren found herself watching Rafe's eyes, wondering what he was thinking. No doubt she'd get a piece of his mind when they were alone again. But then, she had a word or two to say to a man who gave away a gift in front of the giver.

There was a commotion at the door and the owner rushed to intervene. It seemed some folk were insisting on being seated at a table near the "Angel of the River." She was taken aback by the way they stared. She had worried that their itinerary in the Docklands would go unnoticed, but now she worried that they were being noticed too openly.

How could those people know about her? Had the shopkeeper told people the name of the person who had made good his loss? Or did everyone in the East End read penny papers? Surely they had better ways to spend their hard-earned money.

When Jims said he wished his sisters could have been there to eat, too, she had the waiter make up a box of food to send home with him. Then a thought struck her, and she invited him to bring his sisters to the same pub the next day, midafternoon, so she and Rafe could meet them.

The boy was thrilled. The owner was less so when she asked him to reserve a table for their guests the next day. But because they planned to arrive after the midday rush, the pragmatic man considered the extra coin it would bring and agreed.

Their cab dropped off the boy at a row of dreary, odiferous tenements separated by an alley so narrow it should rightly be called a footpath. He cradled the book and box of food with a grin and ran down the worn path toward his home.

"Where to next?" she asked, feeling a surge of warmth at the hope Jims had radiated.

When she turned to Rafe he was staring at her, but giving no indication of what he was thinking. Then he drew a hard breath and grimaced at the smell emanating from the wretched houses.

"I believe we've been public enough for one day," he declared.

"I'd like to make a stop on the way home, if you don't mind."

Piccadilly was the destination she gave to

100

the cabbie. Soon Rafe helped her down in front of a shop called Hatchards, but, knowing the nature of the shop's trade, declined to accompany her inside. She put her arm through his and dragged him along with her through the door. He trailed her through tables of books and stood to the side with a long-suffering expression as she greeted a clerk who called her by name.

"Alcott?" Another woman's voice was heard and a stout, well-dressed woman in a wide, feathery hat appeared from behind a bookcase to look for her. "As I live and breathe, Miss Alcott!" She bustled over, clutching a pair of books to her bosom.

"Mrs. Buffington." Lauren greeted her with less enthusiasm.

"Imagine seeing you here. But then, you are a devotee of the printed word. One should expect to see you in a bookstore. How are you, dear, I've been reading" — she spotted Rafe and paused a heartbeat — "the books you've recommended for the parish school." She nodded to indicate those in her arms. "Excellent choices. Good, moral lessons and adventures to hold the children's attention."

"I'm glad you agree," Lauren said with determined pleasantry.

"And who is this?" Mrs. Buffington turned

her attention to Rafe, examining him thoroughly as he moved up behind Lauren.

"Rafe Townsend. Rafe, may I introduce Mrs. Archer Buffington. She is on the board of the parish school with me."

The woman pinked as she extended her hand, and Rafe clasped it. He said something about being either enchanted or embalmed . . . Lauren was too busy scrambling for mental footing to tell which. From the way she was staring at the pair of them, Mrs. B. knew of her engagement and made no secret of assessing Lauren's marital "catch."

"My goodness," Mrs. Buffington said, her cheeks pinking. "Such a tall and handsome fiancé. I see now why you've been too busy of late for reading hour at the school." She developed a twinkle in her eye. "And when is the wedding, dear?"

"W-we haven't set a date yet," Lauren responded.

"Really? You're only young once, you know," Mrs. B. said with a teasing tone. "You must enjoy it while you can." Lauren could almost feel Rafe's groan at that.

The clerk arrived to ask what she wanted, and Mrs. Buffington hurried off to the counter to complete her purchase. Lauren told the clerk what she wanted and took a deep breath. As she waited for her books to be collected and wrapped, she strolled from counter to bookcase and made another selection. When she looked up Rafe was holding the shop door for Mrs. B., who paused and turned to raise her voice so the whole shop could hear.

"I suppose we will see you at Lord Drummond's, then?"

Lauren was caught off guard, unable to recall what was happening at the Drummonds' home. "Oh, yes."

Mrs. Buffington smiled, gave a finger wave, and exited.

When Lauren and Rafe emerged minutes later she was carrying two parcels, one a tall, thick rectangle wrapped in brown paper and string, and the other flat but similarly wrapped.

Once in the cab and safely underway, she took a deep breath.

"Clearly Mrs. Buffington hasn't read about us. Around the parish, she is known as a rather strict adherent. I doubt she reads scandal sheets."

"Prefers her gossip firsthand, then." Rafe settled back in the cab with a side glance at her. "Did we look betrothed and besotted enough for her to tell everyone from Mayfair to Seven Dials?"

"Only time will tell," she said, handing him the flat package.

He sat straighter, turning it over in his hands.

"Is this what I think it is?"

"Open it," she said as he eyed her offering with dread.

Rafe pulled the string, folded back the paper, and drew a long-suffering breath. Another copy of *Ivanhoe*. She was determined to torment him with the damned thing. When he looked up she was watching him with mischievous pleasure.

"I wouldn't want you to go without, considering how generous you were with young Jims."

"You honestly expect me to read this?" He held it up and looked straight into her eyes. Big, beautiful, blue eyes with feathery golden rings around the very center. He blinked to clear his vision, but they were still the same. He had never seen eyes like hers. How had he not noticed their unusual coloring until now?

"I hope you will. I think it might —"

"Make me more courageous? More *heroic*?"

She paused for a moment, meeting his irritation without flinching.

"It may help you understand why I feel the way I do."

"I already know why you dislike me. I am not one of your grand, mythical heroes — daring to the point of insanity, selfless, and willing to sacrifice life and limb to right the wrongs of the world."

"That is not as naïve and ridiculous as you make it sound," she said.

"Have you ever met a real, bona fide hero?" He narrowed his eyes and realized his face was throbbing. Was his eye swelling again?

"I have . . . read their stories. The Duke of Wellington, Admiral Lord Nelson . . . William the Conqueror . . ."

"Your expectations keep exalted company," he said with an eyebrow raised. "So, you want a warrior, a knight errant, a leader of men and lover of all mankind . . . with the possible exception of Frenchmen."

"I do not expect perfection," she defended herself. "I do, however, believe a man of worth should be interested in the welfare of others . . . in making the world a better place. That means having the willingness to act when one sees trouble or others in danger."

She met his gaze with a resolve so genuine

that he had to credit that she believed it. And she clearly applied that standard to her own conduct. It struck him that she wanted a man who was willing to do what she herself would do. That gave him a moment's pause. In a mature man of the world that would be laudable. But in a young, unmarried female it was . . . unthinkable? . . . absurd?

He scowled and looked down at that cursed book.

Did she honestly believe some sort of spell, some alchemy of the soul was worked by Walter Scott's words? If so, he absolutely refused to read it. He would not have some head-in-the-clouds scribbler puttering around inside *his* soul!

"If you prefer, we could take a picnic to the river and I could read it to you." The smile that accompanied her offer looked like innocence itself. He knew better.

"And me without a horse blanket?" He thrust the book into the narrow space between them and then crossed his arms. "Not on your life."

Barnaby Pinkum watched the Townsend swell escort the Alcott girl to her front door, turn back to his cab, and depart straightaway. There was no lingering press of hands or exchange of touchless cheek kisses common in the upper crust. It was hard to say if the marriage was on or off, but at least he had collected enough evidence for another article. The Alcott chit was a do-gooder through and through, but from the looks he gave her, Townsend didn't share her selfless impulses.

To meet his deadline he'd have to use the "angel" angle again. Angel of the Streets now . . . swooping in to rescue a motherless urchin unfairly accused of theft . . . then seeing to it the nipper had a nourishing meal before seeing him safely home. His own stomach growled and he rubbed it with a frown. Damned guttersnipe ate better today than he did. Well, he intended to remedy that with a story so good it would feed him for a week.

EIGHT

The next day Lauren had planned to begin with a ride on Rotten Row at ten. Rafe had agreed to arrive at that time, suitably mounted, to escort her to the park. Afterward she planned to take him to the parish school for reading time, then to the Seven Sisters to meet Jims and his siblings. It was an itinerary crafted with visibility in mind, and one that was likely to grate on Rafe Townsend's nerves.

Assuming he had nerves.

During yesterday's activities he had remained cool and detached from everything but steam engines. Now, as she watched him dash through the pouring rain and up her front steps in riding clothes — tall, broad-shouldered, and determined — she thought of Aunt Amanda's scandalous musings on his husbandly qualities. What would it take to rouse aloof, self-possessed Rafe Townsend to a display of affection?

108

Seconds later he was in the entry hall, grumbling about the rain and rejecting Weathersby's assistance in drying his water-spotted boots. When she stepped out into the hall, he straightened and handed Weathersby back the towel.

"A fine morning you chose for a ride," he said. "It's pouring."

"I am aware." She made a moue of regret. "I fear we shall have to alter our plans." She paused for a moment. "I was thinking of finding someplace sheltered or indoors. Perhaps an arcade —"

"Or a turn around the Crystal Palace," he supplied. "The gardens there are interesting, and there are plenty of people and places for refreshments."

She considered that for a moment, then agreed it would be a suitable alternative.

Weathersby summoned a cab because the Alcott carriage had been let down for fair weather, and Rafe once again found himself seated close to his difficult intended. She wore a shapely green skirt and jacket with gold trim and another swallow-shaped hat — this one with handsome, gold feathers that played with the lights in her burnished hair. The woman knew how to dress for impact. And *undress.* He forced himself to look out the window and focus on his plans for the morning.

"I opened that blasted book last night," he said without looking at her. He didn't need to look; her image was burned into his mind. "I managed to make it through six whole pages before I fell asleep. That has to be the most somniferous tome ever published."

Surprised, she studied him for a moment. "Well, the first chapter is really background. Sir Walter is something of a historian. The real story starts in chapter two."

"It would have been nice to know that," he grumbled, squeezing his eyes shut, hoping to banish the effects of her appearance. "The man drones on . . . throws in every word he knows . . ."

"Start with chapter two. I usually do."

That made him turn. "You skip some of your precious bard's words?"

"I prefer to get to the meat of the story."

"As do I," he said, studying her face. Lovely skin, pert nose, and those unusual eyes. Something hungry was stirring inside him, but he was determined to resist it.

"At least we have that in common." She studied him the way he studied her. Realizing she was staring, she pressed her lips together and looked away.

What did she see in him that put her off so? He wasn't accustomed to being found lacking. Heaven knew there was nothing lacking in . . . her eyes . . . that feathery, golden circle inside the blue . . . a morning sunrise at their centers. He abruptly redirected his gaze.

They spoke little for the rest of the ride, simple comments on the shops, architecture, and landmarks they passed. He was surprised to find that she had a penchant for Georgian style, which he himself favored. His parents' house was a recent Gothic monstrosity smothered in heavy velvets, stuffed with bric-a-brac and whatever curiosities were in vogue. She surprised him by saying she had found his mother a very warm and engaging hostess. As he turned that over in his mind, they arrived in the plaza of the Crystal Palace and found that the rain had slowed to a drizzle.

He bolted from the cab, took a deep breath, and assisted her down the steps. He found himself reluctant to release her when she reached the ground, and when her hand slipped into the crook of his elbow he felt an unsettling surge of . . . satisfaction? pleasure?

He stiffened, refusing to think of contact with her in such terms.

Yes, he found her attractive; he had from the first time he set eyes on her. But he reminded himself that she was also impulsive, stubborn, and impossible to predict. He couldn't afford to fall into lustful fascination with her. If she was difficult and prickly now, imagine how she would respond when she watched her entire fortune being poured into ships and warehouses instead of being used to feed and clothe hungry urchins.

He paid for their admission and they paused inside the entry to take in the grand expanse of iron and glass that was now filled with greenery, fountains, and natural exhibits. Wooden paths wandered here and there, taking them through collections of ferns, exotic palms, and copses of small trees from commonwealth lands. At the crux of the main gallery and side exhibition halls, stood an English oak that nearly reached the barrel vault of glass that formed the main roof.

"It's remarkable," she said, gazing all around and then up at the distant roof. "A work of engineering and art comingled."

He steered her out of the stream of visitors to a fish pond surrounded by stone sculptures and filled with water lilies. The air was warm and humid, and he noted that her cheeks were sweetly flushed.

"I was here more than once as a child," she said, gazing up at the vaulted roof. "I didn't understand how grand it was. I was more interested in the dinosaur statues outside and the shaved ices than the exhibits." She smiled, and he found himself smiling back. It was the first exchange of genuine goodwill between them. He was caught off guard.

"Do you find it too warm?" He motioned to a stand farther down the main path. "We could get you some chilled water or a lemon ice."

Before she could answer he had her hand in his and was pulling her through exhibits and around knots of well-dressed patrons. He looked around as if searching for something or someone, and then escorted her to the north junction of the grand hall. He halted at an open-air café filled with white, wrought-iron tables and chairs.

"This will be more comfortable, I'm sure." No sooner had he said it than his name boomed from across the café.

"Sink me — if it ain't Townsend! Ain't seen you in a whale's age!"

A moment later Rafe was engulfed in a crushing embrace by an older man with frizzled gray hair and a scruffy face. The fellow pounded Rafe on the back, exclaiming in less than polite terms his pleasure at their meeting.

"You crusty old salt, how have you been?" Rafe seemed pleased to see the old fellow and abruptly invited him to join them at the table Lauren was standing beside.

"An' who's this fair lass?" The old man was thick and compact and missing a leg from the knee down. But the awkward wooden replacement didn't keep him from darting to the table, grabbing her hand, and giving it a much-too-exuberant kiss.

Lauren recoiled from that frontal attack, but too late. Her hand was held captive in the man's bearlike grip and she was taken aback by his leering grin and the smell of spirits wafting from him.

"Captain, meet Miss Lauren Alcott of the East Anglia Trading Company Alcotts," Rafe said, clearly pleased. She had never seen him smile so genuinely. She couldn't take her gaze from the way his face lighted from within.

"Miss Alcott, may I present Captain Harlow Stringer, the hero of Bonasera Bay."

She forced a pleasantry and managed to free her captive hand. When Rafe pulled out a chair for her the captain plopped down in the only other chair at the table, leaving

Rafe to borrow one from a nearby table.

These two, she realized, knew each other well. Her next observation concerned the faded wool and tarnished gold braid of the captain's aged uniform. Crumbs were stuck in his beard and on his coat front, but there were two complete ranks of medals pinned to his chest.

"Imagine finding you here," Rafe said as he settled beside Lauren.

"Where else'd I be?" The old boy licked his lips. "Best damned place in London to see folk and —" he gave Lauren a looking-over that made her shiver — "ogle the pretties. Where'd ye find this slip o' muslin?"

"In my father's ambitions," Rafe answered. "She is my intended."

"Damn me — yer pa's lookin' out fer ye good an' proper." The captain's eyes widened. More ogling ensued.

"When it suits him," Rafe responded.

"Still at odds with th' old man, are ye?" Captain Stringer shook his head, dislodging crumbs in his beard. To Lauren's surprise, he turned to her to explain, "Yer man's square of beam and keel. Not one t' take skiffy orders, even from his pa." He clamped a hand on Rafe's arm as it lay on the table. "Ne'er saw a better midshipman."

Lauren blinked and looked at Rafe. Mid-

shipman was a naval rank . . . a young officer in training. Rafe Townsend had been
in the navy?

He saw the question in her eyes and
answered it. "I went to the Academy. Against
my father's wishes."

"Academy boys — all pisser an' no
bollocks," Harlow declared. "Wouldn't give
a ha'penny fer a score of 'em — 'til this lad.
A crack navigator, he is." He tapped his
temple with a canny expression. "Reads
stars and marks charts wi' the best of 'em."

"You'll turn my head, you old flounder,"
Rafe said with a grin. "And here I thought
all you talked about these days was Bonasera Bay."

"Ahh, Bonnie Bay. Fer that I'll need to
wet me whistle." He gave a sly look, and
Rafe pulled a flask from his inside pocket.

A waiter hurried over to take their order,
and Harlow Stringer downed a pull from
the flask and sighed. "Damned temperance
ranters got it so ye can't get proper grog in
this place." He looked to Rafe with a wicked
twinkle in his eye. "Lucky though . . . I got
friends."

Rafe chuckled and nodded to the old man,
who took it as his cue to launch into his
favorite story.

"I capt'ned a Guard cutter out of Sussex.

Hard work an' dangerous. Smugglers don't give up easy. They'd as soon take their chance of gettin' pinched as dump a valuable cargo." He leaned toward Lauren. "Things got dull after Crimea, so I asked fer postin' to the Coastguard."

He looked down and pointed to four medals on the top rank — one of which had clearly been polished and cared for more than the others.

"A man gets used to action, see. After years of bollocksout battles, fightin' gets in yer blood. Makes it tough to settle down.

"The Battle of Bonasera." He tapped another shiny medal on his chest. "The bloodiest, fiercest fight o' my life. I were in the Baltic, ye see, back in '55. Helped take down the fortifications at Sevastopol in th' Crimea." He huffed. " 'At were a tea party compared to Bonnie Bay.

"Three smugglers aimin' to rendezvous, tho' we didn't know that at first. Frigate-size ships ridin' low — manned by salts wi' the grit to fight to the last dog howl."

Rafe glanced at her and she could have sworn he winked. She sat back in her chair, sensing that this meeting was more than happenstance. He'd brought her here on purpose, to see this gritty old salt and hear his story. Her gaze fixed on the old boy's medals . . . that shiny one was a cross overlaid by a crown and a lion. If that was indeed the Victoria Cross — and what else could it be? — he had to have done something rare.

". . . dark o' the moon . . . smugglers' favorite time . . . with Bonnie Bay set deep inside tall cliffs that made it hard fer the Guard's Coast Riders up top to see. Black as pitch it was — not even a glint of gunmetal t' give us away. In come the first ship — sails slack — lookin' for easy harbor. Just as we were about to set our guns barkin', a second sail was spotted headin' for the bay. Change of plans. We'd have to take the first ship without firin' a shot so the second ship would keep comin'.

"Nineteen men I had — strong swimmers, all." The captain took another swig from the flask. "Eighteen o' us went over the side and swam — blades in our teeth — to the shadows of the rocks. They figured they were safe and let down th' anchor. They were lookin' out to sea and thinkin' about their grog ration and the rendezvous. We come up the anchor chain and took down the watch, quiet as death. One by one, they fell, 'til we got to the crew quarters. Made noise there, I tell ye. Th' capt'n an' his mates come runnin' and we got banged up

118

a bit before we got the bastards bound an' stowed.

"We was feelin' pretty good . . . thinkin' to meet the second ship with our prize's guns . . . when a third sail appeared. Lights blinked from its crow's nest. We hadn't reckoned with signals. When we didn' answer the bastards run out their guns. Next thing we knew, we was in th' fight of our lives!

"Lost track o' how many men we took down and how many volleys we fired. The second ship turned to empty their cannon on us, but we got the first broadside before they could ram their waddin'. Aimed at the water line, we did — old Navy trick — an' them old wooden hulls sucked up cannonballs like spit on sponges. They maneuvered close enough to board us an' soon the decks were slippery wi' blood an' there was bodies floatin' in the water. Th' second bark caught fire . . . th' crew that was left abandoned ship when it started to sink. The third came straight in — don't know why the bastards didn't run. Guess they figured to relieve the first two o' some cargo, once the fightin' was done.

"Hand-to-hand an' blade-to-blade we was — no time to load guns anymore. Past the first volley or two, they didn't' bother wi' cannon either . . . just come streamin' aboard in waves, like rats.

"Fer a time I forgot where I was . . . kept slashin' and roarin' and climbin' over bodies. My eyes burned from smoke and I could barely breathe for the stench of burned gunpowder. My arms an' legs seemed to move on their own.

"Then my boys managed to load our one remainin' gun. Luckiest damned shot ever — hit their powder magazine — it blew an' took out half the deck an' main mast. Got 'em good — splinters an' arms an' legs flyin' everywhere — th' bastards screamin' as they flew over the side. Blew a hole clean through 'er. She took on water, then rolled like a mackerel. A sight I'll never forget.

"By that time the Coast Riders had seen th' light from the fires. They spotted my cutter behind the rocks and set about chasing down the smugglers who made it to shore."

Lauren stared at the mental pictures he painted, stunned by his descriptions of ships being sunk and bodies being torn asunder.

"How did you survive?" she said through a tightened throat.

"Don't rightly know. I come to days later . . . a sawbones had cut off my leg. Had enough laudanum in me to kill a horse." His bravado dimmed as he stared

120

into memory. "Ten of my crew survived, tho' some were torn up pretty bad. A couple o' my lads got burned in th' fires. They stood their ground, tho', an' took down dozens of the bloody bastards." He paused, his face now grave as he saw the carnage afresh in his mind. "I fight it over an' over in my sleep every night . . . tryin' to save my lads."

Rafe took a deep breath and turned to her to explain. "That was the biggest haul of contraband the Coastguard had ever captured. Rum, brandy, gunpowder, mahogany, and pig iron. Some of it had to be raised from where the ships went down. The Coast Riders kept the locals from salvaging, and the bulk of the cargo was claimed for the Crown and transported to Sussex. Miraculously, Captain Stringer's cutter remained untouched. He was decorated again for his extraordinary courage. Three frigate-size ships against a single cutter with a nineteen-man crew — it was a feat worth every honor in the books."

She took another breath, trying to dispel the stark images the old sea dog had evoked with his story.

"Imagine seeing you here!" A male voice burst through the somber mood. She and Rafe both turned and discovered a striking, broad-shouldered fellow in an expensive-looking suit bearing down on them.

"Barclay!" Rafe shot to his feet.

His surprise was matched by Lauren's. The man bore a half-healed black eye, a cut on his lip, and greening bruises that matched the ones on Rafe's face. She rose, causing the captain to scramble to his feet and sway before steadying himself.

"This must be the Angel of the Streets." The man Rafe called Barclay brushed past him to reach for Lauren's hand. She could see beneath those fading injuries a strong-featured face and striking brown eyes. His shoulders were unusually wide and his dark hair was a bit unruly, but every other aspect of his appearance and bearing spoke of gentlemanly status. "Don't just stand there; introduce me to the Angel."

Rafe did not look pleased.

"Miss Alcott, may I present Barclay Howard, grandson of the Earl of Northrup and my sometime landlord. Barclay, Miss Alcott, my intended."

"Bounder," Barclay charged with a smile, then addressed her. "I have never once charged this cadger rent. I just make him restock the liquor cabinet when we run dry." He turned halfway to Rafe. "She is splendid, man. You are blessed beyond words." Then he turned back to Lauren. "If he makes a shambles of this engagement, you must allow me to console you and correct whatever foul impression he might leave of British manhood."

"I have a healthy regard for British manhood, Mr. Howard. Though I cannot help but wonder if you were one of the old chums Rafe encountered a few nights ago." She tapped below her eye. "You bear the same souvenirs."

Barclay glanced at Rafe. "We encountered the same group, Miss Alcott. As friends, we stood together to correct a wrong impression."

Lauren glanced at Rafe, who looked as if he might take a swing at his old friend and landlord here and now. Her heart sank as she realized the fight probably had to do with the impression made by those blasted articles in *The Post* and *The Examiner*. Rafe had paid for her reckless words in pain. Small wonder he had been prickly and difficult with her.

A second later Barclay produced a rolled newspaper from under his arm and slapped it against Rafe's midsection. "Brace yourself, old man. Page two."

Rafe opened the paper, and whatever he read inside caused him to blanch. She stepped past Barclay to his side and saw bold print proclaiming "The Angel of the Streets." So that was why Barclay had called her that instead of mentioning the cursed river.

At that moment old Stringer finished the last of the flask. As Lauren tried to read the article over Rafe's arm, the captain spotted another audience and lurched off with an "Ahoy, mates!" to relive yet again his glorious deeds.

Rafe abruptly folded the newspaper and straightened.

"I believe we should move on."

"What does it say?" Lauren demanded. "I saw only the first few lines."

"The usual. You're an angel of mercy and I am a heartless cad."

Barclay shook his head. "How they get by with printing such stuff is beyond me. Though I can certainly see why they cast you, Miss Alcott, in the role of an angel."

Rafe groaned. "Little do they know. And what brings you to the Palace, Barr, besides spreading cheer?"

"Intentional happenstance. I overheard a certain young lady mention an outing to the Crystal Palace and decided it might be a pleasant morning for an indoor stroll myself." He looked around. "It appears she changed her plans. Still, one should never pass up an opportunity to renew one's acquaintance with parlor palms and giant goldfish."

The mischief in his face made Lauren smile. He was a peach, Barclay Howard. Rafe had interesting taste in friends.

Soon the threesome was walking around the glass palace together, sharing the pleasure of the exhibits. They paused for lemon ices from one of the vendors and perched by the topmost-floor railing to enjoy the sunshine breaking out between the clouds.

"How do you know Captain Stringer, Mr. Howard?" she asked.

He chuckled. "Only by his stories, Miss Alcott. Unlike Rafe, I was never a naval sort. He managed to survive a training stint on one of the old boy's Coastguard ships some years back."

"Quite a character," she murmured, turning to Rafe. "Was the story he told true?"

"Every word and more. You got the short version," Rafe responded, catching her gaze in his. "He is a legend in naval circles. A true hero."

She reddened under his probing gaze. He undoubtedly was wondering if she'd gotten the point of this "accidental" encounter.

"He drinks before noon, is slovenly in appearance and coarse in manner — hardly what one expects of an officer and a gentleman." She realized that her judgment, though spot-on, sounded harsh.

"You prefer your heroes sober, immaculately groomed, and courteous to a fault?" Rafe gave a deep rumble of a laugh. "In the world of make-believe stories, perhaps. In the real world, Stringer is probably as close to a living, breathing hero as you will ever come."

That confirmed her suspicion about why he had brought her here . . . to meet his version of a bona fide hero. He honestly believed she was a pampered schoolgirl with stars in her eyes. Her expression tightened.

"Do you have the time?" she asked of Barclay, having spotted the chain on his vest. "We have an engagement at three o'clock."

Barclay read his pocket watch. "Just past two."

"Then we should have the doorman summon a cab."

"Tut-tut, Miss Alcott." Barclay gave her a glowing smile. "Your intended may be a devotee of public cabs, but I am not. I gladly offer you the use of my personal chariot."

"You have no idea how far she intends to go," Rafe said curtly. He had caught the chill she was casting his way. Barclay, bless him, shot Rafe a wicked grin.

"I would take this fair angel to the ends of the earth if she asked."

Rafe shot him a dagger of a look that drew Barclay's laugh.

She beamed at Barclay as he held out his arm, and she slipped her hand through the crook of his elbow. He led her down the ornate iron steps to the entry. Rafe was left to follow with his face like a thundercloud.

After watching Barclay install his intended in the grand brougham, Rafe scowled and muttered just for his friend's ears, "Boot-licker."

Barclay gave a wicked grin and leaned just close enough to respond. "Don't tell me *you* wouldn't lick those dainty boots if you got the chance."

"What was that?" Lauren asked as they climbed into the carriage and settled, one on either side of her, causing something of a squeeze. The fact that neither would give way betrayed the subtle competition under-lying their friendship.

"Just a comment on boots . . . quite the fashion these days," Barclay said, leaning a bit too close to her for Rafe's liking.

Lauren gathered her skirts and shifted

across the carriage to sit facing the pair of
them, and Rafe smiled.

NINE

"Not this place." Barclay's dismay at the sight of the Seven Sisters wrenched a laugh from Rafe and a smile from Lauren.

"Seven Sisters makes a very tasty pork pie," she said as the carriage came to a halt. "Are you sure you won't join us?"

"Save yourself, man," Rafe said, too loudly to have been meant for Barclay alone. "The place may be infested with urchins."

"Urchins?" Barclay frowned briefly.

"We've invited a new acquaintance and his sisters for luncheon here," she explained, drawing a grimace from Rafe.

"She invited them," he explained. "One of her duties as an *angel*."

Barclay gave Rafe a wry look. "And you're an angel's accomplice now? This I must see."

There was an uncommon amount of foot traffic on the street, which was too narrow to allow a heavily loaded wagon to pass Barclay's grand carriage. The wagon driver shook his fist and snarled about "swells" taking up too much room. But part of the problem was a number of men ignoring the pavement to stalk down the middle of the street in groups, headed in the direction of the docks.

As Rafe and Barclay vied to help her down from the carriage step, the door to the Seven Sisters opened and Lauren's Aunt Amanda appeared in the doorway, along with the restaurant's agitated owner.

"Auntie A, what are you doing here?" Lauren rushed to her aunt.

"You forgot this, dear." She held up a familiar rectangular package wrapped in brown paper and string. "I thought I would bring it and see what you're up to," Amanda said, eyeing Rafe and Barclay behind her. "Quite a bit, I see."

"The books!" Lauren seized the package. "Thank you so much, Auntie A. Are Jims and his sisters here?" Her aunt seemed a bit confused and stepped back to admit her to the pub. Lauren's jaw dropped as she paused inside the entrance to the dining room.

Every chair at every table was filled with a child — no, a ragged *urchin*. And not one of them appeared to be Jims Gardiner.

The owner stammered that he didn't know how many to expect, and when they began showing up he was afraid to turn them away . . . given the piece in the newspaper. Lauren's shock was mirrored by Rafe's as he and Barclay ducked into the restaurant.

"Sweet Jesus." It was half-whispered, and she couldn't tell whether it came from Rafe or his friend until Barclay continued, "Are you running a school here or a soup kitchen?"

Lauren looked in dismay at the score of children turning to her, asking where the food was and if they'd get books, too. Two older girls stood and shushed the others.

"Miz Alcott"–they made awkward bows — "we're Jims's sisters, Polly and Althie. Jims saw the men headin' fer the docks wi' clubs and ran out to see what was happenin'."

"Happening where?" Rafe demanded.

The girls drew back, wary of his scowl, but one finally answered. "The men is grumblin' about no work — th' ships not unloadin' at the docks. They say they're goin' to make the Customs men pay."

Rafe turned to Barclay. "We kept hoping talk was all it was."

"Talk about what?" Lauren asked, touching his arm.

"The men who work the docks don't get paid if they don't unload cargo. And cargo is sitting on boats in the harbor . . . the tariffs were just raised again and some can't or won't pay them." He looked to Barclay. "Stay here. I have to see what's happening."

Before Lauren could ask what he intended to do he was out the door and charging down the street.

"What does he need to see?" She turned to Barclay, both confused and annoyed. "What does it have to do with him?"

"One of the ships sitting off the docks belongs to Townsend."

Lauren froze for a moment, remembering the lowered voices in her father's study saying that business was not proceeding as usual. Now a Townsend ship was sitting in the harbor unwilling or unable to pay the increased tariffs on the goods it was carrying. A sense of urgency she couldn't explain seized her; she had to see what was happening herself.

She turned to Aunt Amanda. "Please, Auntie A, see the children get fed and read them some stories." She dumped the parcel and a five-pound note into Amanda's arms. "Afterward give the books to them — one to each family."

"What? Wait —" Amanda's eyes widened on the restless children.

"You" — she took Barclay by the arm and pulled him out the door — "come with me."

"Gladly," he said with a smile. "Where?"

"Wherever Rafe is going."

A moment later they had dismissed the Howard carriage to wait elsewhere and were hurrying after Rafe.

As they moved toward the docks, more men joined the exodus, talking boldly about the unfairness of the government's scheme. "Protect the rich and to hell with workin' men," one of the brawny crew declared. Tariffs put them out of work and made goods too pricey to sell, they roared. Damn the bloody government for takin' food from their children's mouths!

Twice Barclay steered her into a doorway and blocked the sight of her with his big frame until a rowdy group of men passed. "You should go back, Miss Alcott. This is no place for ladies."

"I'm not a shrinking violet, Mr. Howard. You can go back if you wish." She raised her chin, studying him. "But if you come with me, you'll have to remove that top hat . . . lest one of these fellows removes it for you."

Barclay glanced around them, then did as

she suggested.

"Very well." He frowned. "But if things turn ugly . . ."

"I'll hide behind you," she said with a glowing smile.

That settled it. He straightened, carried his hat under his arm, and gave her his other arm to continue.

Rafe skirted the edge of the crowd filling the street leading to the offices of the harbormaster. He had been to the harbor offices numerous times to meet Townsend captains and pay docking fees. The harbormaster was a fairly reasonable man, caught as he was between the demands of his government superiors and the need to keep trade and commerce flowing through his domain.

It was the greedy politicians and their cronies in banking who caused the panic of '73 and sent the economy plunging. Now, seven years later, business owners and workers alike were still struggling to make ends meet. The tariffs meant to protect British industry and production had been countered by tariffs across Europe and reduced trade across the entire continent. Less demand for British goods overseas meant fewer jobs and higher prices at home. Unemployment rose, and men who had no work found ways to fill their time and make their anger known. The focus of that anger just now was the harbormaster, the most visible embodiment of the government's tariff policy.

The crowd, mostly sinewy dock workers in shirtsleeves, was packed into the brick-paved square in front of the harbormaster's office on the edge of a wharf. From the anonymity of the crowd voices were raised, demanding that ships be allowed to dock and their cargoes be released. Each demand grew louder and the mood of the crowd grew angrier.

Constables arrived, to push the men away from the harbormaster's door, swinging truncheons to clear the way. But their arrival was too late to dampen the crowd's rebellious mood. In fact, as Rafe saw it, their presence and pugnacious attitude only aggravated the situation. There was a fight in the air and these desperate men and their cause would be the losers, no matter who was left standing.

Setting his hat aside and discarding his coat, he pocketed his cuff links and rolled up his sleeves. He had learned long ago, at his bombastic father's knee, that to talk to men in shirtsleeves he'd have to *be* in shirtsleeves. A tall freight wagon of crates and casks, sitting at the edge of the square, would make a perfect platform. He burrowed his way through the mass of men and climbed up on it. He could see shoving in the middle of the crowd and realized the men at the front would soon be propelled into the line of constables now guarding the harbormaster's door.

"Dock workers! Honest, hardworking men!" He paused before repeating his call and then continuing. "I hear your anger and frustration at what is happening in the Docklands. I know your concern for your families and your livelihood. You have much at stake here. Well, so do I!"

The men closest to Rafe turned to him, glaring with suspicion.

"Who're you to tell us what we feel?" one shouted.

"My name's Townsend. One of my ships is out there in the harbor" — he pointed — "waiting for somebody to wake up and realize tariffs hurt us as much as they help us. More, even!"

There was grumbling and wary agreement as the men nearest him quieted others and dozens of skeptical faces turned to him.

"I know what you're thinking . . . I'm a businessman, a fellow who doesn't have an aching back and calluses on his hands. What do I know about you and your work?" Murmuring threatened to explode into agreement. "Well, I'll tell you!" He bellowed the next bit, as a challenge to all who might reject his presence here and his words.

"It's your livelihood, sure as hell" — he jerked a thumb at his shoulder — "but it's mine, too. Every shilling levied as a tariff takes money out of your pocket *and* mine. It forces me to cut expenses and lay off workers. Some of you have worked for Townsend Imports. You know we pay a fair wage for a day's work. And when work is short, we try to take care of our own. We're strong, but we can't force the government to remove tariffs any more than you can."

There was muttering and some agreement among the men, but he couldn't make out whether or not he had established common ground.

"My ship has been out there nine days now — waiting, watching, hoping the government will see reason. I'm frustrated, too. But I also know that storming the harbor-master's or the Customs House won't do anything but harden the government's determination and make them reject every word you utter."

He could see a few nods, and the increasing quiet spurred him to the next logical step.

"You need to make them see what they're doing to the import-export trade and the men that make it happen. You can only do that if you put it in words they understand."

"Don't need no words!" One worker, whose tolerance for talk had long since expired, raised a club and shook it. "They'll understand *this*!"

"Shut yer gob an' listen to th' man!" came a booming voice nearby.

"Shut yer own damned gob, ye toady!"

And the first blow was struck.

A handful of men began wrestling and bashing one another, but those who tried to break up the fight ran into those eager to see it ignite into a full melee. There didn't seem to be many weapons at first, but the moment one overzealous combatant was shoved back by a constable, billy clubs, saps, and lengths of bare wood materialized. No amount of shouting for calm and reason could staunch the rush of anger and the venting of frustrations.

Rafe jumped off the wagon and shoved through the chaos, making for the harbormaster's door, but he wasn't the only one with that destination in mind. A score of men with makeshift weapons were aimed at the knot of uniformed constables blockading the entrance.

Lauren watched, gripping Barclay Howard's arm with icy fingers, as the violence broke out. Rafe had shed his hat and coat and climbed up on a wagon bed to try to talk this hostile crowd into a more reasonable approach. He stood above the men with his sleeves rolled up, looking big and earnest. He tried to make them see that their plight was part of a larger problem, that he shared their goals and their anger. Every word rang of power and sincerity in a way she hadn't imagined hearing from him.

Braving the angry crowd to call for a measured course, he was a pillar of reason. She was mesmerized by the certainty and determination he projected. Then she spotted what she thought was a familiar face in the crowd — a little face.

Jims? Was that Jims Gardiner?

She called his name and started toward him, but there was a flurry of motion in the crowd that blocked the way, and she heard Barclay utter a "damn it" behind her. He pulled her back against a wall at the side of the mob, but they were spotted by angry dock workers who took exception to the presence of "toffs" and "laidies" among them. Broad-shouldered Barclay thrust her behind him, ducked a blow, and then came up swinging.

She was grateful for his vigorous defense, but her attention was riveted on the spot where Jims had disappeared. Was he trapped in the chaos? He was a scrawny little thing — he could be fighting for his life. She had to find him.

Instead of slipping away along the wall as Barclay ordered, she went in the opposite direction — skirting the edge of the conflict, searching for Jims. She called to him again and again as she dodged and darted, keeping to the edge of the crowd.

Then she rose onto her tiptoes to look for the boy and spotted Rafe instead, caught between a rank of constables brandishing clubs and a score of armed and angry workers straining to get to the harbormaster's door.

"You can't get in — the door is barred!" he roared, trying to hold them back. "The time for talking is over. You need to retreat and regroup. The next time you come, you have to come with shipowners, importers, and warehouse managers beside you . . . a united front. We've all got a stake in this. To make the politicians listen, we have to come together!"

Out of the crowd came a burly arm with a club that caught the side of his head and sent him sprawling. She screamed as the mob surged over him and lunged for the constables. Somewhere at the bottom of that mass of fury, Rafe lay wounded . . . perhaps gravely.

Frantic now, she focused on the spot where he had gone down and ducked and shoved her way through the crowd. She found him dazed and struggling to rise.

"Rafe!" She tried to help him up but only managed to get him to his knees. "Get up — you have to get up!"

She dragged his arm around her neck and tried to pull him up with her. He weighed a ton, but he seemed to realize she was helping and put what effort he could into standing. It took her a moment to realize Jims was on Rafe's other side, with a thin little arm around him. She could do nothing but point to the dock at the side of the harbormaster's building. He was leaning heavily on them as they dragged him from the fray, but he managed to make it to the side of the building before collapsing to his knees again.

At least he was out of the main fracas. She released him against the side of the building and straightened. His eyes were closed and

141

his head drooped as he slumped against the wall. She stroked his face and looked at Jims.

"I have to get help. Can you stay here with him?"

"Aye, miz." Jims nodded. "I'll stay by 'im."

Barclay was her only hope, and she had left him on the far side of the square. She looked around for something to stand on and spotted the wagon Rafe had used. She reached it, lifted her skirts, and climbed up on it to search for Barclay.

Dark-uniformed constables now dotted the teeming crowd, but they didn't seem to be trying to restore order — more like cracking the heads of the protesters with abandon. She couldn't see Barclay anywhere and tried calling out to him.

The sound of a woman calling for help shocked some of the men closest to her — those doing more shoving and name-calling than actual fighting. Some were distracted long enough to look up. She shouted to Barclay that they needed him . . . Rafe was injured and they needed help.

Barnaby Pinkum watched from the roof of a warehouse above the square that fronted the harbormaster's office. He had followed his angel and Townsend to the restaurant they'd visited the day before only to have them head on foot to a square near the docks where angry longshoremen had gathered.

When he saw Townsend climb up on a wagon to address the crowd, he pulled out his pencil and pad and took down the toff's words in a flurry. So Townsend was styling himself a friend of the working man, eh? This was a new tactic. Then the reason was revealed: A Townsend ship lay in the harbor because Townsend Imports was unwilling — or unable — to pay the mounting tariffs. The son of wealth and privilege claimed a common interest with the men who handled his company's freight and made his comfortable life possible. And he sounded surprisingly sincere.

This could be a new twist on the editorials *The Examiner* had run denouncing tariffs and demanding that the government withdraw them. A bit of real news. If only he had a chance to write about that, instead of blathering on about a rich female's do-gooder deeds and rocky romance.

Then Townsend was knocked down and he spotted the angel's gold-feathered hat as she braved the dangerous crowd to reach her fiancé's side. They disappeared from view for a few moments, then she re-

143

appeared and climbed up on the same wagon Townsend had used. She began calling and then beseeching the crowd to cease the violence and return to reason. At least that was what he assumed she would be saying. He couldn't make out her words in the din. The men nearest her staggered to a stop and looked up . . . likely shocked that a mere female would demand attention in such a mob.

After a moment she was helped down — or taken down — by the crowd. He glimpsed her golden hat bobbing here and there until she disappeared at the side of the harbormaster's office.

Alarmed, he headed for the drainpipe he had climbed to his vantage point and was soon on the street again. There was still fighting, but additional constables were arriving in numbers to put down the unrest. As their whistles trilled, protesters at the edge of the crowd abandoned the struggle and ran. The fresh crew of constables advanced, pushing the protesters toward the waiting clubs of those guarding the harbormaster's door. More of the protesters dropped their weapons and fled for the safety of side streets or boats tied up along the nearby wharf.

Barnaby was able to creep around the

square to the place he had last seen Lauren Alcott. On the wagon he found Townsend's coat and expensive top hat, which he quickly snatched, but there was no trace of her. Men lay scattered around the square, some groaning in pain, some silent and still where they had fallen. None of them looked like Townsend.

He hid from the constables as they cleared the square and tossed the remaining rioters and victims into the Black Marias that arrived. When all was quiet he climbed down from the crates in the wagon to search for Lauren Alcott and her intended. He hadn't seen them leave and they weren't among the poor blighters arrested and hauled away. They couldn't have gone inside the harbormaster's office; the door had been barred during the chaos.

As he leaned against the side of the harbormaster's office, thinking what to do next, he spotted something on the narrow dock that ran alongside the building and served as mooring for the skiffs the harbormaster and his inspectors used to row out to ships.

Just feet from a ladder that led down to the murky water lay a hat . . . a lady's hat . . . sparrow-shaped, with brilliant gold feathers.

He hurried to pick it up. One side had

been crushed; some of the feathers were broken. He looked up and around, focusing on the ships anchored in protest away from the docks.

Where was she, his Angel of the Streets?

TEN

Lauren struggled against the ropes binding her. She lay in the bottom of a longboat, one shoulder soaking in the cold water puddled along the keel. Four — there were four men in the boat besides Rafe, who lay unconscious between her and Jims. She had thought the men were helping her down from the wagon at first. When she told them about Rafe needing help and they rushed her toward the side of the harbormaster's building. But when she reached the place where she had left Rafe and Jims, she saw them being carried — Rafe bound hand and foot and Jims tussling to break free of his captors — to the end of the dock.

She screamed as two other men dragged her toward the same fate, but her cry was swallowed up in the noise of the fighting. They bound her with rope, stuffed a rag in her mouth, and told her to "shut it" or she'd be dropped in the water. Now she ached from being manhandled and lowered to a boat waiting below. No amount of resistance could possibly overcome the four men in the boat, the ropes binding her from shoulders to knees, and the fact that Rafe and Jims were lying helpless beside her.

They were being abducted and taken . . . somewhere in the Docklands, probably . . . but it made no sense. Why would anyone abduct her or Rafe? Did it have to do with Rafe's speech? Were these men part of the mob he'd tried to divert? Who else could they be?

She strained against the ropes, frantic to find a way out of her bonds and out of the longboat. Her thoughts always came back to the same place: even if she managed to escape, Rafe and Jims would still be in their hands, and she would have no idea where they had been taken. She had to wait to see where they were taking her, get Rafe and Jims to wake up, and find a way to get them all to safety.

They were hauled aboard a ship and dumped unceremoniously on the deck. Rafe was groggy and, from what she could tell, less restrained by ropes than she was. His hands were tied, but he seemed to be struggling to look around and make sense of their circumstances. Poor Jims lay sprawled on the deck looking small and fragile.

"So you're Rafe Townsend," came a voice from nearby.

Rafe looked up and blinked, trying to focus on the man in a dark uniform looming over them. "I am." His voice sounded raspy and unstable. "Who the devil are you?"

"Acting captain of the *Clarion,* Juster Morgan."

"The *Clarion*? Our *Clarion*?" Rafe declared, finally reaching full throat. "Where is Captain Pettigrew? I demand to see the captain."

There was a moment of silence before Morgan responded. Lauren rolled onto her side to look around. They were surrounded by sailors, all of whom wore expressions of concern.

"He's dead."

That took a moment to register with Rafe.

"Dead?" He looked around at the glowering crew. "You mutinied?" That started a rumble of anger in the men.

"Of course not," Morgan declared hotly. "The captain was so overcome by anger at this vile standoff that his heart seized and he fell dead. Afterward a handful of men went overboard — deserting to be with their families. As first mate, it was my duty to assume command and enforce discipline on the rest."

Rafe shook his head. "Pettigrew is truly dead?"

"Aye, sir," came another voice. It was a small, wiry fellow with a grizzled but earnest countenance. "Standin' on the deck not far from here, givin' the harbormaster's office a raised fist an' a royal tongue-lashin.' Clutched his chest, he did, staggered, an' fell stone dead."

"He had no family, so he lies in the deep hold," Morgan continued, "awaiting proper burial at sea."

"Wrapped him up good, we did. Our capt'n — a fine man, he were," offered a tall, stringy fellow wearing a striped, seaman's shirt.

"And what is the purpose of abducting us and hauling us onto a ship that my company owns?" He struggled to sit up and was finally helped onto his sitting bones by that tall, stringy fellow. "Have you lost your minds?" He glanced around and realized she was there, too. "And not only me, but my intended wife and a defenseless child!"

"Not so defenseless," came a low grumble from a burly crewman rubbing his arm. "Th' little sod bit me."

"Unfortunate, that," Morgan said sharply.

"But having them here will make it all the more urgent for those bastards to get matters sorted. Your father is known in the trade for being a tough dealer, but this time he's met his match. To get you and your bride back, he'll have to pay the tariffs, get our cargo to shore, and pay me and my crew."

"If he don't pay, you stay right here." The burly fellow Jims had bitten jabbed a gnarled finger at the deck beneath them.

"For how long?" Rafe demanded. "How long do you think my father and the port authorities will put up with a ransom demand?"

"If he won't pay" — Morgan's eyes glinted — "we'll find someone who will." He turned to his crew. "Take them below. Put them in the brig."

When they removed Lauren's bonds Jims scrambled across the deck and into her open arms. The threesome was taken down the hatch steps to a dark passage that smelled musty and damp and grew worse as they progressed downward through the ship. They were soon shoved into a small enclosure set with iron bars and filled with nautical odds and ends. Apparently they didn't use the space for much but housing rope, lumber, and stacks of spare sail canvas.

151

The wiry old fellow, who the others called Fosse, seemed a bit uneasy about their treatment of her, for he called her ma'am and promised to speak to "Actin' Capt'n Morgan" on her behalf. He made no such promise to Rafe, however, as he produced a ring of keys and locked them in the cell as he left.

"Wait!" she called after him, rushing to the bars. When Fosse turned back she pleaded, "Mr. Townsend's been injured and needs tending. I need clean water and toweling, and whatever medicinals you have on board." When Fosse scowled, she added softly, "Please — he's on your side. He came to the docks to try to find a way to make the harbormaster see reason. You can't just let him lie here in pain."

Fosse looked as if he might speak, but then turned and hurried back up the stairs.

A small lantern just outside the cell provided meager light, and the cell's proximity to the iron hull of the ship meant a serious chill pervaded the area. Lauren shivered and rubbed her wrists, then checked Jims's reddened face.

"Are you all right?" She inspected his bruised jaw and split lip.

"Yeah. Tha' big bugger hits like a kickin' mule." He winced from bruised pride as much as pain. "I tried to stop 'em, miz."

"I know you did, Jims. It was gallant of you. But there were just too many of them." She ruffled his hair, then turned to the stacks of canvas where Rafe sat slumped against a large spool of rope.

"Are you all right?" she said, focusing on the dried blood on his temple and pushing back his hair to determine the extent of the injury. His eyes were closed and she wasn't sure he had heard her. "Are you awake?"

"My head hurts like the devil himself is —" He opened one eye in a pained squint and his voice faded. "I'm afraid I — may — not —"

As his eye closed and his head drooped, she felt his hands and realized he was even colder than she was. The spare canvas stacked around them was too stiff and heavy to provide any warmth. Her main petticoat was wet on one side, but it was all she had. She had Jims turn his head, then raised her skirt and slipped out of the heavy muslin to wrap Rafe in the dry part. Thank heaven his feet weren't wet.

Still, it wasn't long before he began to shiver, and she knew she would have to do more. They needed blankets. She called out to that Fosse fellow again and again without raising him or anyone else.

"When I gets shivers," Jims said, rubbing his own thin arms, "Ma climbs under th' blanket wi' me."

"Body heat." Her smile felt weak as she nodded. Together, they dragged Rafe over to lie on the stacked canvas and she climbed up and curled onto her side around him. She rubbed his arms and shoulders and pressed her body tightly against his, sharing with him what warmth she still retained. When she looked up Jims was sitting on the edge of the canvas, hugging himself and looking miserable. She sat up, took off her jacket, and held it out to him. "Put this on."

He shook his head, but when she insisted he did put it on and wrapped his arms around his middle with a small sigh of relief. "Thanks, miz."

After a while Rafe's shivering eased and she felt his body respond with rising warmth that eased her own bone-deep chill. Fatigue set in and she closed her eyes, giving herself over to it until she sensed movement.

She raised her head to look around and found Jims, struggling to squeeze through the bars of their cell.

"Jims! What are you doing? We're on a ship — you can't escape."

She sat up in alarm as the boy twisted and shoved his rail-thin body outside their

154

prison. "Where are you going? Can you even swim?"

He stood, pulled her jacket tight around him, and pressed a finger to his lips to gesture for silence. A heartbeat later he had disappeared into the darkness and the stacks of crates and barrels that filled the hold of the ship. What was the boy doing? And what would happen to him when the *Clarion*'s crew caught him?

"Be careful, Jims," she said on a prayer. "Heaven watch over you."

She checked Rafe, feeling his head and hands. He seemed warmer and she sank back beside him. She was exhausted. Sometime later she awakened to find her head on his shoulder and her arm curled tightly over his chest. He lay on his back, watching her.

"This is a surprise," he said, his voice husky . . . or maybe just dry. If only they had some water.

"You were shivering. Body warmth was all I had to help you."

He looked down at the petticoat wrapping his shoulders and belly.

"I see you managed to take your clothes off again."

"Only one petticoat. And in a good cause."

"So, saving me is a good cause?"

"In the present circumstances." She gazed

155

into his eyes and felt a strange arousal in her deepest core. It probably wasn't wise to continue this conversation in such close proximity, but the sensation was too interesting not to explore. "I called again and again for that Fosse fellow, hoping to get blankets and some water, but he didn't come and you were so cold . . . I . . . had to do something."

"Most charitable of you. Perhaps I can repay you someday."

"You already have," she said, her voice now oddly resonant. "I was cold and miserable, too. I shared my warmth, you shared yours."

"You didn't find such contact objectionable?" He glanced at her arm, which was still wrapped around his ribs.

"The chill may have affected my judgment."

His smile, at such close range, was mesmerizing. Her gaze slid to his lips as she wondered . . .

Apparently he was wondering the same thing.

He leaned to touch hers lips with his. It felt like an invitation to exploration, and after a moment something inside her relaxed. She responded with the same gentle curiosity, tilting her head and absorbing every nuance of that contact. A flow of something more complicated than warmth began between them, and when the kiss ended she had the odd feeling of that connection lingering.

She drew back her arm and opened her eyes to his surprisingly sober expression. It jolted her. Had she done something wrong? She was not exactly experienced at this kissing business.

He swallowed hard, then drew back a telling inch or two, which brought heat to her cheeks.

She would *not* blush.

"We have to do something," he said, squeezing his eyes shut as if in pain. "We're being held for a ransom my father will never pay."

It took a moment for her to quell her disappointment at the change in him and right her thoughts. "You mean he would truly refuse to pay the tariffs and crew to free us?"

"They're no longer just a crew; they're outlaws. Abducting us, no matter how dire their situation or noble their intentions, has made them criminals. My father is more likely to set the law on them than part with hard-earned coin."

It was a sobering thought, accompanied

by the realization that they could be held on the ship for a long time . . . unless the harbor constables intervened. Would they try to board the ship to rescue two people, even ones from prominent families?

She sat up, grateful for something to take her mind from the awkwardness of their differing responses to that kiss. He obviously didn't think it quite up to par.

"Talk to them," she said, "the way you did to the protesters outside the harbormaster's office."

"It didn't work then. What makes you think it would work now?" He pushed up onto an elbow and rubbed his face.

"I don't know. Perhaps if you say that we understand their grievances and that if they let us go, we will . . . will . . . personally pay the tariffs and wages and won't press charges against them."

He sat up slowly and she scooted back, watching him wrestle with both the pain in his head and their predicament. He searched her face and looked as if he were struggling to summon words.

"The minute my father receives a ransom demand, he will shut down the Townsend accounts. He can't abide being forced into anything — certainly not by those he considers 'underlings.' What about you? Would you happen to have a spare thousand pounds just moldering about?"

"A thousand pounds?" She was staggered by the sum.

"I don't know the entire inventory. Captains have some discretion as to what additional freight they bring on board when there is room. It could be closer to two thousand."

"Two thousand pounds?" She swallowed hard.

Truth be told, she had no idea how much money she had. There seemed to be sufficient funds for dresses, hats, and seaside holidays, but she was always careful not to test the limits of her good fortune.

She did have an inheritance from her mother that was managed by trustees. She had asked her father about it when she turned eighteen and was told that her grandfather had entailed it on her mother and the entailment stood for her as well. Could it be made available to her? Even if it could be, how could she explain the situation and convince the trustees of her need for it while being held against her will on a ship in London's harbor?

"We're in dire straits, I'm afraid," she said, frowning. "What money I have is in the hands of trustees at the Bank of England. I can't imagine them handing over a few thousand pounds to meet the demands of a merchantman's crew that's gone rogue."

Footsteps drew their attention. Fosse was back with an armful of blankets. The tall, stringy fellow he called Gus accompanied him, bearing a wooden box that clinked as if there were glass bottles inside. Fosse unlocked the cell door and ordered them to stay back as the pair entered. They unloaded the blankets on a nearby stack of canvas and set the box on the floor.

"Miz, yer to come with me," he declared, beckoning to her. "Captain says you're to stay in th' first mate's cabin." She stared at the man for a moment, surprised by this abrupt change in accommodations. She turned to help Rafe up, and Fosse added, "Not him, miz. Just you. He's to stay here." He looked around, scowling. "Where's the boy?"

Rafe looked at her in surprise, too. Apparently he hadn't realized Jims had been brought below with them.

"I have no idea. I was tending to Mr. Townsend and must have fallen asleep. When I woke up he was gone."

"How'd th' little sod escape?" tall, skinny Gus demanded, stepping to the door to glare into the gloomy hold outside.

"Blackbeard's bollocks — Morgan'll be sore." Fosse paused to look them over and make a quick calculation. "He can't have got far. We'll find 'im. An' when we do . . ." He tried to usher Lauren to the door without touching her. "On yer way, miz. We ain't got all day."

"I'm not going anywhere by myself. I am Mr. Townsend's intended wife and I won't be separated from him. He's been grievously injured. If I am given better accommodations, he must be also." She watched the pair exchange doubtful glances and continued. "There will be the devil to pay if the *Clarion*'s owner learns his son was mistreated in your care. You have not even provided us with water or food in how many hours?"

As if on cue, Rafe rose and staggered slightly. The bruises on his face and dried blood on his temple reinforced her claim of injury.

She purposefully met Fosse's gaze, and the earnest *please, please, please* in her thoughts must have shone in her eyes. He looked down and shifted his feet.

"Aww-right," he said reluctantly, giving tall Gus an elbow and pointing to the wooden box on the floor. "We'll take ye both up." He pulled an old flintlock pistol

161

from the back of his waist and cocked it. "Ye'd best try nothin.' "

Good as gold, they were, as they climbed two sets of stairs and found themselves admitted to a small, smelly cabin fitted with a narrow bunk, shelves built into the wall, a dusty washbasin, and linen that probably hadn't been changed through several of the *Clarion*'s voyages. She went straight to the small window and threw it open, only to find the smells of the harbor not much of an improvement.

"Here — whaddaya think yer doin'?" Fosse rushed to shut the crusty window and wave his pistol at her . . . which she saw in the better light was badly rusted.

"It smells in here." She straightened, unintimidated, and adopted Aunt Amanda's most emphatic manner. "We need water to drink, fresh air, and clean linen. You need to air that mattress. Bring me a broom, some clean cloths, vinegar, and water for cleaning." She turned to Gus. "If you would be so good as to put the medicine box on the washstand and find us a chair or two . . ."

Rafe watched her take charge as if she'd been born royal. This was a side of her he hadn't imagined, considering her charitable convictions and tender mercies toward the less fortunate. Damn if she didn't have the makings of a dowager duchess inside that nubile frame.

It wasn't long before Gus and a cabin boy they called "Little Rob" returned with a broom, an armload of linen, pails of water, vinegar, and, of all things, a feather duster.

Under her direction the pair set about cleaning the cabin, airing the mattress, and scrubbing the floor. To Rafe's surprise, she seized the feather duster and cleaned the shelves herself, muttering that a Mrs. Beeton would not approve and examining the books belonging to the former occupant. Afterward she hiked her skirts and climbed up on the bunk to wipe down the shiplap walls and take down the lantern for cleaning. Two chairs were provided, and a Delft porcelain washbasin and pitcher and toweling identified as the late captain's soon appeared. After he leaned out the window and determined there were no viable escape possibilities, Fosse grudgingly allowed them to keep the portal open to freshen the air.

As they worked, Lauren asked questions about their recent voyage, their cargo, and the short-lived mutiny that had sent some of the crew over the side. Little Rob, no more than nine years old, seemed fascinated by her and answered every question with

163

more information than was strictly necessary. But when she asked about the boy who came aboard with them — if he'd been found — Little Rob reddened, glanced at Gus, and disavowed any knowledge of Jims. She smiled and asked him to keep an eye out and let her know when he was found. He relaxed and nodded.

Rafe found himself watching her perfect posture, the simple grace of her movements, the smiles that made Little Rob and pole-thin Gus's ears redden. Like them, he watched her every expression, for every nuance of acceptance and approval from her. It should have worried him, this deepening fascination with her. But truth be told, he'd never met or even imagined a woman who would, *could* do the things she did. Everything about her was unexpected, including her self-possession while being abducted and held against her will. Most women would be swooning, weeping, or at the least wringing their hands.

Not Miss Alcott, Angel of the River and the Streets. She ripped off her petticoat and wrapped it and *herself* around him to warm him. Then she demanded — and received — better treatment for them both.

When she spread a blanket over the bare wooden bunk and directed him to lie down and rest, he was so unsteady on his feet that he complied. She searched the box of medicinals and came up with a tincture that she said should help the ache in his head. Even added to the hot tea provided by Gus, it was barely palatable. But she insisted, so he downed it all. A bowl of soup and a mug of ale settled his stomach.

As the medicine took effect, he fell into a restless sleep that gradually deepened.

When he awoke Gus and Little Rob had finished and withdrawn, and the cabin was fully dark. She had draped her petticoat over one chair near the window to dry and pulled up the other chair beside the bunk, which she now leaned against with her head on her arms on the mattress beside him, breathing softly, slowly. She had fallen asleep, too, and for a while he just watched her sleep. After a while she must have sensed his attention. She stirred and sat up, putting a hand to her lower back and stretching up with a wince.

He closed his eyes, but she had already caught that he was awake. "How are you?" she asked.

"I'll recover." He opened his eyes again. "The medicine worked. My head is feeling better."

"Good. Don't go back to sleep." She

rubbed her face. "We have things to do."

"And how do you suggest I stay awake?"

"By helping me plan our escape."

He groaned and raised his head to glance at the locked cabin door.

"I am not up for another round of head-cracking just yet." He sighed and then rolled up onto an elbow to study her. "Here's an idea . . . why don't you try charming them into releasing us?"

She narrowed her eyes. "I doubt Acting Captain Morgan is susceptible to any enticement that doesn't involve money."

"You underestimate your powers of persuasion. You seemed to mesmerize Gus and the boy."

She pulled out one of the drawers beneath the bunk and propped her feet on it. "I was merely being pleasant, hoping to elicit a similar response in return." She cut him a glance. "It doesn't always work."

The implication struck.

"Who doesn't it work on?" From her mood, he felt he knew.

She turned to look directly at him. "You."

He frowned, though the effort caused his face to hurt.

"When were you pleasant to me?"

She scowled. "I was more than pleasant when I sacrificed my petticoat to keep you

166

warm. You didn't even bother to say 'thank you.' "

"I didn't?" He glimpsed a more personal pique behind her upraised chin. "Horrible of me. I thought perhaps the kiss said it all. May not have been up to my usual standard. I'll try to do better next time."

"Next time?" She seemed genuinely unsettled by the prospect.

"We are betrothed," he said. "It's not uncommon for engaged couples to show affection."

"That blow to the head left you addled," she said, her color rising.

"While in captivity we could make good use of the time." He gave a wicked half smile. "It wouldn't hurt to have a bit of practice."

Eleven

"You are without a doubt the most conceited, illmannered man I have ever had the misfortune to —"

"Kiss?" He smiled, as if pleased to have roused her pride. "Who do you compare me to, Miss Alcott? How many men have you kissed?"

"None of your business, Mr. Townsend." Why was he talking about kisses when he — *hadn't disliked their kiss after all.*

"It may become my business if we are forced to" — his handsome eyes searched her defenses — "make our association permanent."

"If we are trapped into marriage, you mean?" She straightened up and crossed her arms. "If it comes to that, you will have to answer for your own qualifications. *Taking* pleasure does not assure that one can *give* it."

He sat up, staring at her in surprise, as

the sound of a bell clanging came through the open window, growing steadily louder.

"What is that?" She shot to her feet and rushed to the window to search the dark harbor for the source of the sound. She heard him slide from the bunk and sensed he was joining her, though she refused to look.

"A fireboat," he muttered, pointing to a small, steampowered vessel weaving furiously between dark hulks of anchored ships toward a plume of smoke at the far end of the docking berths.

"Fireboat?" She stretched out the window to see better. "A boat is on fire?"

"Not necessarily." He pushed his head out the window, blocking her direct view. "The fireboats pump water to put out warehouse fires along the docks, as well as any boats that catch fire."

"I never thought about a boat catching fire. Does that happen often?"

"Once in a while," he answered, craning his neck to see where the smoke originated. "The Docklands are full of decrepit old warehouses — disasters waiting to happen. They're crowded against the river's edge and the Metropolitan Fire Brigade has a devil of a time getting to them. So it's up to the fireboats to pump water from the harbor

169

to see those blazes don't spread."

"But it could be a ship?" she asked, assailed by competing thoughts as she tried to see past him.

Half of her mind was focused on the fire situation and whatever about it suddenly seemed important. The other half was reeling from awareness of his closeness and the sensations that were making her breath quicken and heart race. She could feel heat radiating from him as he crowded into the window beside her and once again felt the surprising hardness of his arm and shoulder pressed against her. His hair was mussed and there was a hint of beard shadow on his jaw. He smelled like musk with a hint of sandalwood and something piquant she wanted more of but couldn't name.

He must have felt her gaze, for he turned slowly toward her.

She looked up into his darkening eyes and felt a rising curiosity that had to be satisfied. Without another thought, she grabbed his shirtfront with both hands, hauled him against her, and pressed her lips to his.

This was no tentative exploration, no impulsive expression of curiosity. This was desire for whatever pleasures a thorough kiss could provide. As her lips pressed his, sensation trickled along her nerves . . .

through her face and down her throat. Her skin tingled in a way that made her catch her breath briefly. It felt like her body — bone and sinew — was hungry for contact with his big, solid frame.

She sank into his arms and into a kiss deeper and more pleasurable than she had ever imagined. She parted her lips as his tongue traced them and soon was returning that teasing flicker of sensation. Her whole body reacted, some parts softening and others tightening with expectation. She wrapped her arms around his ribs and pressed against his length . . . a reaction as natural as breathing and unstoppable as a sneeze.

A new, sensual awareness filled her as his lips wandered from hers, over her cheek, down her throat. She held her breath. His kisses, wherever placed, were just as potent. She traced his back and shoulders, exploring, drinking in sensations, then slid her fingers up his neck and into his hair. Every texture was fascinating, and exploring them somehow heightened the pleasure of his kisses.

She scarcely heard the metallic scrape of the key in the lock and staggered slightly when he released her.

"Brought yer supper." Fosse's voice and

the light of his lantern jarred her back to ordinary time. She squinted, disoriented. It was as if she'd been startled awake in the depths of a vivid dream. She stepped back against the wall for support as cabin boy Little Rob carried bowls of stew to the washstand and the old seaman hung his lantern overhead.

"What is happening?" Rafe asked, investigating the food. "Have you sent word to my father?"

"Capt'n Morgan sent a message ashore." Fosse's eyes narrowed slightly as he looked from Rafe to her. She had to keep herself from covering her kiss-reddened lips. "Ain't heard nothin' back." He paused a moment. "I'll be bringin' the mattress back shortly."

"Any word on the boy Jims?" she asked.

"Slippery little bugger. Ain't seen hide nor hair of 'im."

With that, Fosse and Little Rob exited and locked the door behind them, leaving a prickly bit of tension mingling with the aroma of stew in the air. She stayed where she was, waiting for strength to fully return to her legs. He picked up a bowl and carried it to her.

"I believe you're hungry."

When she looked up he wore a knowing half smile that brought fading color back to her face. She straightened, making herself look up.

"So I am," she said. "And this actually smells palatable."

"Townsend Imports hires the best cooks we can find for our ships. It's the way we keep crews."

"Really? That is clever of you."

"We know our business, Miss Alcott."

"Lauren," she offered. "It seems silly to insist on formalities now that we're prisoners together."

"Lauren." His gaze drifted over her. "Whatever we Townsends do, we do well." She had a feeling he wasn't just talking about imports and commerce. Blasted man.

She took the bowl and headed for the chair beside the bunk. He retrieved his own bowl and took a seat on the bunk.

"I've been thinking about our situation," she said between spoonfuls of surprisingly good beef stew. Tucked into the side of the bowl was a thick slice of dense bread that had soaked up the gravy. She nibbled it and paused to let the flavors fill her head and calm her chaotic thoughts.

She looked up to find him watching her intently. Did he think she'd lost her wits, or that she'd just proved herself a shameless hussy? She was afraid to give him time to

173

consider either.

"You know, if you're correct about your father's refusal to pay, we'll have to do something ourselves. And soon." She forced herself to consider the snatches of information she had garnered about their situation. "This could get out of hand quickly."

Rafe lowered his gaze and blinked. He was scrambling for mental footing here. He took another giant spoonful of stew and chewed. One minute she was reducing him to a pile of cinders with her lips and the next she was talking about escape plans and resolving this mess without open warfare. How could the woman change so completely from one minute to the next? She switched from passion to reason as easily as flipping a coin.

He shook himself, trying to jolt his faculties back to functioning, and realized his headache was gone. A moment later he managed to put together a coherent thought.

"I don't know if you noticed," he said, "but there were men on the decks of nearby ships, watching the protests of the dock workers and even cheering them on. Some have been sitting in the harbor much longer than the *Clarion*. If the harbor police or

Coastguard are called in to board this ship, they could ignite a wholesale battle for control of the harbor."

She nodded, raking her teeth across her lip as she thought.

"By now your father has received their ultimatum." She paused, considering what action might counter an assault on the ship. "I don't suppose we could get a message to him, asking him to delay any action from the harbor police until we can find a way to escape?"

"And just how do you propose we do that? Bribe the cabin boy?"

She straightened, put her half-finished dinner aside, and looked at him with delight. "Rafe Townsend, you're brilliant."

"I am?" He was both puzzled and annoyingly pleased. "You realize that is the first compliment you've ever given me?"

"You're not exactly one to hand out plaudits yourself," she said, turning toward the bookshelf and searching the spines of the books she had dusted earlier. "Here." She pulled a tall, thin volume and opened it to scan the contents. "Exactly what a boy growing up at sea would like."

"What?" He came off the bunk to peer into the book with her.

"Tales of the sea," she said. "Stories of

heroic captains and valiant crews. Great tempests and deadly perils. Foreign lands and exotic ways."

His jaw dropped.

"You propose to *read* him into cooperation?"

"There isn't a boy born who can resist a good yarn." She looked up at him. "I bet even you are susceptible, being a lover of the sea."

"Oh no." He straightened and glowered. "Not me."

"But you were a navy man — a midshipman at the Academy."

"*Were* being the operative word. I am not —" He broke off that thought and raised his chin. "And if we were able to get a message to my father or yours, what then? How do you plan to defuse this standoff and get us out of here without mayhem?"

"I'm sure we'll think of something," she said with determination.

"Because we're so good at putting our heads together?" He looked straight into the golden rings in her eyes and was seized by the urge to pull her against him and demonstrate. The color rising in her cheeks said she sensed his double meaning, and he could have sworn she was suppressing a smile.

"That is yet to be seen, but I have reason to hope."

Quiet settled over the ship as the crew's daily duties were done and the evening meal was finished. Music from a harmonica floated in the window, and when the mattress was returned and made up, Lauren began reading a story to Rafe and invited Little Rob to stay and listen. Surprised, he climbed onto a chair between her and the bunk, curiosity glowing in his eyes. He had heard plenty of sailors' stories, he said. The crew told tales as they smoked their pipes of an evening.

But the story Lauren read was something different . . . a story of pirates taking a prize and sailing to a special island in the Caribbean. There was treasure, betrayal, and heroic action enough to light the boy's eyes with desire for an adventure of his own. Sensing the time was right, she asked if he had seen the sights of London . . . if he ever went ashore. He said there was a provisions boat that went at dawn to avoid the Customs patrols and once in a while they took him along. She looked sad for a moment as she spoke of her fear that her family would be frantic over her disappearance. Little Rob sank fully under her spell.

"I got a ma. I miss her, too."

She looked at him, seeing in his face a genuine longing.

Just then the door flew open and Acting Captain Morgan barged in to order Little Rob out of the cabin and cuffed his ear. Then he scoured his former quarters and its inmates with a glare of suspicion. Lauren gasped when he snatched the book from her hands.

"Don't think you'll be charming my crew into helping you. You're going nowhere until we see the tariffs paid and our pay chest delivered." He strode to the shelves and filled his arms with the books. "You'll not be needing these. You're not on holiday here."

He charged out with the books and barked an order for Gus to lock the door and keep watch to see no one went in or out of the cabin. The last thing Lauren saw as the door closed was the cabin boy peeking ruefully around Gus's dolorous form.

She turned to Rafe with a breath of relief. "There goes our plan."

"Miserable bastard," he said, scowling at the door. "When this is over that is the one man I want to see charged." His face and voice both darkened. "Now I'll never know how that pirate story came out."

When it struck Lauren couldn't help laughing. A minute later Rafe joined her, and she couldn't help thinking that his laugh was unexpectedly lovely to hear.

The kitchen door of Alcott House stood open to the evening air, and Barnaby Pinkum waited behind the metal bins for one of the manservants to exit with the kitchen leavings. It took a while, but a man he recognized by the name of Rupert exited with a huge pile of leftover food. Barnaby sprung up and gave him a shock.

"What're you doin' here?" the fellow demanded.

"Rupert, right? Say, is that roast chicken?" He gestured to the great platter the man held. "I'll give ye a sixpence for the rest of that bird."

Rupert glowered, looked over his shoulder at the darkened kitchen, and then nodded. When the bird was wrapped in newspaper and in Barnaby's possession, he had one more offer to make.

"There's another waitin' for th' answer to a question."

"I ain't sayin' nothing bad about the Alcotts," the man said firmly.

"Ain't askin' ye to." Barnaby grinned "Just want to know if Miss Alcott is home tonight.

179

Did she and her man come back this evening?"

The fellow studied both him and the question as Barnaby bit into a chicken leg and watched for a response.

"She ain't home," the fellow finally said. "Went off with Mr. Townsend this mornin' and ain't come home. Missed dinner, an' Miz Perrix and Mr. Alcott were worried off their feed. Then Old Man Townsend came — boilin' mad." The man was warming to his tale. Like most house servants, he was eager to talk about the goings-on in the family they served. "Him an' Mr. Alcott and Miz Perrix talked in the drawin' room wi' the doors closed. Miz Perrix come out in tears and went straight upstairs. The master sent for brandy and him an' Townsend talked longer."

"And she still hasn't come home?"

The man shook his head. "Miz Perrix's in a state."

Barnaby flipped Rupert a second sixpence and headed for the park across the street to finish his supper and have a think. Later he hitched rides on the rear of cabs and made the rounds of taverns that catered to dock workers and sailors. There was dismal talk of the day's rout, but nothing about his angel.

180

Now on the same rooftop he had perched on during the protest, he wiped his hands on his shirt and pulled the Angel's hat from his rucksack. He sat holding it for a time, staring at the lights of ships in the harbor.

She was out there somewhere. Likely with Townsend. He pulled out a candle lamp and notepad and set to work on the piece he owed *The Examiner* in the morning. Her whereabouts were going to have to remain a mystery.

Well, why not? Readers loved a good mystery. The Angel and her fiancé had come to help quell the riot; Townsend made a valiant effort and was beaten for it. The Angel of the Streets had gone to his aid and disappeared. Had she been taken during the riot?

Barnaby wrote for an hour straight, then sat back to look over his work and rub his hands together with unabashed pleasure.

This could light a fire in the troubled Docklands.

TWELVE

"The laws of salvage?" Rafe scowled, thinking he was hearing things. "How the devil do you know about those?"

"I read. A lot."

He lay on the floor in the darkened cabin, having insisted he felt fine so she would take the bunk. They had vermin-free blankets and feather pillows secreted from the old captain's cabin. Strangely, the darkness around him seemed filled with *her*.

"I just wondered what would happen if a ship caught fire and the cargo was tossed overboard."

"Well, the law says that the ship must be in clear danger of sinking for the right of salvage to apply. And why would anyone think a ship in a harbor was sinking?"

"Just asking." She rolled onto her side and propped her head on her hand. "The *Clarion* has an iron hull, right?"

"She does. She has a coal-fired engine for

the paddle wheel, and triple masts and sails for ocean-going. She's a transition ship, actually . . . halfway between sail and steam. Screws and propellers are the thing now. More efficient, and they take up less space — more room for cargo. That was what I was investigating at Upton Hall. I want to gradually refit our ships with them. We have to stay competitive. The company with the fastest ships gets commodities to the market first and sets the price."

"Refitting sounds expensive."

"It will be," he said. "But we have to do it if we mean to survive in international trade. If Townsend Imports doesn't make it, there will be hundreds of men out of work on three continents."

She nodded, then fell silent for a time. "Are you still awake?" she finally said.

"Afraid so," he answered, trying not to think of the reasons for it. Spending the night with her in a locked cabin had worked its way to the top of the list. She had kissed him with such passion earlier, leaving no doubt that she wanted a response from him. Not only did she rouse a response, she'd left him wanting more. He should be alarmed by his pleasure at her physical interest in him, but for some reason he couldn't summon a shred of concern. Kissing her was different from any experience he'd had with a woman. It was all-consuming and utterly . . . *satisfying.*

"How long until dawn, do you think?" she asked.

"Hard to say. A couple of hours perhaps."

"So about four o'clock?"

He could somehow feel her mind working.

Moments later she sat up and started taking down her hair . . . only to freeze at the sound of a key in the lock. She slid to her feet. and a moment later he was standing beside her, staring at the opening door.

A small, crouched figure crept inside from the darkened passage. The moment the door closed behind him, Rafe lunged for the intruder.

"Aaaay —"

He clamped a hand over the boy's mouth and dragged his wriggling form to the window, where the light was somewhat better.

"Jims?" Lauren gasped as she hurried to them. The boy slowed at the sound of his name and then quit struggling. She knelt and grabbed him by the shoulders. "Where have you been? I was so worried."

When Rafe released him, she pulled him into a hug and he buried his face in her shoulder. "I been lookin' for you an' the mister." He took a shuddering breath of relief. "I thought ye was gone."

She looked up at Rafe, who was leaning a shoulder against the window. Setting Jims back to look him over, she decided he was none the worse for wear.

"We wouldn't leave without you. You're all right?"

"Yeah." He straightened with a confidence that wasn't entirely convincing. "I crawled all over th' ship an' watched an' listened. The men — they ain't good with ye bein' held prizner. They jaw a lot . . . an' they don't like that capt'n feller much."

"A reasonable bunch, then," Rafe said, giving the boy a nod.

"How did you get in here?" Lauren asked. "The door was locked."

"That other lad — he caught me snitching food from th' galley, and because I was s'posed to be a prizner anyway, I talked 'im into coppin' the keys and lettin' me in."

"So you've had something to eat?" she asked. When he nodded the tension in her shoulders eased. "You've had quite an adventure."

"I saw all kinds o' stuff in that big hole with th' barrels and crates." His eyes widened. "The barrels is sealed up tight, but

185

there was a couple o' wood crates I got open. They got bales, too, an' big bolts o' cloth an' wood chests wi' drawers that smell real good."

She looked up at Rafe. "Chests that smell good. Spices?"

"Very likely," he answered.

"Some smelled like tea." Jims was clearly awed. "Ma, she had some give to her. I didn' take to it, but Ma an' the girls liked it fine."

She thought on that for a minute, then took a breath and lifted the boy's chin. "You've been as brave as a knight in armor, Jims Gardiner. Now you should rest. I would read you to sleep if we still had a book."

As it turned out, he didn't need much coaxing to fall asleep. She had him climb under the blanket on the bunk and then sat beside him stroking his unruly hair. When he relaxed and began to breathe softly she moved to the floor beside Rafe, who sat with his back against the bunk.

"The crew is unhappy with their new captain," she said softly, settling closer. "Maybe they need another leader."

"That's mutinous talk," he said, drinking in her presence.

"I'm a prisoner. I'm allowed to mutiny."

He chuckled silently and felt his shoulder move against hers.

"I bet if you gave them a speech like the one you gave on the dock, they'd listen," she said.

He sighed. Did her mind never stop working? "You heard that?" He turned his head to look at her.

"Every word." She looked up at him. "You very nearly had them."

He searched her face in the dimness. "You're just full of compliments today," he said with a wry smile.

Soon her eyes closed and her head drooped against him. He put an arm around her to support her, and before long his cheek rested on the top of her head. With a smile he inhaled her scent and closed his eyes.

He roused a bit later with a crick in his neck and stretched it while trying not to disturb Lauren. She must have felt the change, for she stirred and sat up straight.

"I didn't mean to wake you," he murmured.

"It's good that you did. It will be daylight soon." She rubbed her face. "I've come up with a plan to get us out of here *and* solve the tariff problem. I'll need your help."

"Does it involve mayhem, bloodshed, or swimming?"

"No."

"Then I'm in."

"We lost Little Rob, but we've got Jims back," she said quietly. "He's obviously good at moving around unnoticed. He can sneak ashore on the provisions boat that runs just before dawn. We'll need some men on the dock . . . with gaffs and plenty of brawn."

She rose and headed for the door, searching through her hair.

"Longshoremen?" He was puzzled.

When he stood up and joined her, she was squeezing a hairpin together, and she soon inched it into the lock.

"Where on God's green earth did you learn to do that?" he said, watching her finesse the wire into the door lock.

"There are times a household key may be misplaced or a cupboard or storeroom must be opened without a household official's presence. Mrs. Beeton was quite adamant that this household tip must never be used for nefarious purposes."

"Who is Mrs. Beeton?" He was incredulous. "And why would she think lock-picking would be used for anything *but* nefarious purposes?"

"She is an expert on household management and economy. I was trapped with her book of advice and admonitions for days. It turns out some of her advice is actually useful."

With a click and the turn of a knob the door was open. She looked up at him with a grin and he was compelled to return it . . . before it occurred to him that he had no clue what they were about to do.

"Bring the lantern," she said softly. "And we'll have to find another lantern or two and some matches."

All of her questions about the cargo . . . salvage requirements . . . kerosene lanterns . . . longshoremen with gaffs . . . He stopped dead in the quiet passageway and grabbed her arm.

"I think you'd better give me the details of this brilliant plan of yours," he said with hushed urgency.

She stepped close to him in the darkness and whispered, "We're going to set the ship on fire."

She was insane, he told himself. Abduction and imprisonment had pushed her over the edge.

"We most certainly are *not.*"

"Oh, not the whole ship," she assured

him. "I'm thinking just the cabins. And perhaps something in the hold. We'll start with the mattresses . . . they'll smoke terribly and hide our activity at first. We had one catch fire once and it filled two whole floors with smoke. It took forever to air out the house."

Once past the first shock he realized that she was too damned calm as she talked of torching — *hold on* — longshoremen and gaffs?

"Wait." He pulled her to the junction of steps in the passage and dragged her into the darkest corner he could find. After a moment he realized his arms were around her and her hands were once again gripping his shirt. In the dark her quick breaths sounded sensual and the press of her body against his was threatening to seduce his skepticism.

"Explain," he ordered through a tightening throat.

She did. And despite his misgivings, by the time they returned to the cabin they had two more lanterns and a box of matches pilfered from the galley.

"This is the craziest thing I've ever done," she said as she dragged their mattress into the hallway at first light.

190

"Somehow I doubt that," Rafe responded as he reluctantly added their blankets to the pile. They had managed to wrestle a mattress and pillows from the captain's cabin into the passage. Old newspapers and some packing straw from open crates served as kindling.

They had only an hour to secret Jims ashore and convince Fosse and Gus of the need to start tossing the cargo overboard. The two had been appalled at first to find their prisoners had escaped, but Rafe's emphatic assurance that if they helped with the plan they would be cleared of responsibility for the abduction brought them around. While the sleepless acting captain stalked the deck and snarled at the night watch, Fosse and Gus gathered a number of the crew below deck to hear Rafe's invitation to be part of the plan. The men eyed him warily at first and glowered at Fosse and Gus.

"No ransom is coming," Rafe declared forcefully. "I know my father; he's stubborn as a mule. He won't pay you a penny. More likely he'll set Scotland Yard and the harbor police on the lot of you. They'll storm the ship and you will be declared accomplices to criminal acts of abduction and imprisonment. Serious charges. Years at hard labor."

191

The men muttered angrily, torn between distrust and despair.

"But there is an alternative." His face glowed with determination. "A way to save your hides as well as the *Clarion*'s cargo." He took a breath and announced, "If the ship were to catch fire, who could blame us for ditching the cargo overboard?"

"Where the hell is Lawrence?" Horace Townsend bellowed as he barreled past a shocked Weathersby into the entry hall of Alcott House. "The *Clarion* is on fire — the ship holding Rafe and your daughter!" he declared as Lawrence Alcott rushed out of the dining room with a napkin still tucked under his chin. "Get your hat, man!"

A minute later Lawrence had shed his napkin, grabbed his hat from Weathersby, and was climbing into Horace's carriage. They raced through the fog-cloistered streets toward the harbor while Horace explained that a runner from the harbor police had brought the news a quarter of an hour earlier and he'd called immediately for his carriage. He had no word on how the fire had started or how much it had spread.

Lawrence tugged up his tie and noticed that Horace hadn't shaved or bothered to change his clothes from last evening. He looked positively gray with concern. Was that for their children or their cargo?

"I never wanted to pay the bloody tariffs or give the bastards wages," Horace reminded him. "It was you who refused to go to the authorities last night. What would they do to our children if we refused payment or brought the law into it? you said. Well, the time for that is over. I sent word to Scotland Yard as soon as I heard of the fire. Officers will be at the docks by the time we get there."

"Of all the miserly, pigheaded —" Lawrence snapped, furious at Horace's betrayal of their agreed-upon course. "Some things are more important than money. I want my daughter back. I'd have given whatever I have to get her back safe and sound. If that meant paying the scoundrels, I'd have sold my winter woolies to make it happen. Can you say the same?"

Horace looked struck by the accusation, then angry, and he turned to the window with a growl. A moment later his knee started to bounce with tension.

They rode the rest of the way in silence and found the Docklands near the Customs office in turmoil. People had turned out of nearby lodgings into the foggy dawn and bobbies were drawn to the docks to discover the source of the smoke that mingled with the fog. Horace sent the carriage away and they rushed on foot to the edge of the dock. They spotted dim flashes of light in the smoke and could hear the distant crackle of flames and the frantic shouts of sailors, punctuated by loud splashes.

"Where're the damned fireboats?" Lawrence roared with frustration.

A second later they spotted shore boats carrying men with gaffs who seemed to be guiding barrels floating in the water to the dock. Horace stalked down the quayside, shoving bystanders aside, to get a look at what they were doing. Other men were on the stone steps leading down into the water, seizing drifting barrels and hauling them to wagons waiting above.

"Those are my barrels!" he shouted, rushing to the men at the top of the steps. One turned to him with a wry expression.

"Yeah." The man's face was familiar to Horace, but he couldn't have put a name to it to save himself. "We was told you wanted 'em saved."

"B-but . . . how . . . who told you that?"

"A boy come to th' warehouse an' said to get Townsend workers down to th' docks."

"What boy?" Horace scowled, thinking of his son.

194

Large crates were being hoisted up to the dock by men with a cargo net, and smaller crates and barrels were being carried up the steps by pairs of burly workers. Horace had to step back to let them pass, and a few recognized him and nodded. He was so astonished, he scarcely noticed when Lawrence fought through the crowd to join him.

"Dear God —" Lawrence gasped as he realized what was happening. "They're tossing the cargo overboard."

Together, they searched the outline of the ship. Through the fog and smoke they glimpsed occasional flames and made out human forms rushing back and forth.

"My Lauren," Lawrence choked out. "What is happening to my daughter?"

"It's good and thick," Lauren said, trying not to cough as she stood out of the way of the main hatch with her arms around Little Rob. Her eyes were watering, and she found it hard to keep track of how many barrels and crates had been tossed or lowered overboard. She'd lost count somewhere around thirty barrels and over two dozen crates. Most of the men had tied kerchiefs over their noses and mouths and now looked like the outlaws her father would think they were. Little Rob began coughing again and she moved him as far as she could from the smoke that billowed out of the main hatch and passageway.

At center deck a second energetic plume rose from the cargo hatch, fed by straw used to pack crates and every bit of spare canvas they could find. Then she turned toward the sounds from the dock and was pleased to make out a handful of boats and men urging crates and barrels toward the landing. She could hear the rumble of voices from shore and shrill whistles, as well as the thud of wood and clop of horse hooves. Hopefully that meant they had brought wagons to collect the cargo. She prayed that all was going according to plan.

The most worrisome part was the fact that Acting Captain Morgan was now on deck and raging furiously that someone had "overturned a damned lantern" and caught packing material in the hold on fire.

"What the blazes are you doing? Sound the damned alarm!" he ordered his crewmen, and when they continued rolling barrels across the deck to the water, he charged into them, shoving and striking, trying to make them obey. "Stop, this minute — that's an order!" With a curse, he grabbed a spar from the main mast and went for Fosse.

"They're rescuing the cargo." Rafe rushed

to confront him and draw his ire away from Fosse and the men unloading cargo.

"What the bloody hell are you doing out of —" He grabbed the nearest seaman by the shirt and shoved him toward Rafe. "Seize him and get him below deck!"

"Into that?" Rafe gestured to the smoke and flames pouring from the main hatch. "You want to add murder to your crimes?"

Morgan's eyes bulged and his face flooded crimson with fury. "What the hell have you done to my ship?" He rushed Rafe, fists clenched.

"Think, man," Rafe said, trying to fend him off.

Lauren cried out as Morgan landed a blow that made it past Rafe's outstretched arms. It sent Rafe staggering back. Unloading stopped as the men watched their acting captain attack one of the owners of the ship. After that first blow Rafe's entire frame came alive with anger and he began to return blows with real force. Morgan staggered but righted himself and committed furiously to a battle for control of his vessel.

Praying Rafe could hold his own, Lauren told Little Rob to stay put and rushed across the deck to encourage the men to continue dumping the cargo into the harbor.

"Hurry — keep unloading," she called.

"We don't have much time before the harbor police arrive. We must get as much of the cargo ashore as we can before they stop us."

Her words seemed to break a spell and they turned to hoist crates and roll barrels with renewed determination. She turned away from the fight to see how their smoky cover was faring and didn't see Morgan lurching backward . . . toward her. By the time a crewman shouted a warning Morgan had already knocked her over the edge of the deck.

Her scream was cut short as she entered the water.

She had no time to take a breath, and now in the cold, suffocating darkness, she had to fight her skirts, her hair, and the churned water to find which way was up. When she breached the surface she gasped for air and realized she had to rid herself of the water-logged skirts that threatened to drag her down, but the ties of her petticoats were swollen with water and her cold fingers couldn't seem to find the hooks at the back of her waist.

She kicked furiously against her restraints to stay afloat but quickly realized that she was in trouble. The dock was too far to reach with dangerous barrels and crates bobbing in the way. Behind her the ship was a long, smooth wall of iron.

Time seemed to slow as Rafe watched her go over the side. It was clearly an accident, but fear for her and fury at the acting captain combined in explosive blows that laid Morgan out on the deck unconscious. Panting and bleeding from a cut on his face, Rafe staggered to the opening in the railing where Lauren had disappeared and searched the churned surface of the water.

"Lauren! Lauren, where are you?"

His calls went unanswered. His heart seemed to stop until her head popped above the water. She was struggling to stay afloat and choking on water as she tried to steady herself. When she succeeded her call for help was alarmingly weak.

Fosse, Gus, and a couple of other men rushed to see what had happened. He told them, and himself, that she could swim like a fish. But dread still squeezed his gut and worked its way up to his throat. He had to do something — had to save her.

"A ladder — I need a boarding ladder."

The men looked at one another in dismay.

"The captain tossed 'em overboard when some of the crew deserted," Fosse declared, his eyes widening on Lauren's struggle.

Frantic, Rafe looked around and spotted the heavy cargo net the men had been using to haul freight up to the deck and pointed. "That! Get that net over the side and secure it."

The net was dropped over the side, and several men braced to hold it while Rafe climbed down it to the water level.

"Lauren, swim to me — I'll pull you out!" When she just floundered for another minute he continued. "Come on, Lauren, swim. I know you can do it — I've seen you do it! Swim to me!"

Had she hit her head on something? She was thrashing, and he realized she was struggling to move. He climbed down to the rows of the heavy rope net that hung in the water and made himself continue downward. A surge of panic filled him as he sank and the water closed around his feet and rose to his knees. He steeled himself and called to her again and again while leaning out, extending his arm as far as he could while holding fast to the rope of the net. With every breath he found himself praying that the men above had a firm grip on that net.

He saw the change in her when she realized he was nearby and offering help. She focused and began to swim, but her strokes were short and frantic, as if she were fighting for every bit of distance she closed. It seemed a small eternity before she was near enough to reach. Relief energized him as he grabbed her hand and then her arm. Pulling her waterlogged form out of the water required every bit of strength he possessed, but he soon had an arm around her and was lifting her up onto the net and into his arms.

She gasped, trembling with relief as she clung to him and buried her face in his shirt.

"Thank you, thank you, thank you," she muttered, tightening her arms around him.

"You're all right." He freed a hand to cradle her head against his chest while she caught her breath. "You're safe."

Moments later he called for the men on the deck to begin to haul them up. With the help of Fosse and Gus, he lifted her back onto the deck and then climbed aboard himself. He'd never been so glad to have a deck beneath his feet — even if it belonged to a ship on fire. He had Little Rob find a blanket, wrapped her in it, and guided her to a seat on the nearby bridge steps, out of the worst smoke.

She looked up at him with a shivering smile that warmed something chilled in his core.

"I couldn't get my skirts off."

Relief poured through him and he laughed.

"There's a first time for everything."

THIRTEEN

On the dock the bystanders heard a scream, followed by a splash. Someone had gone overboard — a woman, from the sound of it.

The next second Lawrence was searching frantically for a boat and harbor officers to row out to the ship. Horace joined him in the boat and they were halfway to the *Clarion* when a fireboat arrived and hailed the master of the ship. Through the fog and smoke they heard voices, but the roar of the water and the racket from the fireboat's pumps soon drowned them out.

Lawrence was beside himself, certain that the scream had been Lauren's and that she was in peril. "God knows what they're doing to my sweet girl."

Horace cut him a glance and muttered, "Whatever it is, it's probably not half of what she's doing to them."

When the fireboat repositioned to the far

side of the *Clarion,* they were able to maneuver closer and called out to the ship, demanding to speak to the captain and to see Rafe Townsend and Lauren Alcott. Moments later Rafe and Lauren appeared at the railing above, and the sight of them was both a reassurance and a shock. Rafe had blood on his face and Lauren was disheveled and appeared to be dripping wet.

"You're here. Good!" Rafe called down to them. "You can give us a ride back to shore. Things appear to be well in hand here."

"Well in hand? The damned ship is on fire!" Horace bellowed as Rafe disappeared above them. He turned to Lawrence with a look of outrage, but he was staring up at his daughter, demanding to know if she was well.

"I'm fine," she called. "Just wet. And cold." She appeared to have a blanket around her. "I . . . fell in." Her voice was higher than usual and uneven . . . she was shivering. "What is happening on the dock? Is the cargo being saved?"

"It is," Lawrence said, finding new reasons for anxiety, and turned to the officers in the boat. "We have to get her to shore — she's freezing."

Rafe pulled a couple of the crewmen away from rescuing cargo to rig the boarding swing, and as soon as she was aboard, he stepped onto it beside her. Together they were lowered, and Lawrence nearly upset the boat as he rushed to reach her. He hugged her and set her back to look her over.

"My little girl — what have they done to you? I'll see the wretches in chains, I swear."

"I wasn't looking and was knocked overboard, Papa. It was an accident. I just need a good, hot bath and some dry clothes." Her words were brave, but her teeth were chattering and she was paler than usual.

He scowled at Rafe. "It seems every time you two are together my daughter comes home looking like she's been used for bait."

Horace, on the other hand, greeted his son with a stiff nod, then ordered the rowers back to the dock. "I'll have an accounting, boy." He settled opposite Rafe and gave him a searching look. "Were you or were you not being held for ransom?"

"A full accounting in due time," Rafe answered. "Is the cargo being taken to our warehouse?"

"God knows," Horace said, rubbing his face. "Though I saw men I recognized from our warehouse in the mix. Where is that scoundrel Pettigrew? I would never have taken him for such a conniver. He always struck me as a dependable fellow."

"Pettigrew is dead," Rafe said, watching Lauren lean her head on her father's shoulder. "Didn't they tell you? Of course not. The one who took over as acting captain, Juster Morgan, is responsible for our detention."

"Pettigrew, dead?" Horace was stunned by the news. "Then how did you get free? And how did the blasted ship catch fire?"

Barnaby Pinkum crept through the crowd on the dock, watching the strange tableau of the burning ship unfolding. It was called the *Clarion,* and the crew, in an effort to save some of the cargo, had started tossing it overboard. It was being salvaged by enterprising dock workers and whisked away, though its destination was a mystery. None of the men involved would say where it was being taken. Then he spotted Horace Townsend and crept close enough to hear him insisting it was his cargo and quizzing the longshoremen rescuing it.

Lawrence Alcott joined Townsend, wringing his hands over his daughter's safety. That was all Barnaby needed to fix on the pair, and when they heard a woman's scream amid the splashes coming from the burning ship, his pulse jumped and his newswriter's instincts came alive. Was that his Angel? Was she in trouble? And what the devil was she doing on a burning ship?

He watched as Alcott commandeered a boat to go out through the fog and smoke to the burning ship. Soon the clanging of a fireboat and the roar of water from hoses masked all other sounds. Was this a rescue mission? Waiting and watching for whatever happened next, he told himself this was the best chapter yet of his Angel saga. He was going to make it a dilly.

Lauren was wet, bedraggled, and chilled to the bone, but her discomfort was balanced by the knowledge that her plan — *their* plan — seemed to have worked. Seeing officers in the boat, she and Rafe put off sharing the details of their misadventure and focused instead on the riot, the injury Rafe sustained, and her decision to go with him and take care of him. Horace seemed confused, and when he demanded details she closed her eyes and leaned into her father's arms, while Rafe rubbed his face and complained of fatigue and hunger. When they reached the dock and saw the waiting crowd, she realized they had yet another gauntlet to run.

Onlookers crowded close, threatening to

block the way as her father helped her up the steps. At the front of the spectators she spotted a fellow in a bowler with a pad and pencil in his hands. Something about that hat and the fellow's diminutive stature seemed familiar.

While they waited for the carriage to arrive, questions flew at them from every quarter, including from a pair of serious-looking men from Scotland Yard. They had received a report that Lauren and Rafe were being held against their will aboard the ship that was now on fire, and they wanted clarification from the supposed victims themselves.

Rafe's stiff posture masked alarm that she might have shared if she hadn't already thought of an explanation.

She told them about Rafe's speech to the workers protesting the tariffs and how he was struck in the riot and rendered unconscious. Several men from the ship *Clarion* were in the crowd, recognized him, and came to his aid. They carried him to the safety of their ship and she naturally went with them to tend his injuries. There was no time to or means of notifying their families, for which both she and Rafe apologized.

"Captain Pettigrew was a gracious host," she told them with an eye on the bowler fellow who was straining to hear what was said and seemed to be taking down every word uttered. "But he blamed Rafe's injury on the intolerable tariff situation and grew more and more furious. At daylight he was in the main hold inspecting the cargo when his heart seized. He must have dropped his lantern in a pile of loose packing."

To her surprise Rafe joined in with, "He managed to make it up to the deck and collapsed there. In their hurry to reach the captain, someone knocked over a lantern in the passage, and suddenly there was fire all around. We barely made it out of the cabin in time."

"And the cargo floating in the harbor?" one of the Scotland Yard men demanded. "What about that?"

"First Officer Juster Morgan feared he would be held responsible for the entire cargo going up in smoke," Rafe added. "He ordered the men to begin heaving what they could overboard. Men at the docks decided to haul them in."

"Now, if you don't mind" — Lauren's father pulled her protectively against him — "I must see to my daughter's health. If you have more questions, you know where to find me."

As she was ushered toward the carriage,

she heard a voice ask, "How did the Angel get wet? Did she fall from the ship? Or did she *jump*?"

She paused to glance back over her shoulder at the little man in the bowler. He'd called her "the angel." From his knowing look she realized he was indeed the one who'd started those stories about her.

"What is it?" Rafe paused, too, and followed her gaze to the man.

"I think that's him," she said, nodding toward the fellow with the bowler and writing pad. "The one writing those pieces about us in the papers."

Rafe made a move toward the man, but the little scribbler shrank back into the crowd and was quickly lost from view.

She sighed silently as she clutched the blanket tighter around her and mounted the carriage steps.

Now he had one more tale to twist to make her life difficult.

Rafe watched her fall asleep on her father's shoulder when they were safely in the carriage and felt that stirring in his chest again. This time — shockingly — there was no alarm. She was so damned confusing. Canny and determined one minute and soft-eyed and yielding the next. What lay at

210

the heart of the woman? What did she truly want . . . besides universal literacy and better nutrition for urchins everywhere? He stared at her face, the feathery crescents of lashes against her pale skin. She was exhausted and disheveled and he'd never found her so appealing.

"What the devil were you on about back there?" His father broke through his thoughts. "Pettigrew is dead and his idiot first mate panicked at the fire and ordered the cargo overboard?"

"Captain Pettigrew is indeed dead, of a heart attack," he said. "Juster Morgan took over and decided to force the issue and hold us for ransom. When the ship caught fire I convinced the crew to toss some of the cargo overboard — it seems we got at least a quarter of it, perhaps more, ashore underneath the Customs officers' noses."

Horace appraised his disheveled son. "Damned enterprising . . . taking advantage of the situation to save our goods." His gaze darted back and forth as he assessed the situation. "You can bet the Customs men will be at the warehouse first thing tomorrow morning." He grinned. "We'll have some explaining to do, boy."

There were tears aplenty from Aunt

Amanda when Rafe carried her through her front door, wet and shivering. He had picked her up, despite her father's protest and his own father's insistence that she still had two good legs to walk on. Rafe carried her up the stairs, deposited her on her bed, and then stood for a moment looking down at her with an unreadable expression on his face. Aunt Amanda hurried into the bathing room to light the water heater, leaving them alone for a minute. He picked up her hand and gave it a squeeze that sent a shiver through her.

"We made it." His voice seemed husky and his gaze lingered.

"We did." She smiled. "Did you think we wouldn't?"

He gave a chuckle. "I confess I had a doubt or two." His gaze dropped to their hands and he stroked her skin gently.

"I didn't," she said softly. "I knew you could convince the crew."

He paused for a moment. "All I did was give them a reason to do the right thing."

"That's all some people need," she said softly.

She caught his gaze, and for a moment her heart skipped several beats. She watched his broad shoulders sway as he released her hand and exited.

He might not know it, but he was in grave danger of letting his head and heart join forces to make him into something truly wonderful.

As Lauren stepped into a tub of hot water in her bathing room, Aunt Amanda insisted on checking the water temperature and bringing her French toweling, scented soap, and rose oil. Lauren would have been happy to have some time to herself, but her disappearance and homecoming had overwhelmed Amanda. She insisted on staying close and sharing her worry over Lauren's disappearance.

"We were beside ourselves," she said, dabbing her eyes. "Your father nearly wore ruts in the floors with his pacing and I didn't sleep a wink for two nights, fearing what was happening to you. I was so relieved when that Townsend fellow carried you —" Her voice cracked and she dabbed her eyes again and blew her nose.

When Amanda recovered she insisted on having the details of Lauren's abduction and subsequent escape. "Tuts" and gasps aplenty greeted the tale of what had happened to her and Rafe at the harbor. There was no need to hide that she and Rafe had been held prisoner before they secured the

213

cooperation of the crew and hatched a plan to escape and salvage what they could of the cargo. She saw no cause to mention how the fire actually started. When she finished she reached for the toweling and climbed out of the tub.

Clothed in a warm gown and tucked into bed, Lauren asked about Amanda's time reading to the children and how they had liked the books she had chosen for them. Amanda was happy to report that the children were wide-eyed, attentive, and thrilled to be given books of their very own.

"I confess, I rather enjoyed reading to them." She smiled. "I might be persuaded to join your reading hours at the parish school." Then her smile faded. "Speaking of reading . . ." She produced a newspaper and read aloud a piece about Lauren in yesterday's edition of *The Examiner.*

The published description of her heroics was accompanied by details of Rafe's attempt to bring reason to the mob of angry dock workers. The accompanying drawing, however, showed only her angel depiction pleading for peace as the protesters throttled one another around her feet. The writer declared that after she called for restraint, she had disappeared in the violent crowd and hadn't been seen or heard from since.

214

He concluded the article with a dramatic appeal to Fortune to return their generous Angel to London's needy streets.

Aunt Amanda lowered the spectacles on her nose to study Lauren. "Clearly he knew you were missing. How could he have known?"

Lauren shook her head, then laid back against a bolster. "He must have heard Rafe's words firsthand because he wrote them exactly." She sat bolt upright. "He was there this morning." Her eyes widened. "He's spying on us, *following* us."

In the silence that followed she sank back against the pillows.

"Did it really happen the way you said?" Amanda asked quietly.

"Of course." She felt a twinge. "Why would you ask that?"

"Why indeed? When you were held prisoner with Rafe Townsend, day and night, unchaperoned. Heaven knows I'm no prude, but . . ."

Lauren reddened with annoyance. "All I did was tend him after he was injured." She burrowed deeper into the covers. "They threw us both into a freezing cold cell, and I insisted on better conditions and that I be allowed to care for him. He slept forever. When he awoke we talked. He actually lis-

tened to me." She saw Amanda's eyes widen. "Something of a shock, I know. There may be a dormant bit of humanity in him after all."

She studied the canopy over her head, but saw in her mind's eye how he looked and listened and the surprising charm of his laugh.

"He was convinced his father would never pay the ransom, and we tried to think of ways to raise the money ourselves."

It struck her. "Auntie A, what do you know about my inheritance from Mamma?"

Amanda seemed startled by the question. A blink later she was all benevolence and concern once again.

"I have no head for money matters, dear. I leave such things to my brother." She reached out to pat Lauren's hand as it lay on the coverlet. "He is the one to ask. Now get some rest while I see about dinner. Oh — I meant to tell you." She turned back. "Lady Drummond called the morning before I brought your books to that Seven Sisters place. She didn't stay long, but she seemed keen to confirm that you and your intended will be attending their dinner party this Saturday. She said nothing about the story in the papers . . . but then she wouldn't, being a lady of breeding and sensibility. Will you be up to it?"

"Saturday is three days away." Lauren sighed, feeling exhausted. "I suppose I will be recovered in time, but I can't vouch for Rafe."

Amanda gave her a reassuring smile as she opened the door.

"Strapping fellow that he is, I'm certain he will be fine. I'll let Lady Anne know we still plan to attend. Don't fret . . . I doubt the Drummonds live and die by the nonsense in gossip papers."

The Drummonds might not, Lauren thought as she lay in the quiet of her bed, but others who attended might. Lady Anne's visit to make certain she and Rafe would be there could only mean that she wanted their gossip-worthy presence to help make her night a success.

She groaned, already dreading it.

Amanda found her brother in his study with his head resting against his chair and his eyes closed. He had been beside himself with worry when word came of Lauren's abduction. Now that she was safe at home, exhaustion had taken over.

She cleared her throat twice, then said his name.

He started awake and for a moment

seemed disoriented before focusing on her.

"I hate to disturb you, dear, but there is something you should know. Lauren just asked me about her inheritance from her mother. Apparently this ransom demand made her think of accessing it."

Lawrence sat up sharply, rubbing the sleep from his eyes.

"What did you tell her?"

"To speak to you, of course." She gave him a wry smile as she turned to go. "Everyone knows I have no head for finance."

218

FOURTEEN

Flowers — huge bouquets of pink and white — arrived the next morning, just ahead of Caroline Townsend. The upstairs maid appeared at Lauren's bedroom door carrying a vase of them for her bedroom and a summons from her aunt to come and greet her future mother-in-law.

Fortunately Lauren had risen early enough to breakfast in her room, dress, and tame her hair into a simple chignon. She paused just outside the grand parlor doors to take a deep breath and then entered to find her aunt and Caroline Townsend chatting amicably.

"There you are, my dear." Caroline patted the settee beside her and Lauren felt obliged to accept that invitation. "I was so worried about you. Forgive the intrusion, but I had to see that you're recovering from your ordeal. I tried to get details from Rafe, but . . . well, you know how men are."

"Thank you for your concern. The flowers are lovely. And I am feeling well enough," Lauren said as Caroline took her hand and patted it with what could only be called affection. "I might ask the same of Rafe. He did suffer a nasty blow to the head."

"He slept well and long, I believe, but his father has him up and about now. He has always had a strong constitution. They went to the warehouse to check on some cargo or other. I tried to get him to rest and leave business for another day, but he insisted." She smiled. "He can be a bit stubborn."

"I've noticed." Lauren returned her smile. "Though sometimes what is called stubbornness is merely determination mislabeled."

She noticed the way Caroline softened. "That is kind of you to say, considering your recent differences."

She sighed. "I think our conflicts come from the fact that we are more alike than different."

Caroline's smile broadened. "He has a good bit of his father in him. I have always believed he needs someone spirited enough to withstand his many opinions and natural authority." She paused and produced a knowing smile. "I think you may be just the ticket."

After Rafe's mother left Lauren sat for a while in the parlor, relishing the quiet and thinking. His mother was a dear. His father was a nightmare. Little wonder that Rafe turned out to be so puzzling. Strong, opinionated, intelligent, and willing to trade physical blows when the occasion called for it. He was determined and principled and not quite the selfish son of privilege she had believed. Aboard the ship she had found herself enjoying his company and their prickly banter. Not to mention the kisses. Was that closeness merely the effect of having to join together against adverse circumstances? Now that they were back in their usual world, would he remember that time as warmly as she did? Would he think about those kisses and recall the feel of their bodies touching?

To keep from dwelling on that part of their adventure she rose and headed for her father's study. She had questions that needed answers.

Lawrence was standing behind his desk gathering documents into a leather folder when she entered the study. He glanced up and smiled at her.

"Papa, I have a question for you," she said as she came to lean against a nearby chair.

"How are you feeling?" he said, pausing

with documents in his hand. "No fever or stomach complaints? Harbor water is so filthy . . ."

"No, I'm fine. Just tired," she answered, straightening.

Reassured, he went back to stuffing his folio with documents.

"I want to know about my inheritance from Mamma."

"Yes? What about it?" he said, slowing but not looking at her.

"Well, what are these entailments it contains? Some time ago you told me there were conditions, and while we were aboard ship I realized I know nothing about them. Do you have some documents or papers I can read?"

Her father stopped sorting and closed the folio sharply.

"I have no idea. I mean, I am certain our solicitors keep copies of them." He glanced around the study. "I doubt if I have anything here. We would have to check with Willingham and Boswell. The funds themselves are in the hands of trustees at the bank." He expelled a heavy breath.

"Honestly, I don't have time just now. I have an important meeting in a short while." He checked his pocket watch and seemed jolted by what it read. On his way out he paused to give her a kiss on the forehead as he had when she was a little girl. "Be sure to get some rest."

She frowned as she watched him leave. He didn't remember the details of her mother's inheritance? He was a consummate businessman, a titan of commerce. Surely he would have taken an interest in his wife's financial resources. But then, it had been a stressful few days, and she knew he was deeply concerned about matters affecting his business merger and their finances. An unsettling wave of insight broke over her as she drifted out of her father's study.

She watched him take his hat and gloves from Weathersby and stride out the front door into a world she hardly recognized.

For the first time she realized the burdens he carried as a father, a man, and a force in the world of business. With that awareness came an abrupt and somewhat disorienting expansion of the world she had known. Suddenly she understood how he saw her concerns about child welfare and universal education and fair wages. Causes that had always seemed such a simple and obvious good to her no longer seemed as simple or as obvious. As he dealt with laws, institutions, and the immovable weight of nations and governments, she began to understand how her concerns and causes must seem small and inconsequential.

Then she thought of Jims and his family, to whom she now owed a debt. She thought of his sweet face, his curiosity, his game way of engaging a bruising world. How could his hopes and welfare not matter?

Why didn't others care about — she stopped with a hand to her head.

Here was something she didn't like thinking: others like her father were busy thinking about the wider, messier world outside the necessities of children's empty bellies and bare feet and need for schooling. Someone had to think about those wider things, she supposed. But why couldn't they spare a bit of time for more personal good — for kindness and sharing — for making the world better for real, individual people?

Her head was spinning and her stomach started to churn. She dragged herself up the stairs to rest, wondering if she had swallowed more harbor water than she realized. But deep in her core she sensed it was more than just fatigue or stress . . . something deeply personal and vital in her had just shifted, and she wasn't sure if it was for good or for ill.

The kitchen cooked for two that evening, because her father had declared he would be working late and would have a bite of dinner at his club. On her way downstairs to the morning room where she and Amanda took simple suppers, Lauren saw Amanda standing in the upper hall. Her aunt was staring with a puzzled expression on her face through the doorway of the upstairs parlor.

"What is it?" She paused beside Amanda and tilted her head to learn what had absorbed her aunt's attention.

In the brief silence she heard voices and moved into the parlor.

"There are people in front of the house," Amanda said as she followed Lauren to the front window. "Some seem to stroll by, others have paused. Some left flowers at the gate and one even lighted a candle."

"A candle? Whatever for?" she said, sinking onto a knee on the window seat as she watched one lady near the gate bow her head.

"I believe it's for you," Amanda said in a constricted voice.

"Me?" She looked at her aunt in dismay.

225

"You've been declared 'London's Angel.' "
Amanda turned to her needlework chair and
returned with penny papers in hand. "And
by recent accounts you're missing."

"That's ridiculous." She sat down on the
window seat with a plop and took the
papers. Each was open to an article that had
been circled . . . an article announcing that
the beloved Angel of London had disappeared during the riot on the docks and
hadn't been seen since — even by her family.

"Rupert brought one to the house, saying
they were all over town. When I read this
one I sent him out to find some others."

Lauren held up one particularly lurid account in disbelief.

"I was gone two days and they make it
sound as if I died."

She froze for a minute, then looked at her
aunt and down at the people lingering
outside their gate. They believed the stories
and they'd come to . . . pay respects? . . .
mourn?

"This is intolerable. I cannot let them
continue to think such a thing for a minute
longer." She rose and tossed the papers
aside.

"What are you going to do?" Amanda
stepped in front of her.

"Tell them I'm home and safe . . . to go home and not believe anything they read in those blasted papers!"

"Wait." Amanda grasped her shoulders. "They may not understand that you're not responsible for those stories that call you a saint or claim that you're missing and in peril. Let me go and see what can be done to send them off." She turned back at the door. "Whatever happens you stay here. You've already been in one riot this week."

Lauren rushed down the back stairs to tell an anxious Weathersby that her aunt would deal with the group at their gate and that she suspected dinner would have to be held for a bit. She spotted parlormaids at the front window watching the people but didn't bother to chide them because she was bound back upstairs to do the same.

She spotted Aunt Amanda's favorite shawl when her aunt emerged from the alley beside the house and strolled through the knots of people keeping vigil on the pavement. Across the street several others stood in the park, watching and pointing at the house. She lowered herself on the window seat and peered at the scene from between pillows.

Amanda paused to chat for a moment with each small group, and Lauren watched

227

her work her considerable charm on them. With a few words, a touch on the arm, or a smiling nod, she sent them off toward their homes. Soon the score of folk wishing for the Angel's return were gone, except for one lone woman by the gate.

Whatever the woman said to Amanda, she could see it had an effect on her aunt. She held her breath, waiting for the woman to leave. Instead, Amanda took the woman's arm and led her to the alley and down toward the kitchen entrance.

What the devil was Auntie A doing?

Lauren hurried down the main stairs and through the house to the kitchen stairs, where she found her aunt escorting the woman up to see her.

Spotting her confusion, Amanda quickly introduced them.

"Lauren, this is Mrs. Trimble. I'm not sure if you recognize her, but she says you saved her and her daughter's lives not long ago."

Lauren was thunderstruck. The woman's face was familiar, but the strain the widow had suffered since their meeting seemed to have etched additional years onto her face. The widow twisted a handkerchief with reddened hands and had trouble meeting Lauren's eyes.

"Of course I remember." Lauren nodded

and managed a smile. "Has something else happened? Why have you come?"

"I heard you were . . . I was afraid . . ." The handkerchief now looked like a rope. "Maybe I'm being a foolish old woman . . . but when I heard something had happened to you . . ." She looked from Lauren to Amanda, as if for help. Whatever she had come to say had to be difficult indeed.

Lauren took charge and ushered her into the main salon, where the gaslights were turned low and the atmosphere was more conducive to a personal exchange. She settled Mrs. Trimble on a settee and squeezed her hand. It was cold. She rang for some sherry, and after Amanda pulled a chair over to join them, the woman relaxed a bit.

"What troubles you enough to bring you out alone and after dark?" Lauren asked.

"I was worried about you. And your family." She took a deep breath and her chin quivered. "You know I am a widow. My dear husband died in an accident three months ago. Since then, I find it difficult to sleep, and I walk the floor at night."

"I am so sorry for your loss." For a moment she shared the woman's feeling of grief. "But why would you worry about me, Mrs. Trimble?"

"Four days ago I had a visit from Gilbert's head clerk. What he told me makes me think things are not right at Gilbert's company. And I know that Gilbert was worried . . . before his accident." Her eyes watered and she dabbed them with her tortured handkerchief.

Just then Weathersby arrived with the sherry. He poured three glasses and offered the first to the distressed widow. She took a deep breath, sipped, and produced a sad little smile. When Weathersby exited Lauren urged her to continue.

"Gilbert said some odd things in his last days . . . about . . . if anything should happen to him, we would be taken care of. I thought he was just overly tired and lacking sleep. He was sometimes called out in the night to admit goods and cargo to the warehouse."

"What was Gilbert's position?" Lauren asked, glancing at her aunt. The mention of "cargo" and "warehouse" focused her attention.

"He was the warehouse manager of Consolidated Shipping. They have facilities down by the docks. He was always diligent in his duties and kept meticulous records. But Merrell Hampstead, his head clerk, recently told me that he had been troubled by goods that appeared where they shouldn't and other goods that disappeared before they'd been sold. Their tallies were in shambles and it was giving Gilbert ulcers."

Lauren looked to Amanda, who nodded, acknowledging that "cargoes" and "warehouses" were too much of a coincidence to ignore.

"Mr. Hampstead told me that we were supposed to have Gilbert's pension from the company. There was to be a death benefit, too. A lump sum . . . which was never paid to us. Merrell brought me some papers showing that Gilbert had indeed arranged a surety for us, but the company won't even talk to me about it." She took a ragged breath. "I don't think these new owners are honest.

"Worse still, Merrell seemed anxious himself. He has been given many of Gilbert's duties and was told by the owner's agent to be less 'particular' than Gilbert in his handling of cargoes. That they didn't want him 'having an accident,' too."

Lauren leaned closer to Mrs. Trimble. "Who are these new owners? Do you know their names?"

"All I know is that it is a group of men who each put up funds to buy the business."

231

She struggled to remember as she took another sip of sherry. "He didn't know their names, just the agent who brings orders from them. A Mr. Murdoch. Obadiah Murdoch." She gave a shiver, as if the very name fouled her mouth, and finished her sherry in one gulp. When she put her empty glass on the tray her hand was shaking.

"How can I help you?" Lauren asked, intercepting the widow's elusive gaze. "I can give you the names of honest solicitors to help you get the money you are owed."

Mrs. Trimble's shoulders sagged. "That is wonderful of you, Miss Alcott, but I" — she looked down — "don't have funds for a solicitor."

"I'm sure we can arrange something. I can contact them about taking your case."

"That is generous, but that is not really why I came." She glanced to Amanda and back. "I was worried about you. And your young man, that Mr. Townsend. I know you weren't happy with him that day on the river. Is he still your intended? The papers weren't clear about that."

"We are still betrothed." Lauren frowned, surprised by her mention of Rafe and her desire for clarification of their relationship.

"Well, Mr. Hampstead — Merrell said that these new men who bring in goods and unload wagons, they're imbibers. And when they drink they talk. He heard them laugh about the Townsends, saying 'they think they're so smart.' One said, 'How smart can they be when their warehouses are piles of dry wood?' "

"Why would that — implying that wood is —" Lauren stiffened. "Dry wood is vulnerable because it *burns*? Was that a threat?"

Mrs. Trimble winced. Clearly she and her husband's head clerk considered it so, and the weight of that, combined with her financial distress, had disrupted her sleep for days. "I vowed if I could find you, or your intended, I would ask you to tell him to be watchful."

Lauren took both of the woman's hands in hers.

"Thank you, Mrs. Trimble. You've done the right thing, bringing this to us. If there is a threat to the Townsends' warehouses, they can take measures to prevent it." She struggled for composure. "Now, I want you to go home, get some rest, and see our solicitors as soon as possible. I'll write a note this very night to let them know you're a friend and should be shown every courtesy."

Teary-eyed again, Mrs. Trimble ignored

the bounds of propriety to hug Lauren tightly and mutter, "Bless you, dear angel. God bless you."

Lauren went immediately to her father's study for pen and paper to write down the names of the solicitors for Mrs. Trimble. She had Weathersby call for a cab to take the widow home, bade her goodbye, and then hurried back to the study to write two notes, one to the firm of Willingham and Boswell and the other to Rafe, telling him that she urgently needed to speak with him.

Before she sent the second note she paused to think of Rafe's reaction to such a request. Would he just dismiss it as her overactive imagination? Perhaps if she went in person she could convince him of the seriousness of the threat.

FIFTEEN

Rafe stood at the top of the steps outside the warehouse office of Townsend Imports, looking out over huge stacks and shelves of goods from around the world. This was the newest and largest of their locations, the hub of their expanding enterprise. On the floor below constables in their dark uniforms and distinctive helmets stood watch to ensure that none of the cargo was removed from the premises.

His father had been spot-on two days ago to predict that Customs officers would be pounding on their doors the morning after the "rescue" of their cargo. Inspectors from that office arrived in force the next morning and bulled their way past the old watchman to search for contraband. They demanded to see the warehouse records and checked every container in the warehouse for signs that they had been in harbor water.

Barrels and crates that showed the slightest moisture were dragged into the center of the floor and stacked where they could be examined and cataloged. The chief Customs officer said this inventory would be checked against the manifest his inspectors had taken from the *Clarion*'s captain ten days before. Horace blustered and threatened legal action and the chief officer countered with a threat of criminal charges for smuggling contraband and evading lawful taxation.

Now they were stuck with police guarding their cargo from them.

A commotion at the main door sent him down the stairs and rushing through aisles of stacked bales and crates. He stopped dead at the sight of his mother and Lauren Alcott in the double doorway. Each carried a large, cloth-covered basket on her arm and they were trying to convince the officers at the door to let them enter. Rafe arrived in time to either prevent or participate in whatever mayhem lurked behind his intended's smile.

"What are you doing here?" He pulled his gaze from Lauren to address his mother.

"We knew you were keeping watch," Caroline said, sailing past two officers, "so we thought we should do our part and bring you sustenance."

"You refused to rest sufficiently after your head injury," Lauren said, following her inside, "but at least we can see that you take proper nourishment." She glanced at the scowling constables.

"Really, officers, do you think these two ladies capable of making off with tons of disputed cargo in a hamper?" He turned to Caroline, relieved her of her basket, and offered her his arm. "Father will be delighted."

Lauren followed them through a warren of shelving and stacks of goods and then up a long run of metal stairs that rang under their feet. The warehouse office was furnished with a desk, a polished meeting table, filing cabinets, and imported curiosities. It was clearly intended to create an aura of substance and success for the sales part of the company.

They found Horace dozing, sprawled in a chair with his feet propped on an ottoman. He started awake at Caroline's touch, sighed at the sight of her, and rubbed his face briskly.

"I brought you some food . . . knowing you neglect yourself when there's business brewing," Caroline said as she set the basket on a nearby desk. "Cook packed your favorites: roast chicken, rosemary potatoes, cucumber sandwiches, and pear and strawberry tarts."

He started to smile, but caught sight of Lauren.

"What is she doing here?" He sat up straighter.

"She is my accomplice," Caroline said with a wink in her direction. "Or I'm hers. It's hard to say which."

Rafe looked at Lauren quizzically and she gave him a determined smile. "Your mother was planning to bring you some food when I arrived to see you. She invited me to come along." After they opened the baskets and a bottle of wine she edged closer to him and said, "I need to have a word with you."

He paused in the middle of heaping his plate.

"That sounds ominous." He picked up a glass of wine and headed for the door. She followed, and he settled on an upper step in a way that made room for her. She sank beside him and for a moment watched him eat. He groaned with appreciation as he tore into a splendid piece of roast chicken and washed it down with wine. After a moment he turned to her. "What is this word you want?"

"I had a visitor earlier this evening. Mrs. Gilbert Trimble."

He gave up trying to recall the name,

shrugged, and took another bite of chicken.

"She and her daughter, Meredith, were the ones whose boat overturned . . . that day . . . on the river."

He stopped chewing and made himself swallow.

"So, she came to pay homage to the angel who saved her?"

"Not really." Her face colored at that half-truth. "She came to tell me that things are not right at her husband's old firm, Consolidated Shipping."

"Consolidated?" That name he did remember. The world of London's shipping and import-export firms was not so large that companies didn't know their competitors, large and small. Consolidated was a modest-size company that had been sold twice in recent months and was becoming known for undercutting customary prices on commodities.

"You know the company?" she asked, watching him make connections.

"By reputation. It's changed hands lately, but I can't recall any specific owner associated with it now."

"That may be because it's owned by a group of investors. Mrs. Trimble says her husband was concerned about some of the goings-on in their warehouse. He was the manager of it and was killed in an accident."

"Ah, yes. The widow and the daughter." He straightened, realizing Lauren might have some interesting news. "What kind of goings-on?"

"Something about cargo and materials appearing in the warehouse out of nowhere and then disappearing again without bills of sale."

"That doesn't sound good. Customs officers take a very dim view of 'ghost cargo.' They expect proper documents on every tin of tea and slab of teak. Goods that don't flow through proper, well-taxed channels get companies into trouble." He waved a hand at the mound of goods stacked in the middle of the warehouse. "Case in point."

"What's happening?" she asked, following his wave to the sight of the stacked cargo. "There are constables at the door and standing watch outside. Your mother said your father is determined to take the government to court if necessary to prove that salvage was necessary."

"There will be a legal tussle, but our solicitors say we have a good chance to make our case. At worst they expect we will be forced to pay the damnable tariffs." He studied her for a moment, sensing something more was involved in this late visit.

Word of sketchy practices at a competitor's warehouse might be news, but it was hardly reason for an evening visit like this.

"So what do the late Mr. Trimble's book-keeping troubles have to do with us?" He propped an elbow on a step above and leaned closer, catching a faint scent of roses.

"The new owners manage Consolidated through an agent and a crew of men he brings with him. They're crude and drink a lot. Mr. Trimble's old head clerk heard them laughing and saying that Townsend ware-houses are old and made of *dry* wood."

He searched her eyes, seeing in them a disquiet he now understood. Talking about a competitor's properties in such terms was bad form at best — an ugly threat at worst.

"So she thinks they might decide that our warehouses are conveniently flammable?"

She nodded. Those sunrise eyes of hers were plateglass windows into her soul. She was genuinely concerned for him. The thought sent a wave of pleasure through him that he hoped didn't show.

"Why are you bringing this to me to-night?"

She looked as if she'd been accused of high crimes.

"I . . . I . . . was afraid if I just sent a note you wouldn't take it seriously. And I care about everyone's welfare and safety."

But he could see he'd caught her off guard.

"I'm not just 'everyone.' I'm a man you kissed twice."

"You counted?" she said.

"They were memorable. It wasn't that hard to keep track."

"That's interesting. I'd lost count."

He laughed quietly. He wanted her to admit it . . . was almost desperate to make her confess the same tension and expectation he felt. He stroked the side of her face with his knuckles. She was sleek, rosy-warm, and her pupils were dilating.

"I . . . just wanted to warn you . . . mischief . . . may be afoot." She was staring at his lips and he returned that attention in kind. A moment later she pulled her gaze from him to look out over the warehouse. "This has brick walls. It should be safe."

"Walls do not keep you safe." His voice grew husky as he leaned closer. "They may give you a feeling of security, but inside every stone fortress there is something that can catch fire." He leaned closer still, turning her face back to him. "Wherever people are, no matter how fortified they are, there will be weaknesses and vulnerabilities." He saw her lips part and realized her breath

242

was coming faster, too. "Have you ever caught fire, Lauren?"

"Have you?" she whispered on a breath.

"Yes," he whispered back. "Just now."

His lips touched hers and those three words became both a confession and a prophecy. He had caught fire the day he woke in the belly of a ship with her petticoat and her arms around him. He had continued to catch fire every time he came close to her, every time he touched her. And he would continue to do so because he was combustible in a way he had never realized, and she was the unique spark that ignited him.

Rafe Townsend . . . scholar, businessman, and fortress . . . wanted a woman. One specific woman.

Her.

And for this moment his arms were around her and he was kissing her and she was kissing him back. God, was she kissing him. His whole body, every fiber and sinew was awakening to —

The sound of the office door opening above brought him crashing back to reality and she jerked back as he released her. His mother's voice was a douse of cold water.

"I was telling Horace about the woman who came to see you, Lauren. I'm afraid I may have left something out. Perhaps you should come and give him the particulars."

Lauren rose and followed her inside. A moment later Rafe followed, bringing his food with him. She found Mr. Townsend behind his desk, feasting on tarts that smelled heavenly. She recounted for him what happened during Mrs. Trimble's visit and the news that Consolidated Shipping was now owned by a group that operated through a disagreeable agent. When she revealed the agent's name he frowned.

"Never heard of him," he said. "Still, it wouldn't hurt to poke around a bit."

"There was talk about Townsend having old, dry wooden warehouses," she continued. "And the men saying it were not exactly the sort you want talking about your business."

"*Agreed,*" Horace and Rafe said together, almost in the same breath.

They looked at each other in surprise, and Rafe snatched one of the delicious-looking tarts and bit into it while his father sputtered.

"There is one thing more," she said, looking at Rafe. "This whole business of what happened aboard the ship. Wild stories about my disappearance have made several newspaper editions, and my 'reappearance' may cause more comment. That, combined with news of an inquiry into Townsend Imports and constables at your warehouse, may cause even more public interest."

She looked at Rafe. "I believe it is important that we continue to appear in public and make it seem everything is proper and expected. Lady Anne Drummond actually paid my aunt a call a few days ago to make certain we would attend her dinner party."

"Lady Anne called on you about an invitation? That is unheard of." Caroline looked to her husband. "We were invited, you know. I accepted."

"I'm not budging from this warehouse until this thing is settled and Ledbetter and his government toadies can't lay a finger on my cargo," Horace declared, jabbing the papers on his desk with a finger. He glared at Rafe and then at Lauren. "You two started this mess. You'll have to get us out of it."

Caroline sighed and Rafe looked as if he wanted to punch his father.

"I think we've done all we can here, Lauren," Caroline said coolly. "We'll leave the hampers. I suspect my husband will be eating out of them for some time to come."

She took Lauren's arm and turned her

toward the door. Lauren glanced at Rafe as she exited, but he was locked in a staring match with his stubborn father. She and Caroline were in the carriage and underway when Rafe's mother spoke again. "Don't mind Horace. He's a donkey's rear sometimes, but he'll come around."

"He didn't seem overly worried about this news," Lauren said.

"You have to understand, he's met many challenges and faced difficult situations before. He's not easily rattled, but that doesn't mean he's not concerned."

SIXTEEN

Lord Theobald Drummond held a title and
small estate in Ireland but was better known
in England for woolen mills he had mecha-
nized early on and produced a significant
fortune for his family. His home in Belgra-
via was nothing short of opulent and his
wife, Lady Anne, was a renowned hostess.
Their dinner parties were occasions not to
be missed.

At any other time Lauren would have been
delighted, even honored to attend, but just
now she had a lot on her mind. She spent a
difficult night thinking of all that had happened on the *Clarion* and worrying that she
had managed to fulfill Rafe's worst expectations of her during their time together. Early
on he'd thought her stubborn and impetu-
ous. Had her solution to their captivity and
cargo problems merely confirmed that opinion?

Fires, he'd said. He had kissed her on the

steps, but the things he said made it seem more lustful impulse than true affection. She thought of her own response . . . kissing and wanting to have his arms around her, his body against hers. There was clearly a dose of lust in her, too. But she was beginning to think there might be more than desire. Perhaps a lot more.

She finally had to admit that she wanted him to join her at the Drummonds' because she wanted to see him, wanted to know him better and to have him understand there was more to her than progressive ideas and outrageous behavior. She wanted him to *like* her.

Thus it was a tremendous relief to enter the Drummonds' grand salon and find Rafe there in handsome evening dress, chatting amicably with their host and hostess. Beside him was his friend Barclay Howard, also in fine evening clothes and even finer spirits. The moment she and her father and aunt appeared in the doorway, the Drummonds spotted them and smiled. Rafe excused himself and made straight for them, drawing the attention of the guests already present.

"My dear Lauren, lovely as usual."

Her heart skipped as he leaned close to drop an air-light kiss on her temple. Leave it to him to manage the perfect public greeting for making an impression of prenuptial bliss. The bruising on his face was gone and his light hair fell in tapered layers over the cut still healing on his forehead.

Every aspect of his appearance seemed calculated to draw the eye, and — *sweet mercy* — how it worked. She couldn't take her gaze from him.

Her pulse picked up.

He offered her father his hand, her aunt a gallant kiss on the hand, and herself his arm as an escort to greet their host and hostess — but not before Barclay presented himself for a greeting and a kiss on the cheek that even she thought too familiar.

"Miss Alcott," he said. "I see you have recovered from your ordeal. Sakes, you are more ravishing than ever."

Signaling his annoyance with a heavy breath, Rafe tried to steer her away from Barclay toward the Drummonds and his mother Caroline. Before they had taken two steps a familiar face appeared in their way.

"Miss Alcott, how good to see you again." Mrs. Buffington, wife of Admiral Archer Buffington and a fellow member of their parish school board, was looking her over as if she were goods in a hat shop window. "What *ordeal* did that young man just reference? Has something happened?"

Clearly Mrs. Buffington had missed the gossip altogether.

"It was nothing really." Lauren cut Barclay a sharp glance. He would bring up the very stories they were here to lay to rest.

"Nothing?" Barclay was not deterred. "It was an adventure of the first order." He turned to the matron. "Once again, Miss Alcott has —"

"Has yet to greet our host and hostess," Rafe intervened, trying to rescue her from what promised to be an interrogation.

"There you are." Lord Drummond arrived to thwart their escape attempt. Lady Anne took Lauren's hand and drew her close for an airy kiss on the cheek.

"So glad you're well enough to attend. And I look forward to hearing all about it."

"About what?" Mrs. Buffington was truly interested now, having caught a whiff of something important. "Have you been ill, Miss Alcott?"

"Have you not been following the papers, Mrs. Buffington?" Lady Anne said with a twinkle of mischief. "Miss Alcott has quite a following in London for her uncommon deeds. Most recently she was thought to have disappeared for two days during the riot at the Docklands."

Marigold Buffington's mouth gaped. Lauren would have enjoyed it if she hadn't known the trouble it presaged. Rigidly pious Marigold was as tightly laced as the queen's corset.

"I'm afraid it was my fault," Rafe inserted with the good sense to look chagrinned. "I went charging down to the docks to try to talk some sense into that mob and left her in the care of Barclay Howard . . ." Rafe indicated Barclay, who smiled and gave a half bow, before he added, ". . . which turned out to be a horrible idea, knowing how vulnerable he is to any suggestion from a lady. Apparently Miss Alcott was afraid for me and insisted he escort her to the docks, too. Things got a bit rowdy, and I was injured. Crewmen from one of our ships in the harbor recognized me and carried me out of harm's way. Miss Alcott, being a most intrepid and determined young woman, insisted on attending me." He sighed. "I was literally senseless at the time and in no condition to object."

Grateful for Rafe's intervention and surprisingly self-effacing manner, she took over the story with as much candor as she could manage.

"It was harrowing, I will say," she continued, "being surrounded by that riotous mob. But my first concern was Mr. Townsend's health. When he was injured, I was desperate for help and called for Mr. Howard. He had gone with me but was across the quay, fighting his way through the crowd." She gave Barclay a glowing smile that he acknowledged with a nod, somewhat mollified. "I finally found help in those crewmen from the *Clarion,* a ship which happened to belong to Townsend Imports. With their crew's help I was able to get him to safety and help him to recover."

Rafe, at her side, looked at her with what appeared to be adoration.

"Hip hip hooray for London's Angel," Barclay said with a grin, lifting his glass to lead a toast. To her chagrin, the other guests followed his lead. She blushed so thoroughly that Rafe stepped in.

"I was fortunate to have such a capable nurse," he said. "Unfortunately my luck did not extend to the *Clarion* and her captain. Poor man suffered a heart attack and set the ship ablaze with a lantern as he fell." He took a deep breath. "We were forced to flee a burning ship."

There were gasps and murmurs at that, and sympathy all around. Lauren was soon busy sharing the details of how they came to be near the docks: the children waiting for them at the Seven Sisters. Out of desperation, she pulled Aunt Amanda into the narrative, emphasizing that her aunt had taken care of the children while Lauren went to see what happened to Rafe. While Amanda told them about the hungry children — how they gobbled up food and stories with equal eagerness — Lauren was able to escape the attention and join Rafe near an open terrace door. The cool evening air coming from the garden was a godsend.

"What do you think? Have we convinced them?" she asked.

"If I hadn't been there," he said with that wry smile she found so irresistible, "I would believe every word we said."

She laughed. It felt so good to be with him, sharing the secrets of all that transpired in the last two weeks. She looked up and was enveloped unexpectedly in his gaze. There was something between them now, something more than kisses and body heat. This was a part of her life she would share with him and no one else. He knew it, too, she could see it in his eyes as he reached for her hand.

A stir went through the salon as a late-arriving pair of guests were shown into the company. A short, balding man with prodigious muttonchops and fierce, dark eyes was accompanied by an excessively slender woman whose plain, dark gown and doleful expression gave the impression of deep mourning. They were announced as Mr. and Mrs. Creighton Ledbetter to curious looks from the assembled guests.

Lauren felt Rafe stiffen at her side and looked up to see his face set and his gaze intent on the newcomers.

"Who is he?" she whispered.

A muscle in his jaw flexed as he dipped his head to answer. "The Undersecretary of Tariffs and Other Bad Ideas."

It was more judgment than identity. She knew too well Rafe's opinion of tariffs and knew his father and hers felt the same. When she looked around for her father, she found him beside Lord Drummond and being approached by Ledbetter. He was forced by decorum to accept the man's offered hand.

Barclay Howard appeared at Rafe's elbow and uttered quietly, "This is a surprise. I didn't think the old boy ever left his office."

"He doesn't," Rafe said a bit too calmly, ushering her toward the other guests. "Unless he has business to do. Which begs the question . . ."

Moments later the undersecretary was

standing before them with a twist to his mouth that resembled a smile.

"How interesting to meet you, Miss Alcott," Ledbetter said, ignoring Rafe's presence. It was a cut that Lauren feared might require an answer. "I have read so much about you in the papers."

"I am surprised to find that you would bother with such accounts," she said, forcing a smile. "Surely you have more pressing matters to occupy you."

His amicable mask slipped for an instant; if she had blinked, she would have missed it.

"My wife is to blame," he explained with a sardonic laugh. "She is a devotee of the 'evening wheezes.' Always scouring the gossip rags."

Lauren glanced at the severe-looking Mrs. Ledbetter, standing awkwardly beside their hostess, as silent as a post. To Lauren's eyes there never existed a woman less likely to enjoy reading, even for the vicarious thrills of gossip and scandal.

"And you may know my fiancé, Rafe Townsend." She smiled up at Rafe and found his face set like granite.

"I know his father, of course," Ledbetter said with a purse to his mouth that was pure condescension. "And I've seen young

255

Townsend's name bandied about of late . . . something about that debacle down by the docks. Got the worst of it, I heard." He tut-tutted. "Well, you seem to have gotten over it. It has yet to be seen if your father will do as well."

That provocation landed on the air just as dinner was announced and Lady Anne called for all to accompany her into the dining room. She took Lawrence Alcott's arm and Lord Drummond took Mrs. Ledbetter's. For a moment it looked as if Ledbetter might offer Lauren his arm, but Barclay Howard stepped in to rescue her and lead her into the dining room. She gave Rafe a glance over her shoulder and was relieved to find him offering his arm to his mother, who seemed equally relieved to accept.

The seating seemed strangely ordered. Her father was seated at Lord Drummond's right hand and across from Lady Anne, who found herself beside the disagreeable under-secretary and his silent wife. Down the table a ways, Rafe was seated opposite Lauren, between his mother and a lady who was introduced as a cousin of Lady Anne, and she found herself bracketed by Barclay and a rotund gentleman who turned out to be an MP from a country borough. She still had a knot in her stomach from the near incident with Ledbetter and was glad to see Rafe engage in pleasantries and small talk. By the time the fish course was done she had the sense that his attention was focused mostly on the talk at the head of the table.

It wasn't long before conversation around her was flowing along with wine, and Lauren found herself making acquaintances and deflecting more questions about her "recent work," with answers focused on the St Ambrose parish school and her recent encounter with other children who needed a school of their own. The others' curiosity about her abated as her information grew ordinary and the rest of the courses flew by. Barclay's talk grew bolder and louder. Wine apparently had a lubricating effect on him and the people around him. Despite his imposing presence, there were smiles and occasional laughter as he described his most recent adventure — a riot at the harbor, near the Customs House — in amusing terms.

Thus, it took until the dessert course for her to notice that conversation at the head of the table had ground to a halt. She noticed Rafe staring at the head of the table and leaned forward to look past Barclay. Her usually amicable father was red-faced and glaring at Undersecretary Ledbetter.

Lady Anne seemed flustered and Lord Drummond was clearly displeased about something. When Lady Anne rose, drawing the men to their feet with her, and declared that the gentlemen seemed ready for their brandy and cigars, there were discreet scowls and the occasional indrawn breaths. The foot of the table had just been served their cherry compote and some seated there had not even had time to taste it.

Lord Drummond tossed down his napkin with a "Gentlemen" and a directional gesture. The men excused themselves to follow him. Shortly, Lady Anne invited the ladies to accompany her to the salon for coffee. As Lauren entered the hallway, intending to catch up with Rafe's mother and learn what had happened, Rafe caught her arm, and she looked up into his darkened eyes. The last two ladies moving to the salon saw him delay her and smiled knowingly. When they were alone in the hallway Rafe leaned close to her ear.

"What was the name of the agent who runs Consolidated Shipping?"

That took her aback for a moment. "Why would you need to —" The intensity of his gaze stopped her. She frowned and tried to think. The name finally bubbled up from memory. "Mur— Murdoch."

"You're sure?"

"I believe that's it. Why do you —"

But he planted a kiss on her cheek, turned on his heel, and headed for Lord Drummond's study.

Rafe slipped into the spacious study to find talk subdued despite the determined congeniality of their host and the mellowing influence of excellent brandy. The guests had unwittingly divided into two camps: one fairly neutral in the conflict between Lawrence Alcott and the undersecretary of Trade and the other clearly in Lawrence's camp.

Ledbetter, given license by the influence of spirits and feeling the importance of his position, began to speak loudly about the "lawlessness" emerging in the country.

"As I was saying, we have laws regulating commerce for a reason — especially when it comes to the import of foreign goods. But there are those who scheme to grow fat from the protection the government provides without paying their rightful share of the cost." He looked straight at Lawrence, clearly including him in that group, and there was a perceptible intake of breath around the room. Lawrence's control seemed to be hanging by a thread when

Rafe spoke up.

"No true man of commerce would deny the proper authorities payment of reasonable charges," he said boldly, claiming the room's attention. His arms were crossed and he leaned a shoulder against one of the bookcases, intending a show of certainty and ease.

He recognized Ledbetter's pattern of discourse, the petty pricks and subtle accusations that were denied the moment they were called out. For all his diminutive stature, the undersecretary was a practiced bully. What was he doing here? This was not a social event he or his long-suffering wife would enjoy. He had come for something . . .

"Docking fees and standard inspections have stood for centuries without complaint," he continued. "But since the imposition of these tariffs, our ports have seen fewer ships carrying commodities we need to import, and our ships carrying English textiles, copper, tin, and wheat abroad pay higher and higher fees to access overseas markets.

"The effectiveness of tariffs has long been a matter of debate in academic circles. It is a simple matter of record that when one country levies tariffs to protect their markets, they all do. Then we're back to where we started, and the only thing we get is higher prices everywhere." He picked up a glass of brandy and sipped, making a show of appreciating the aroma. "Lovely brandy, your lordship."

"True men of commerce indeed," Ledbetter said with a sniff. "Clearly some who claim to be obedient and loyal to the Crown are *not*. They try to sneak goods into the country through illegal means."

A murmur went through the room.

"And what means would that be, sir?" Rafe asked, straightening and taking one step toward the diminutive undersecretary. "What nefarious tricks allow a company to lower its prices, undercut the market, and still make fat profits for its owners?"

"That is not for me to say. And if you know such scoundrels, you are duty bound to bring it to the attention of the authorities. What companies do you know that flaunt our just and necessary laws? Name one that deserves such a scurrilous reputation and merits severe scrutiny."

"I know of only one that routinely undercuts the market for imported goods." Rafe leaned slightly forward, knowing that he risked but not yet knowing how much. What price would he pay for revealing the name of the agent who had threatened Townsend's warehouses? "You would have to ask Mr. Murdoch about the particulars."

"Murdoch?" Ledbetter stiffened back an inch. "And who is that?"

"Someone who knows how the game is played and can name the players." Rafe let his smile resume. "So I was given to believe."

"By whom?" Ledbetter narrowed his eyes.

"Ah, but that would be telling. And I believe we have all had enough of dreary laws and politics this evening." There were nods of agreement around the room. With a smile, Rafe turned to Lord Drummond. "Now, tell all about this horse you've taken such a fancy to, your lordship. Where do you intend to race him?"

Scarcely a minute later Undersecretary Ledbetter set down his glass and bade their host good evening, mumbling something about his wife's frequent megrims. He did not look as if he had gotten what he came for, but he was not quite finished. He paused by Lawrence Alcott on his way out.

"A word to the wise," he said in a whisper that Lawrence had to lower his head to hear. "That merger with Townsend — I wouldn't count on that. Horace Townsend has too many troubles of his own."

Rafe heard the last part as he went to

Lawrence's side.

"And you," Ledbetter said in a voice meant to be heard by others. "I would congratulate you on your upcoming marriage — a clever move indeed — but I suggest you not count your fortune just yet. If your intended doesn't know why you're marrying her, she soon will." The little undersecretary turned on his heel and exited before Rafe could respond.

He turned to Lawrence, his gut tightening.

"She doesn't know?" he demanded.

Lawrence looked down at his glass, and his silence was all the answer Rafe needed.

For a moment he watched Lauren's father avoid the question of her understanding of why the match was required and what would happen to her fortune the moment they spoke their vows. Damnation! He thought she knew . . . was sure that was the reason for her standoffish behavior at first and later for her continuing prickliness and difficult attitude.

But she didn't know. And her father didn't seem anxious to tell her that they would be creating Townsend-Anglia Trading with her inheritance . . . starting the moment she exchanged vows with him.

The impact of Ledbetter's final words

became clear. It was a threat that someone would tell her. Soon. Spurred by the thought, he headed for the door and navigated his way to the salon doors. In the entry hall Ledbetter was receiving his hat and walking stick from the butler. Hearing rushed footsteps, he looked back over his shoulder. At the sight of Rafe, he smiled broadly enough to show his teeth. Like a hyena over its prey.

Rafe entered the salon, searching for Lauren, and saw her standing with her aunt in urgent conversation. When her aunt saw him and alerted her to his presence, she turned to face him. Her face was pale and her eyes were pools of confusion.

He knew approaching her in front of so many women was risky, but he had to speak with her now. This could not wait.

She didn't resist when he asked to speak with her. She didn't refuse him her hand when he took it on the way out of the salon. She didn't object when he led her to an alcove created by the elaborate curve of the staircase.

"What did the bastard say to you?" he asked, feeling a tightening in his throat.

"The money, my inheritance, is the reason for the marriage." She looked up at him.

"And that it is not — never really was — mine."

He saw the ramifications of it sinking into her.

"My mother died so young, I hardly knew her. She left an inheritance for me . . . something that was hers . . . for me. It was . . . comforting."

He seized both of her hands, feeling a roil of emotion that he sensed must be part of what she was feeling. Confusion. Loss. A sense of betrayal. It shocked him to feel the hurt she experienced. But then, part of that could be guilt on his part. He was the central piece of a plan to take something important from her and use it to settle his company's debts and continue his family's legacy in business.

"There is an entailment. You only inherit upon marriage, and then the funds will be controlled . . . by . . . your husband."

"But they passed a law . . . about property for women."

"Earnings. From work. And small inheritances . . . gifts, really."

"So my gift from my mother . . ."

"Is considerable. The law specifically excludes sizable estates."

That took a moment to settle.

"So silly women won't squander it all on hats and jewelry and other such fripperies," she said, though there was little heat behind the words. They rang as hollow as she felt. "Clearly I misunderstood."

She pulled her hands from his. She suddenly wanted to be anywhere but a social evening filled with people who probably saw her as a frivolous young woman who needed to be managed by a husband.

"I want to go home," she said, refusing to look at him.

He took a step back, then another and another.

Suddenly her aunt Amanda was there with an arm around her, and moments after that her father appeared. Lawrence made their excuses to the Drummonds and called for their carriage.

She scarcely remembered the ride home. As she paused at the foot of the stairs, her father said she needed rest and they would talk tomorrow.

She had never felt less like sleeping in her life, but she prepared for bed because it was the most normal thing to do. When the lights were turned low she lay in her bed thinking of her mother, of the framed photograph on her vanity, of the memories she had clung to over the years. Her mother had always been there, in the background and texture of her life, in the knowledge that she had left something of her own behind for Lauren. Knowing she had means had always given her a sense of agency and possibility that she carried with her. Now it felt as if that part of her world had been revealed to be a theatrical backdrop . . . to be rolled up and put away when the performance was done.

She should have asked more questions, should have insisted on knowing more about the family business and her own resources. But she had been too occupied with her charity work, her devotion to education and children's welfare. Her father, for all his recent grumbling, had been content to let her direct her own time and think her own thoughts. She had always assumed she would marry someday, but he seemed in no hurry to shuffle her off into a life of her own . . . until the last few months.

Thoughts she had been avoiding couldn't be forestalled anymore. Rafe Townsend, with his tall, perfect form, dry wit, and delicious kisses, had known from the start that she was the key to a cashbox. To his credit, he hadn't exactly tried to charm her into wanting to marry him. But then, she hadn't been much of a charmer herself.

She was distant, cool, and resentful of his arrogance and high-handed approach to what was supposed to be their courtship. It took jumping out of a boat in her smalls and towing two drowning women to shore to make him see that she was not and never would be a simple, biddable female. And it took puncturing his pride in front of London's reading public to make him see her as a person instead of a profitable commodity labeled "bride."

What did he think of her now?

Was she less in his estimation somehow now that she knew he was marrying her for her money? Why had he come to pull her from the salon to talk to her about it? More importantly, where did they go from here?

She had been open and truthful with him in all their dealings . . . even in their kisses. Could she continue to be? Could she trust him with her mother's inheritance? With her future? With her heart?

It was a long night. More than once she punched down her pillows as if they had muttonchops, a smirking mouth, and dark, beady eyes. By morning she was exhausted, but much of her anger was spent. When she descended to her father's study she had questions for him and was determined to have answers.

Her father met her in front of his desk and took a chair facing her, practically knee to knee with her. The change of customary positions bespoke a change in his attitude and a burden on his heart.

"Lauren," he began with his hand up, "I know it is a lot to ask, but please let me speak. Afterward whatever questions you have, I will answer as fully and honestly as I can." When she nodded his shoulders relaxed, and she understood that this talk was as hard for him as it was for her.

"When I married your mother she came with an inheritance that had been entailed by her father. He had approved of the match, but he was ill and knew he hadn't long in this world. He wanted to protect her. She was not one for worldly matters and she had a sizable sum . . . more than I realized at the time. I vowed to her father and to her that I would not touch it, that it would remain hers and become a legacy for our children. I put it in a trust of the Bank of England and kept my word. I have not touched a penny of that money.

"My company, East Anglia, has always done well and provided us a comfortable income. But the last few years have drained our capital and strained our accounts. When Horace Townsend approached me about a merger I did some investigating and was surprised to learn that Townsend was struggling as well.

"You might well imagine what it cost Horace to admit such a thing, but it is no secret that there is little capital available in the financial markets. Our former investors are busy keeping their own heads above water. Together, merged into one company, we would become the largest import-export company in England and could set both prices and standards. The question was how to fund the merger and make it solvent from the start."

"That is where the marriage came in," she said quietly.

He nodded. "I was astounded to learn how the trust had grown. There was enough to satisfy our debts and even fund the innovation needed to carry Anglia-Townsend into the future."

"Why didn't you talk to me about it? How large is this account?"

He took a deep breath before answering. "Several hundred thousand pounds."

She sank back in the chair, grateful for its support. That was a fortune indeed. And her father, a man of principle and scrupulous honesty, had not touched the funds in all those years.

"How many is 'several'?" she demanded, thoughts whirling.

He swallowed hard. "Six, plus a bit."

"Six . . . hundred . . . thousand?" She almost strangled on the words.

He nodded gravely. "You see why I was worried. It was incumbent upon me to find a man of strength, good sense, and integrity for you. If the size of your inheritance had gotten out, you would have had money-hungry ne'er-dowells dogging your every footstep. As it was, no one knew about it but our lawyers, our banker, and me.

"When you reached your majority," he continued, "my parental control ended. But there was the entailment, which your mother and I left intact, and which was passed down to you. When I met Horace Townsend's son Rafe and had him investigated —"

"You had him investigated?" She leaned forward.

"I did. Do you think I would trust a man I knew nothing about with my only daughter?" He leaned forward, too, his face softening. "It turned out the singular drawback to the man was his pigheaded father. So I proceeded to explore the notion with you, and you were not opposed to it."

"Silly me . . . swayed by thoughts of long,

romantic walks and deep discussions of books and the mysteries of life. And I thought of children — a house full of little ones. I imagined you bouncing them on your knee as you once did . . . me."

Liquid collected at the corners of his eyes and he gave it a swipe. It was a moment before he could continue.

"Your mother and I had such a wonderful life . . . though our time together was cut short. I had hopes that you and young Townsend would come to like each other and make a good marriage. I had no idea things had gotten off to such a dismal start."

"You were right," she said, laying her hand over his.

"About what?" he said, looking up with surprise.

"That I was being a stubborn twit and he was being a horse's arse." She gave a pained smile. "We were both at fault." She squeezed his hand, seeing disappointment in his eyes. Was that for her behavior or his own?

She slid from the chair to her knees and put her head on her father's lap as she had when she was a child. It was forgiveness personified. He laid his hand on her head and stroked her hair.

"Tell me about the merger. What do you intend to do with the money?"

He took a deep breath and told her about East Anglia's debts and the two ships Townsend had sunk too much capital into . . . sitting in the London shipyard, unfinished. He spoke of building a fast cargo fleet that could navigate the Suez Canal and revealed Rafe's desire to start right away by refitting some of their current ships with better propulsion. That was the project he had in mind when they went to see the exhibition. It was an ambitious plan, an exciting course into the future for them and security for the families of the men who worked for them.

And all of it depended on her.

After they sat in silence for a while she looked up at her father, her mind clear on what must be done.

"I suppose there is only one thing for it now."

He frowned. "What is that?"

"I'll have to marry the man."

Though it was exactly what he had wanted to hear, Lawrence found himself strangely reluctant to celebrate those solemn words.

Lauren sent Rafe a note saying that she would be at the St Ambrose parish school the next afternoon for story hour and hoped he would join her there. She had lost track

273

of whose day it was to plan activities — as if that mattered now — but took the initiative and hoped that he would be accommodating enough to join her. Perhaps afterward they could take a walk in St James's Park or visit a tearoom and talk. She wasn't sure what she wanted to say, but she knew she had to talk with him.

She had the cab driver let her off at the gate of the garden between the gray stone Church of St Ambrose and the building that housed the parish school. It was one o'clock and there were lines of children and teachers moving along the path from the rear schoolyard toward the main doors. St Ambrose subscribed to the notion of educating the whole child, which included moral training and healthful exercise. Each day the children spent some time outside in games and physical activity intended to teach right conduct and fair play.

As she entered the main doors, some of the older children called out to her.

"Got another Round Table story for us, miz?"

"Not knights" — another boy elbowed the speaker — "cowboys an' wild horses, miz. That's the ticket. Got any of them?"

"Not today," she called as she threaded her way through a sea of sweaty young bodies and glowing faces. "But I'll look for some books that have them."

The headmaster's office was usually bustling with activity at that time of day but seemed less so just now. When she approached the school secretary's desk the woman rose with a start.

"You're here," Miss P said, and smoothed her hair toward her bun with a fluttering hand. It wasn't like Miss Pringle to primp or ever be at a loss for words. She seemed downright unsettled as she informed Lauren, "The headmaster and school committee are meeting in the rector's office. They asked me to have you join them as soon as you arrive."

"Thank you, Miss Pringle." Lauren set the stack of books she had brought on a nearby counter. "I'll leave these here for now. I'm so excited to start a new story today. I think the children will love it."

But on the way to the rector's study, she thought about the secretary's odd demeanor. There was no customary smile and no question about the books she had brought for the school's growing library.

The door to the rector's study was open and she could see one man and three women seated before the reverend's desk . . . the headmaster and the rest of the commit-

275

tee. With her now present, the whole committee was assembled. But it wasn't time for their regular monthly meeting and they hadn't contacted her about the need for a special session.

"There she is now." Mrs. Buffington rose when she entered and stepped behind her to close the door. The only chair available was the one Mrs. B had vacated and Lauren looked around in confusion.

"I should get another chair."

"No need." Mrs. Buffington stepped in front of her. "Take mine. I would just as soon stand."

Lauren protested, but Mrs. B insisted. The others watched intently as she took the seat and smoothed her dark gray skirt over her lap and adjusted the collar and tie of her starched blouse. When she smiled at them they looked away.

"I had no idea there was to be a meeting today. I would have brought my pad to take minutes —"

"No need for that, Miss Alcott." The rector waved her concern aside. "This is an informal session." He looked down at his desk and folded his hands on some papers there. "A situation has been brought before us concerning a member of this committee. It appears there have been some — unfavorable reports —"

"Scandalous ones," Marigold Buffington corrected, moving to the side of the reverend's desk and looking pointedly down at a batch of newspapers under the reverend's elbows . . . identified by their grayish tone as cheap penny papers. Most were rumpled from reading and she could see that some articles had been circled.

Lauren's stomach knotted at the sight. They were meeting about a committee member mentioned in the penny papers, the "evening wheezes." This could only be about her. When she looked to her fellow committee members only one of the four would meet her eyes.

"We have read these stories with discernment, trying to apply the most charitable interpretation of events," the rector declared. "But even by the most forgiving standards, we have found them to be . . ."

She had looked to him, hoping for some semblance of fairness in recognition of the earnest work she had done for the school. But the silver-haired rector's face was set in a way she had never seen it: authoritative and judgmental. When he glanced up at Mrs. Buffington she realized the woman's face shared that expression.

Pieces came together in her mind. The

dinner party the other night . . . the demands for details of her "misadventure" at the docks . . . Mrs. Buffington's shock at hearing that she had been aboard a ship for days with Rafe and a crew full of *men.* She remembered now that afterward the woman had scarcely looked at her. At the time she had been preoccupied with the undersecretary's ugly comments and boorish behavior.

"Not only were you staying aboard a ship in the harbor with a man you are not married to," Mrs. Buffington said sharply, "but after a brief investigation we discovered your previous behavior has shown a shocking lack of propriety and common decency." Her nostrils flared. "You stripped yourself *naked* to go swimming in a river."

SEVENTEEN

Lauren was so shocked by the way Mrs. Buffington's accusation was framed that it took her a moment to form a rebuttal.

"I–I was not naked, Mrs. Buffington. I had merely shed my skirt and petticoats before diving in."

"So you admit that you undressed in public to go swimming. And on the Lord's Day," another committee member said in dismay.

"I admit to swimming . . . to an overturned boat and two women who were floundering and would have drowned if I hadn't ferried them to the riverbank. Did you *read* the story in the papers? I believe they reported what took place."

"They were quite clear about your behavior," Mrs. Buffington declared, "including your betrothed's condemnation of it. You called him a coward afterward, and stalked off without clothing or a proper escort. A humiliating incident for your family and intended."

"I dressed as soon as I could and I made sure the women were taken care of . . . found them a conveyance home."

"And scarcely a few days passed before you were plucking a dirty little street thief from the hands of justice," Mrs. Buffington continued, her voice and accusations sharpening. "Making yourself out to be some sort of 'angel' while engaging in profligacy and lawlessness."

"That's blasphemy, that is." The headmaster, the only male member of the committee, finally screwed up the nerve to reveal his opinion. "Making out you're on the level of the angels. That's sinful pride, that is."

"I never claimed to be an angel." Her heart was now racing and her hands, despite her gloves, were icy. "Surely you know that I am not responsible for anything in those papers. A newswriter seized upon the incident and turned it into something lurid and sensational."

"We thought we knew you, Miss Alcott." One of the other members, Mrs. Jacobs, had tears forming in her eyes. "Trusted you with the minds of young, impressionable children."

"I doubt any of them read scandal sheets,"

she said, feeling a restraint in her giving way. "And apparently you have only read the most lurid parts. After my work on the committee and in the school, how could you believe I would ever be a corrupting influence on the children?"

"What else would you call a woman who sneaks off to spend days dallying with a man aboard a ship?" Mrs. Buffington charged. "Under the guise of tending his injuries. More of that 'angel' nonsense when you were undoubtedly engaging in an *unconsecrated* union. As an unmarried woman who sits in services every Sunday, you knew better, and still you did it. Fornication alone is grounds to remove you from this committee and from the school."

"Our staff must be above reproach," Mrs. Owens, wife of a philanthropic supporter of the school, declared. "You know full well the contract we have with our teachers . . . 'no dancing, no contact with the opposite sex, no music except hymns on Sunday, no whistling, no reading worldly novels or foreign books or attending any theatricals . . .' "

"Our staff is expected to live modest, circumspect lives," Mrs. Buffington broke in. "How can we expect them to abide by our standards of righteous living when one of our committee members flaunts her indecency and immorality for all to see?"

With each word delivered against her Lauren's spine grew straighter. She was astounded by the vengeful attitude of the woman who had brought the charges against her. What had she ever done to offend Marigold Buffington? She turned to the rector, who now sat with his fingers templed, watching the woman berate her with self-righteous vigor. She shoved to her feet, determined to defend herself but struggling for words.

"Surely you, Reverend, must see that the reports in the papers and the incidents brought before the committee are not the whole story. These writings are half-truths and fabrications, meant to sell papers and titillate the susceptible. And you must see that in passing unfair judgment on me, you open yourselves to a more righteous judgment."

There were gasps at that.

The rector's head jerked as if he'd been slapped.

"Unrepentant sinners face a hellish eternity," he growled as he shot forward and pounded a fist on the papers. "It is because we so earnestly wish to save them that we must pass judgment in this mortal realm.

To do otherwise would leave our world at the mercy of sin and evil influences."

She had to steady herself on the desk. She was now condemned as an unrepentant sinner?

"But in the interest of fairness, we give you the opportunity to set the record straight," he continued. "Tell us what you think we have wrong, Miss Alcott. Did you or did you not spend days aboard a ship in London's harbor with a man not your husband?"

"I did. Two days," she said. "But only to tend Mr. Townsend, my betrothed. He had been hit on the head during the dockside riot and was unconscious, unable to help himself. When the men from the *Clarion,* a ship which Mr. Townsend's company owns, offered to carry him to safety aboard their vessel, I gratefully accepted. I stayed to tend him because I considered his health to be in danger. I believe any young woman of decency and compassion would have done the same for her intended husband." She glanced to Mrs. Buffington, who narrowed her eyes in disbelief.

After a moment the rector continued, finally making the real problem clear. "You have admitted to shedding your clothing and jumping into the river to swim . . . a brazen and shocking act. You have interfered with the workings of justice and let a criminal go free to prey on others. And you now claim to be an angel of mercy only interested in the health of your intended husband. All of which you say are misinterpreted in these wicked publications." He gave the papers littering his desk a dismissive wave.

For a moment she felt a glimmer of hope, which he quickly dashed.

"But this latest piece," he lifted a copy of *The Morning Post,* "declaring you have returned from tending a victim of brutal rioters and are at last able to return to your work at St Ambrose Church School, is most damaging of all. Whatever the truth of these unseemly events, they have been laid at the feet of our congregation. Your hedonistic behavior taints our school and the pupils given into our care. To ignore these charges is to allow them to serve as excuses for others to do the same and worse. The reputation of our school must not suffer for the thoughtless actions of one misguided and intemperate girl."

His voice had grown louder and he rose to face her across his desk.

"We must ask for your resignation from this committee and revoke your access to our students and facilities." He stretched his neck above his clerical collar and stared down his long, narrow nose at her. "Whether you decide to stay on the rolls of St Ambrose's congregation or not is up to you. But I counsel you to take time and *distance* to think about your behavior and its effect on our ministry to a sinful world."

She stood for a moment, grappling internally for control. She wanted nothing more than to snatch those wretched papers from his desk and use them to thrash the sanctimonious Mrs. Buffington and the compassionless reverend about their hypocritical heads. They cared nothing for the truth . . . nor would they believe it if she were to pour out the shocking details of her abduction and imprisonment aboard the *Clarion.* That much was clear. Even clearer was the preordained outcome of the farcical "hearing" they had arranged.

They didn't want to hear her rebuttal or to entertain facts inconvenient to their prejudices. They wanted her gone . . . swept from the school the way homeless beggars were swept from the church steps every Sunday morning. She headed for the door, but turned back with her eyes ablaze.

"I take it you would like my father and aunt to stay . . . along with their sizable contributions to the church coffers. Well, I believe I can speak for them when I say, 'Take the beam from your own eye,' Mrs. Buffington. The ugly thoughts that lurk in your mind are worse than anything I have done. And you, Reverend, I believe you have just failed our Lord's greatest commandment . . . to do unto others as you would have others do unto you. Heaven help you if someday you are treated as you have just treated me."

She strode out through the sacristy and then the side doors, pounding her heels against the stone floor with every step. Her hands were clenched, her jaw clamped tight. She pulled in ragged breaths, feeling that if she didn't scream she would burst. But some vestige of self-control channeled that hurt and fury into energy that propelled her through the garden and she began to run. Out on the pavement beside the street she ran — literally — into Rafe.

"Lauren!" Rafe caught and righted her, and saw she was breathing fast and her face was red. "What's wrong?" She resisted being held at first, but he said her name until it penetrated her anger and she calmed. He held her by her shoulders, looking her over, and was shocked by the fierce emotion radiating from her. She turned her head to avoid his gaze, but he could feel her trembling. "I just called to you three times."

She looked up as the fact of his presence penetrated. "You came?"

"What happened?" he asked again.

"I–I have been suspended" — the words seemed to stick in her throat — "booted out of the school and the church. The committee had a meeting and Marigold Buffington produced those articles that were written about me." Each word came faster and her voice grew louder. "The committee read them and declared I am an unfit example for the children . . . a blasphemer who calls herself an angel . . . a stain on the church and the school's good name."

He realized a couple of people had stopped on the pavement to stare at them. With one arm around her, he turned to flag a nearby cab with the other.

She allowed herself to be bundled into the cab and sat, spine rigid, hands trembling, as he gave the driver instructions to "just drive." He took both of her hands and seized her gaze with his. "Tell me. All of it."

"Mrs. Buffington . . . the woman from the dinner party . . . went out and collected every penny paper she could find with an article about me and took them to the rector, Father Nickerson. They called a meeting of the school committee and surprised me when I came for story hour this afternoon. They accused me of dallying with a man — you — in an 'unconsecrated union' while on the *Clarion*. And they said some awful things . . . that I'm tainting the school, and even that I'm claiming to be an angel. They said I stripped off my clothes and was naked that day at the river just to go swimming. They said that even you condemned me for my wicked behavior and that I called you a coward."

"Well, to be fair, you did use that word." He hoped to lighten her mood. It didn't.

"Then consider this your final apology: I'm sorry I said that and I wish with all my heart I could take it back . . . and avoid all of this . . . this . . ." She pulled one hand from his and made an encompassing circle with it before dropping it into her lap. The full weight of the encounter descended on her. "They truly believe I'm a terrible person . . . so vile and wicked that I mustn't be permitted around the church or the children."

Her shoulders drooped and the fight drained from her. Her face paled and her eyes grew luminous. He lifted her chin to catch her gaze in his.

"Surely that's not what they said."

"Oh, but it was. They were quite specific." She swallowed hard. "I am a bad influence on the children, and my infamous behavior is already bringing shame to the congregation. There was another article . . . one I haven't seen . . . about me returning home after our stay on the *Clarion.* I have no idea what it said, but it had to be horrible for them to pass judgment on me and turn me out."

Rafe watched her sinking deeper into despair and felt helpless to counter it. When she looked up at him tears had formed and she blinked repeatedly, trying not to let them fall. Time and gravity had their way, though, and as they slid down her cheeks, something in his chest began to sink along with them. There was such misery in her face, such pain in her voice and in her earnest heart . . .

God Almighty, he was a sinner plain and true, for at that moment he wanted to thrash a minister of the Church of England within an inch of his hypocritical life!

Even more, he wanted to take the pain of that betrayal from her. He would have given anything to bring her back to that stubborn, caring, impetuous spirit he had seen rescuing drowning women, dirty street urchins, and arrogant fiancés who tried to insist she stay in her place.

She was that one-in-a-million who didn't faint or weep or shrink when things got difficult. The one who demanded decency and fairness and wanted all children to be able to read and think for themselves, and wanted their lives to be the better for it.

It was in that moment he realized he —

Aww, hell, he was falling in love with her.

He sank his arms around her, pulled her against him, and melted internally when her arms clamped desperately around him in return. When he felt her sob he held her even tighter.

This feeling, he realized, was the thing poets were obsessed with and ancient Trojans went to war over. It was taking him over, invading and hulling out his reason, filling him instead with a need to remake the world, to right wrongs, to eliminate injustices. Noble impulses were pouring out of the marrow of his bones. Because of her. *For her.*

In an instant he glimpsed just how narrow his world had been before she strode into his life. It was all business deals and hard-fought negotiations, whiskey and cigars over decks of cards, and rowing at a punishing pace to burn off the aftereffects of tension and the sense that there wasn't much left of the man he had started out to be. There was a whole world out there that he'd forgotten until she put her foot down and made him see it.

He felt the tremors that went through her as he cradled her head against him. He wanted to do battle for her, wanted to rescue her heart and her hopes. But just now all he had to give her were words.

"Lauren, sweetness, you're not wicked or depraved or a bad influence on anybody — much less the children at that blasted school." He stroked her hair. "In the last few weeks I've seen you rescue drowning women, feed starving children, give books to urchins and one disdainful bounder, nurse an arrogant cad back to health, and figure out a way to free captives and salvage overtaxed cargo. You're nothing short of amazing."

She pushed back in his arms and wiped her face with her hands before looking up at him with a tentative expression . . . as if she didn't believe what she was hearing. How could she see the good in others so clearly but doubt the goodness in herself?

He released her just long enough to capture her face between his hands. Gently, he stroked her damp cheeks with his thumbs, hoping for the first time that his feelings were showing in his eyes.

"Even in those first days, when you were annoying the thunder out of me, I knew you were remarkable. You surprised me at every turn and I had no idea how to make you and me fit together."

"I was willful and far too outspoken," she said, lowering her eyes. "The things I said to you —"

"I deserved." He spoke from his heart in a way he hadn't in years.

"I was stubborn and arrogant and opinionated . . . still am, I'm afraid. You, on the other hand, think of others constantly and go out of your way to help them . . . people you don't know, people who can't possibly repay or benefit you in any way." He lifted her chin so she would meet his gaze and see that he was utterly sincere.

Her eyes were red, her nose a little swollen, and her face blotchy. He couldn't resist pressing a soft kiss on her lips.

"You stand up for what's right and good, and you expect the best of people. It never ceases to amaze me, the way you bring out the good in others."

"Today I didn't," she protested. "I brought out venom and judgment."

"That was theirs, Lauren, not yours. You

didn't cause it, any more than you caused Juster Morgan to seize us and throw us in the belly of his ship. People have their own good and bad parts . . . like Fosse and Gus and Little Rob . . . one minute they're clapping you in a cold cell . . . but the next the warmth and goodness in you is drawing out the good in them. Bringing out the best in others is a rare quality.

"Don't let those jealous, small-minded idiots at St Ambrose convince you that you have sullied their sanctimonious company and damaged their precious church. You haven't. They are much poorer for your absence. God knows it, and someday they will, too."

EIGHTEEN

In the silence that fell Lauren reached up to stroke the plane of his cheek and trail her fingers along the edge of his hair. Who was this man picking up the pieces of her broken heart and putting them back together with perfect words and a touch as gentle as spring rain? Minutes ago she was drowning in despair and he took her into his arms, sheltered her wounded spirit, and repaired her heart with pieces of his own.

He wasn't a man to flatter or curry favor. He believed in straight talk and rational discourse. Even now he cited evidence for the conclusions he had drawn about her . . . offering her his confidence and clarity until she could find her own.

He was caring for her.

He cared for her.

The idea sent a wave of much-needed warmth through her. There was hope for her and for them . . . for a marriage that was more than contracts and bank balances. The softness in his eyes — she had never seen them like this . . . open and warm . . . giving. The longer she looked into them the more she understood that this closeness, this revelation of his thoughts and feelings was new to him as well. And welcome.

He didn't try to pretend it wasn't happening or wasn't important to him. In his eyes there was an invitation to more, an expectation that made her heart rise and filled her with a much-needed sense of possibility.

She laid her head against his chest again with a sigh that expressed the release of the tangle of thoughts and purpose inside her. Her feelings were still bruised and would take some time to heal, but she understood now that she would survive. And she prayed that he would be with her as she did.

When he called up to the driver to give him an address, she didn't recognize it but wasn't concerned. She sensed now that whatever he did would consider her and whatever was growing between them. It made another pair of tears slip down her cheeks. Hearts were very strange things, she thought, able to be so content in the face of such uncertainty.

After a while the cab slowed to a deliberate pace and Rafe stirred and leaned to peer at their surroundings. She looked around as he released her to give the driver further directions. Aged wooden buildings with padlocked doors crowded the streets and there was a change in the air — smells of salt, rusty iron, and damp wood. They had to be somewhere near the docks. He called out to have the driver stop in the middle of an intersection of the street and an alley. She sat straighter as she realized there were children in the street kicking a ball around.

Rafe bounded out of the cab with a "Stay here" and headed for one of the boys. The others saw him coming and scattered, but his target had picked up the ball, turned, and stared wide-eyed at approaching doom.

Lauren gasped at the sight of Rafe barreling down on the boy and scrambled for the cab's steps.

Rafe grabbed the boy by the scruff of the neck and dragged him on tiptoes to the doorway of a nearby building. There he leaned down into the boy's face. Lauren arrived in time to grab Rafe's arm and try to pull it away from — Jims!

"What are you're doing?" she said frantically.

The boy grinned at her. "Hey, miz." Then he looked up at Rafe. "Ain't nothin' stirrin' here, guv."

296

"Good." Rafe responded with a smile. "And the others?"

"All quiet. We're keepin' a good lookout."

Lauren's jaw dropped and she looked at Rafe. "They're . . . you're having them . . ."

"Watch the warehouses," Rafe responded. "I meant to tell you. Jims here recruited a few lads to keep an eye on our wooden warehouses."

"He give us a ball to play with," Jims said, proudly showing the rubber ball as he pushed sweaty hair from his face. "We get box dinners t'carry home. An' we get a whole shillin' a day."

"It looked like you were about to beat him black and blue," Lauren said to Rafe, pressing a hand to her heart.

"It was supposed to," Rafe said, grinning at Jims. "If anyone is lurking around our warehouses, we need them to think the boys are just playing. Who better to keep an eye on the warehouses than children no one would suspect?"

"Yeah, like us," Jims said. "We're always in th' street. Like the guv said, nobody looks twice at us."

Tears came to her eyes as she looked at Jims's grin and Rafe's mischievous smile. She kissed Jims and then Rafe on the cheek.

Rafe smiled as he turned to look up at the

roofs and the gray, smoky sky. "It'll be getting dark in a little while. When you see the night men climb up on the roofs, head to the side door of the Seven Sisters for your boxed dinners and then go straight home."

"Aye, aye, guv."

When they were settled in the cab once more she turned to him.

"I'm sorry, Rafe. I honestly thought you . . . you . . ."

"I know what you thought. I meant to tell you about the boys, but I thought it might help you to see them at work." He covered her hand with his. "We settled on it yesterday afternoon and it seems to be working out. We have to put on a show. The boys understand . . . even kind of enjoy it."

"Still, after the way you . . ." She was disappointed in her own reaction. "I should have had more faith in you."

He laughed. "Crazy woman. You're going to have to start believing the evidence of your own two eyes." He leaned closer to her. "I was pretending, but I was still acting like a horse's arse. You had every right to think I'd lost control."

She punched him in the arm and he feigned hurt with an "Owww!"

"Are you pretending now?" she demanded, narrowing her eyes.

"Mostly," he said, breaking into a smile.

A moment later he put an arm around her and drew her against his side. During the ride to Alcott House, he explained that some of their dock workers would be watching the older warehouses at night. They were armed with bells to sound an alarm if it appeared someone intended mischief. He bemoaned the lack of streetlamps in the area but was grateful that their main warehouse was well-lighted at night.

He called for the cab to stop when they came to an intersection with newsies on every corner calling out the headlines of the day. He left the cab to inquire at a newsstand and returned with copies of the most recent *Examiner* and *Evening Post*. She scanned the first paper over his arm as he searched its contents. Her eyes widened on a cartoon drawing of an angel descending on great wings from a ship festooned with garlands and hearts . . . with a handsome fellow in her arms.

She choked on a gasp.

The pair in the drawing were kissing.

"This must be what the committee saw," she groaned.

He read aloud the flowery prose that insisted the Angel and her fiancé had rekindled their *amour* after a stay on a ship in

299

London's harbor. " 'Reliable sources tell us that Miss Alcott's fiancé, Rafe Townsend, was gravely injured in the tariff riot and was recognized and carried to a ship called the *Clarion* by some of the ship's crewmen. London's blessed Angel went with them to nurse her handsome intended, and by all accounts spent day and night at his bedside. What more might have occurred between the pair at that bedside is anyone's guess. But their affection and familiarity were clear to all and sundry as they arrived on the dock to face a barrage of questions . . . especially about what had started a fire on that ship that morning. Those watching the pair of lovebirds speculated that it might have been their blazing passions. Does this mean the wedding is finally in the offing?' "

"Blazing?" She looked at him. "They think we set the ship on fire?"

"Well, actually, we did," he said with a wry expression.

"But not with our . . . you know . . ."

"Passions?"

"Kisses," she said, embarrassed to sound so missish.

"I bet we could light up Trafalgar Square if we tried," he said, lowering the paper and his eyelids in speculation. She could almost see the heat building in him. He traced the

300

edge of his teeth with his tongue and her pulse jumped.

"Holy buckets," she muttered and grabbed his face between her hands. Her lips were suddenly hot and she could have sworn she heard a hiss of steam when they met his. It was pure heaven, feeling his lips massaging, teasing, sometimes commanding hers. He tasted a little salty, a little tangy — like every savory flavor she had ever enjoyed rolled into one sensation. It was male and strong and gave her gooseflesh in the most extraordinary places.

She parted her lips and ran her tongue over those handsome teeth of his, exploring their sharp edges and finding it deliciously stimulating. Arousal seared its way from her lips to her breasts to her sex. Her whole body was aquiver as he pulled her onto his lap and wrapped his arms tightly around her. She reveled in the sensation of being held. She wanted to move, to explore his strong, hard body and revel in the weight of it against hers. For the first time she realized how much more there must be to the pleasure and completion of passion between a man and a woman. Sweet Temptation — she could see why there were so many sinners in the world!

"You could be right," she murmured

breathlessly when he finally released her lips. "About Trafalgar Square." He was as out of breath as she was, but he managed a few words as he nuzzled the hollow of her throat.

"I was thinking too small. I believe we could do all of London."

Upon taking Lauren home and helping her explain what had happened at St Ambrose School, Rafe was relieved to see that she was able to talk about it with greater composure. It was her aunt Amanda who needed to be talked out of both vapors and vengeance. At length Lauren called for tea and sandwiches to help calm her aunt's nerves. He could certainly see where Lauren got her feisty sense of right and wrong. Amanda Perrix was something to behold when it came to her beloved niece's reputation.

A resilient English matron, Amanda recovered enough to insist on presiding over the teapot herself. But several times as she poured and passed sandwiches and cakes, outrage got the better of her.

"How dare the holier-than-thou bastards accuse you of such things? After all you've done for the school and that money-grubbing hypocrite of a rector! Care for another cream cake?"

Rafe looked to Lauren with widened eyes, and she could only shrug.

"The bishop must hear about this. He'll have a word or two for that blathering arse. And I have a nine-inch hatpin I'd love to introduce to the sanctimonious prat's bum. A warm-up for your tea, dear?"

When Lawrence Alcott arrived home to the news of his daughter's removal from the church's school committee, he was just as outraged as his sister. He would call the bounder out . . . he would sue . . . he would take that den of hypocrites apart brick by brick! But in the end Lauren's determination not to seek redress finally penetrated his anger . . . as did the fact that she was seated close to Rafe Townsend and he held her hand through it all.

Something had happened between the two of them, he realized. Whatever it was, it seemed to steady his daughter and help her weather what had to have been a tremendous blow. For the first time in weeks Lawrence felt the knots of tension in his gut loosen. His hope that the pair would see the good in each other and come together willingly was rekindled. He invited Rafe to stay for dinner and they spent time afterward telling stories about their family and Lauren's mother. Lawrence was pleased to give the fellow both his hand and his heartfelt thanks as he departed.

Afterward, as Rafe headed for Townsend's main warehouse, he thought about Aunt Amanda's shocking words. By the time he arrived he was trying to recall whether his father still played cards with that fellow he always called "that sneaky son-of-a-bishop."

He had the cab let him off at the front door and used his key. As soon as the door closed behind him, he turned and found himself facing a tall, hard-looking fellow with one ear missing.

"Cavender." The shock of Jake Cavender's sudden appearance set Rafe's heart pounding. "What are you doing here?"

"Your father called me and some o' the lads to watch the wares."

Rafe frowned and leaned to look past the imposing fellow to where their "salvaged" goods were stacked. The places where coppers had stood guard were empty. Further on he glimpsed another face he recognized, Willie Evers.

"What happened to the harbor police and Customs men?"

Cavender shook his head. "Yer pa said they just up and left. He sent a runner for me and I called my lads." His grin showed a big, healthy set of teeth. "Good to be back at work."

Rafe nodded. "Good to have you back. Where's Bullsworth?"

"Makin' coffee." Cavender chuckled. "He says it'll be a long night."

"Likely it will." Rafe gave a wry smile. "Just not for him." The old watchman would soon be having a nap somewhere on a stack of burlap bags and packing straw. Rafe gave the big man's arm a clasp conveying confidence and headed through the stacks to the stairs leading up to the warehouse office.

His father was dozing on the couch and there was an open hamper on the desk with the residue of lamb stew, soft rolls, and berry buckle visible inside. The situation in the warehouse certainly hadn't put his father off his feed. And the old boy hadn't seemed overly concerned about the Customs hearing scheduled for the following morning . . . as evidenced by his snoring.

"Father," Rafe said as he stood over Horace's unconscious form. Repeating it was not effective, so Rafe shook his father's arm and barked his given name. How many times had Horace awakened him the same way over the years? Turnabout was fair play.

"Wha–what?" Horace shot up with eyes

wide open and hair practically on end. "What's happened?"

"That is what I want to know. The coppers are gone."

Horace swung his feet to the floor and sat rubbing his face. "I went down to the floor at about six o'clock to see if your mother had sent some dinner and found them gone. My first thought was that the lawyers got Customs to call it off. But when Boswell came by this morning he didn't say anything about such a possibility. I got a bit concerned and sent Bullsworth to the tavern to find Cavender and collect a few of our men to secure the place. Just in case."

Rafe went to the inner window and stared down into the warehouse. "Why would they pull their men off now? With the hearing tomorrow?"

"I have no idea. It made me uneasy, the coppers leaving without a word, just up and disappearing. Can't say as I'll miss them, but still . . ."

Horace rose and gave his chest a good scratching. "How about a brandy?" He poured and Rafe perched on the side of the desk while his father took the chair behind it.

"Boswell came this morning? What did he have to say?"

"No one seems to know the identities of the members of the syndicate that purchased Consolidated. Which is truly strange. But he did find the location of their warehouse . . . one was listed under 'assets.' And where do you think it is?" He nodded meaningfully. "Cutter Lane."

Rafe lowered his glass without taking a sip. "Our Cutter Lane?"

"The very same." Horace looked thoughtful. "Explains how they knew about our 'old wooden warehouses.' They're settled within spitting distance of them."

Was that a coincidence? Rafe considered that for a moment. It bore investigating.

"Who do you know at the Bank of England?" he asked his father.

"I have an acquaintance or two. Why?"

"Someone there has been passing confidential information to Ledbetter. Given the things he said at the Drummonds', he knows more than he should about Lauren's inheritance. He couldn't have gotten that information anywhere but Alcott's lawyers or the trust officials at the bank." He paused, thinking. "Why is he so intent on disrupting the merger?"

"Who knows? He's always been angry that he wasn't born to a life of wealth and privilege. Even at school he was always jealous and greedy," Horace said. "It beats me why anyone would choose him for a post in government. The man's a weasel."

"There's your answer," Rafe said with a wry expression. "Weasels are useful in government. They do things cabinet ministers and party leaders won't sully their hands with."

Horace conceded that with an unhappy nod and then recalled Rafe's request and scoured his memory. "Let's see . . . Silas Hedgeman is head of commercial accounts at the old girl on Threadneedle. Reliable man. After the hearing tomorrow I'll pop by and have a word with him. You need to be at the Customs House to give your side of the story. The lawyers told Alcott to have his daughter there as well. She seems to have a way with people — being an *angel* and all."

Rafe ignored the sarcasm to think about that. Would their latest notoriety help or hurt the case? Interestingly, she hadn't mentioned her inheritance today — too distracted by the pain of being accused of things she hadn't done by people she cared about and respected.

"I meant to ask," he said as his father added to the brandy in his glass, "do you still play cards with that 'sneaky son-of-a-bishop'?"

Nineteen

Barclay Howard's elegant town house was unnaturally quiet as Rafe let himself in through the front door later that night. The servants had retired and the gaslights were turned low in the main hall. The only other illumination came from the book-lined study, where he found Barclay in shirtsleeves and sock feet, reclining on a tufted leather couch. He was so absorbed in a book that he didn't notice Rafe's approach.

This was certainly new, Barr Howard reading something besides racing forms and sporting news. Rafe bent to look at the book's title and snapped upright with a scowl.

"Ivanhoe?" He growled, startling his friend into dropping the book and lurching up to a sitting position. "Tell me you aren't reading that."

"You damn near gave me a heart attack," Barclay said, clutching his chest. "And I can't tell you that because I *am* reading it." He grabbed the book and drew a deep breath. "Cracking good story. Top-notch writing."

Rafe glowered, flipped back his coat, and planted his fists on his waist. "Is that my copy?"

"I assumed because you weren't reading it . . ."

Rafe shook his head. He could never quite predict Barclay Howard. One minute his friend was a threatening mass of muscle that made people step out of his way on the street and the next he was teary-eyed over a piece of music or an abandoned puppy.

God only knew what reading novels might do to him.

"Put on your shoes and grab a coat and cap. I need your help."

"Now?" Barclay winced, clutching the book to him. "But Ivanhoe is just striking a deal to raise the king's ransom."

"Damn it, Barr, there are fortunes at stake here."

"Whose?" Barclay straightened, suddenly serious. "Miss Alcott's?"

"Hers. And mine."

"Oh." The book was tossed aside and Barclay began scrambling into his shoes. "Why the hell didn't you say that?"

Rafe fidgeted as Barclay tied his shoes and reached for a coat hanging on the back of a nearby chair "Oh, and you wouldn't happen to have any weapons? Knives, truncheons, guns?"

Barclay shot him an insulted look.

"Of course not," Rafe muttered as they headed for the door. "Why would *you* need a weapon?"

Moments later they were on the street and striding for a nearby cabstand as Rafe explained their mission . . . investigating a warehouse at the docks that belonged to a competitor who had made veiled threats against Townsend's storehouses.

"Where did you get this information?" Barclay wanted to know as they climbed into a two-seater and Rafe called their destination.

The driver insisted he'd go no further than one of the main intersections leading to the Docklands. There was no need to ask the reason. The Dockland streets and alleys were dangerous, and cabbies often refused to venture into those unlit precincts at night.

Once they were underway Rafe explained that the information came via a woman Lauren knew. Barclay frowned, and Rafe realized he'd have to explain the connection.

"All right — a woman she rescued from drowning."

"The widow in the river?"

"The same," Rafe said, bracing for a ribbing.

Instead, Barclay produced a small, satisfied smile.

"So it really does have something to do with the Angel."

"Would you not call her that?"

"Why?" After a moment's thought Barclay gave a low, annoying chuckle. "Oh, the lust thing. Feeling guilty, are we?"

"Bugger off," Rafe snarled.

That brought a full-out laugh. "Touchy, too. Fine. Then tell me what we're going to do once we get to this worrisome warehouse."

Before long they were being let out beside the last glowing lamp post on the largest street leading into the Docklands.

They headed on foot toward Cutter Lane, hands in pockets, shoulders hunched the way men did on these mean streets. In the darkness, caps drawn low over their eyes and coat collars up to cover their white shirts, they could have passed for "any man" in the shadows of the harbor district. They skirted occasional taverns and the bung-eyed patrons the drinking establishments belched onto the street at such an hour.

The streets grew narrower and darker as they progressed and they kept to the shadows of the buildings crowding the pavement. After a while Rafe grabbed Barclay's arm to halt him beside a looming wooden structure with large, padlocked doors. He pointed up, and Barclay flashed a grin when he made out the faded white lettering that said it belonged to Townsend Imports. They moved farther down the lane, and near the end of it they spotted activity at a brick-and-wood structure that backed onto a dock where a ship was berthed. It was hard to see what was happening inside until a door opened briefly, and the light inside gave them a glimpse of men moving crates and barrels toward the dock and vessel beyond.

Rafe signaled for Barclay to follow and led him to a narrow alley several buildings back. There was a set of rusty iron steps leading up to a flat roof and they were soon climbing across rooftops to look down on what had to be the Consolidated warehouse. They lay down on the roof, and from that vantage point the ship was mostly visible. The rear doors of the warehouse were open and a gangway had been laid between the dock and the ship.

Rafe studied the vessel. "Smaller than the

Clarion, but large enough to carry a decent size cargo," he whispered to Barclay.

"Why are they loading in the dead of night?" Barclay whispered.

"Only one reason I can think of," Rafe said. "They don't want their cargo to be seen."

They watched and listened, though it was hard to hear what the men said. It became even more difficult to hear with the arrival of a big wagon heaped with containers and covered with canvas. Who covered a wagon filled with crated goods unless it was pouring rain? The night sky was overcast but not threatening.

They shifted position to watch the wagon roll right up to the warehouse's open door and stop partway inside. There was cursing and grumbling as the workers blamed the drivers for stacking the wagon's contents too high. While the irritable drivers unhitched the horses and led them out into the street, men from the warehouse rolled back the canvas cover and set about removing the crates and barrels that wouldn't clear the opening.

After a while the men were able to roll the wagon into the warehouse and close the doors. There were scuffling, sliding sounds and the clap of wood thudding against a stone surface. Activity shifted to the dock and Rafe and Barclay shifted, too, venturing closer to the edge of the roof than they had previously dared.

"They're loading it straight onto the ship," Rafe said quietly, scowling. "Must be some of that ghost cargo the widow spoke about."

"Ghost cargo?" Barclay looked puzzled.

"Goods that appear and disappear without papers or taxation — like ghosts in the night."

Barclay nodded, then tried to read the ship's name. *"Cor-man-dant?"*

Rafe squinted and followed his gaze to the lettering on the ship.

"Cormorant," he said. "It's a bird. Big, hooked beaks and webbed feet. They dive into water to fish. I saw them do it when I was stationed aboard old Stringer's cutter. Old sea dog knew every waterbird there is."

Below, on the *Cormorant,* a man in a frock coat and top hat appeared on the ship's deck to give orders and enforce them with snarls and shoves. He was dressed like a gentleman, but no one could mistake his behavior for belonging to a genteel class.

"Bet you a fiver that bloke is Murdoch," Rafe said. "The man the widow said is the owners' agent."

Barclay watched the fellow closely. "Whoever he is, he's in charge down there." He tilted his head, observing. "He stays on his toes and pivots with his fists ready — I'd bet he's been in the ring."

Rafe wagged his head in wonder. Barclay was a true observer of humanity, as well as a knowledgeable patron of bare-knuckle fighting. Because of his size and muscular frame he had been entreated to step into the ring himself. He always declined, saying he only fought when he couldn't do anything else.

After a while the activity in the warehouse slowed and the lights dimmed. Several of the workers departed, talking loudly about ale and wenches as they headed for the taverns.

"You think that was their last load?" Barclay looked to Rafe.

"Could be." Rafe looked up at the moon peeking through the clouds. "We'll give them some time to settle in, then go down and have a look."

Barclay nodded and they watched in companionable silence until the light from the dockside doors disappeared. Later, the man they supposed to be Murdoch came out the front doors and stood talking to another fellow for a few moments, then he strode off down the lane while the man he had spoken to went back inside and closed the big doors. Still they waited, watching the light from a pair of small, high windows gradually grow dimmer.

"So, you are going to marry the Angel, right?" Barclay said out of the blue.

"It will save the business and both our reputations. It seems the rational thing to do."

"Lauren Alcott deserves more than the 'rational thing.' " Barclay stared off into the darkened street. "An angel like that comes along . . ."

"*Not* your concern," Rafe said sharply, shutting off the unsolicited advice he sensed was coming. He did not need advice in romance and marriage from a man who frightened off every woman he looked at. Literally. Barclay Howard was the big bad wolf of London's eligible bachelors.

Besides, his feelings for his bride-to-be were his and his alone to deal with . . . once he sorted them out. What he did know just now was that he was furious at how she'd been turned into a spectacle by some ha'penny news hack and was treated like a tart on a street corner because of it. She deserved better. A hell of a lot better.

Whether she'd be getting "better" if she married him was the question cycling relentlessly in his head. He didn't much like the answers it raised.

Too many things had gone wrong these last few weeks. Newspapers sniping at his character, a stream of ridiculous stories about them, kidnapping, a burning ship, rescued cargo that embroiled them in legal proceedings, and Ledbetter poking around in his bride's financial situation. Now the gossip rags had plumbed a new low — spreading hints of a premarital dalliance that sullied Lauren's name and got her barred from working at the school that was one of her heart's passions. It was just one bloody calamity after another. And what had he done about any of it?

"So, tell me about this *Ivanhoe* book," he said, hoping to change both the subject and his own mood. "What makes this fellow such a hero?"

Barclay turned to him with a grin.

As they lay on the roof watching the warehouse lights go out, Rafe couldn't tell if it was the book itself or the enthusiastic way Barr related the story that made it sound so interesting. He found himself picturing the action Barclay described, and after a while he looked at his friend with fresh appreciation.

"Someday I may have to read that book,"

he said. "Hurry and finish it so I can have it back."

Lauren accompanied her father to the Customs House the next morning for the hearing regarding the Townsends' salvaged cargo. She had been advised by her father's lawyers to say as little as possible and look as fresh and sweet as a morning in May. To that end, she had chosen a coral silk dress with swirls of white lace on the bodice that had always reminded her of a candy box and topped it with a white picture hat with matching coral ribbons. Her father looked her over as she came down the stairs and he pronounced her the prettiest young woman in all of London.

It was an exorbitant compliment, but it warmed her heart and bolstered her confidence as they took their carriage to the London seat of the customs agency of Her Majesty's Government. Her plan was to answer questions put to her as simply as possible and to volunteer nothing of importance. She had learned that selective truth was sometimes necessary in a complex world, and so was silence. Being too talkative or opinionated allowed for your words to be recalled out of context and used against you.

Tension weighted the atmosphere of the Customs House when they entered, and she felt the stares turned their way had nothing to do with idle curiosity. As they mounted the stairs to the second level, they saw clerks and uniformed harbor police in the hallway and heard angry voices pouring out of a chamber down the hall. Every step closer made the nature of the conflict and the identity of the men engaged in it clearer.

"Ahoy, miz!" a young voice came from the far side of the crowd.

She looked around and found Little Rob heading for her with a broad grin. She opened her arms in surprise and hugged him. Behind him were Fosse and Gus, wearing their best seamen's coats. All three were freshly bathed and had hair slicked down with pomade. In their faces she read both pleasure at seeing her and anxiety at what was happening inside.

"You look pretty as a picture, miz," Fosse said, fingering the cap in his hands. Gus nodded shyly in agreement.

Her father looked taken aback by their familiarity, so she introduced them and explained that they had helped her and Rafe aboard the ship.

"What are you doing here?" she asked, squeezing Little Rob's hand.

321

"Mr. Townsend sent for us, so's we can say what happened aboard the ship," Fosse answered. "But a copper turned us away at the door."

She wasn't sure how helpful their testimony would be, especially if it was factual. But she trusted Rafe's judgment and insisted to her father that they come inside with her.

Lawrence cleared a path for them through the doorway, but once inside they stopped dead at the sight of a furious Horace Townsend, arms held by harbor police, facing Undersecretary Ledbetter.

"What in blazes is going on?" Lawrence rushed forward but was stopped by uniformed officers from reaching his would-be partner's side.

"I'll tell you what," Horace roared. "This double-dealing miscreant arranged to start the hearing *early*. The inspectors presented their entire lot of evidence before my lawyers and I even arrived!"

Ledbetter's eyes glinted with satisfaction as he claimed, "The head of the Customs House asked that the hearing be moved up. Your lawyers were notified."

"By a note delivered yesterday at closing to our office . . . in a packet of other correspondence." Hayden Charles, head of chambers at Horace's legal firm, was almost as outraged as Horace himself. "It wasn't seen until minutes before the hearing started. We rushed here, but the damage was already done."

"Surely, Your Honor," Lawrence addressed the magistrate, "this is most irregular. Allowing one side to begin giving evidence and starting a hearing before the other side even arrives —"

"Are you questioning the integrity of this hearing, sir?" The portly magistrate rolled forward in his chair with a glare that shocked Lawrence. "This may not be the Old Bailey, but it is still a legal proceeding, and I will not have my decisions nor the objectivity of my judgment questioned. Sit down or be barred from this hearing altogether." He pounded the gavel as if it were an axe splitting wood.

Lawrence clamped his jaw shut and turned to the head of Townsend's legal team, who held up a hand urging compliance and then waved them to the rows of chairs provided for principles and witnesses.

It was only after her father settled into a chair beside her that Lauren looked around for Rafe and found him standing at the center of a group of burly constables, looking as if he'd turned to stone. She recognized that look; he was furious and trying to control it.

The magistrate ordered the door closed and everyone involved in the case into seats . . . except Horace and the men restraining him. Ledbetter sat down in a chair at the side of the room, separate from the accused and witnesses. The nod he gave the chief customs inspector made it clear he was involved in some of the decisions here.

"With your permission, Your Honor, I call Rafe Townsend to answer the court's questions," the head customs official said.

The constables parted, allowing Rafe to move forward, He righted the overturned chair in front of the judge's table, then sat down.

"I am prepared to relate the circumstances behind the fire on the *Clarion*," he said, "and the subsequent —"

"We have heard an account of the story you gave Scotland Yard," the chief inspector declared. "What evidence do you have that your injury — your supposed reason for being on the ship — did in fact happen?"

Rafe seemed surprised, then angered. After a moment he pushed back his hair to reveal the still-pink laceration on his forehead. "It did happen. I was knocked senseless and was carried — without my knowledge — aboard a ship owned by my company. There I was tended by Miss Alcott, my betrothed." He glanced over his shoulder at Lauren. "She can testify to my state at that time. There were crewmen assigned to help us, Ben Fosse, August 'Gus' Perkins, and Rob Little, who is known aboard ship as Little Rob. I have asked them to be present to give testimony should that be needed." He looked over his other shoulder and the three rose, ready to step forward. "They can attest —"

"Testimony from *deckhands* is hardly reliable," the customs officer protested.

"Beggin' yer pardon, Yer Honor," Fosse spoke up. "But only one o' us is a deckhand. I'm *Boatswain* Ben Fosse. And Little Rob here, he's cabin boy. We come to tell the truth, yer lordship."

"That will hardly be necessary. We already know the truth —" Ledbetter started to rise, but a scowl from the magistrate stopped him.

"*I* will decide what is truth here and what is not," the magistrate snarled at Ledbetter. "Step forward, Boatswain — tell us what you know."

TWENTY

Fosse stepped forward and with some coaxing came to stand between Rafe and the magistrate.

Lauren held her breath, but under questioning, Fosse told a surprisingly coherent version of the story she had created that day on the dock. With the exception of the timing of Captain Pettigrew's death and the origin of the fire, it was surprisingly accurate. She watched Gus and Little Rob nodding in support of every word.

"And this acting captain, Juster Morgan, who decided to throw the cargo overboard, where is he?"

"Don't know, yer worship," Fosse declared truthfully. "He got scared when the coppers and customs men boarded us, askin' questions, an' he took to 'is heels. Ain't seen hide ner hair of him since."

The customs officer looked to Ledbetter for a reaction.

"I have it on good authority that the men of Scotland Yard spoke with Acting Captain Morgan on the day of the illegal offloading of the cargo." Ledbetter sprang up to face the judge. "He told them the fire was set intentionally by none other than Rafe Townsend. And that it was Townsend who directed the men to throw cargo overboard as an attempt to escape tariffs."

"Well, since neither Scotland Yard's detectives nor the acting captain are here to offer such testimony, I will have to disregard it. Hearsay is admissible in only the most extreme circumstances, such as the death of the witness. Do you have evidence that this Juster Morgan is deceased?"

"I–I do not. However, this is not a proper court of law." Ledbetter inhaled, inflating his chest and flaunting the full weight of his ministerial appointment. "As such, the requirements for evidence must be . . . less exacting."

The magistrate's face grew strangely calm as he studied Ledbetter and the customs inspector, assessing the pair and their assertions.

Lauren held her breath and reached for her father's hand.

"And with respect, Your Honor" — there was a snide edge in Ledbetter's voice —

"the proof of their attempt to avoid lawful taxation is the fact that now the cargo at issue is missing from their warehouse."

That caused an intake of breath around the hearing chamber.

"What?" Horace yanked his arms free and advanced to stand by Rafe, who was now on his feet. "That's a lie. The cargo they inventoried is still there. I have had men guarding the place since the harbor police mysteriously withdrew yesterday."

The magistrate looked at Horace and Rafe with a discerning glare.

"You say the cargo is there, while you" — he turned to Ledbetter — "say it is missing. And no one seems to know where this Juster Morgan fellow may be." He paused to mull over those facts. "I am here to serve justice and Her Majesty's law." His eyes had a flinty cast as he turned to the chief customs inspector.

"You have the manifests from the ship and the documents from the inventory done at the warehouse?" When the customs officer answered in the affirmative the judge pushed up from his chair and ordered his aide to call for his carriage.

"I want to see for myself whether this cargo is in place. Now."

Turmoil erupted in the chamber as the

judge pointed at Lauren and Horace, declaring that they would ride with him. The others would have to find their own transport.

Lauren met Rafe's alarm with a determined look that seemed to relieve at least part of his tension. He took a deep breath and turned to her father to ask if there was room for the crew from the *Clarion* in his carriage.

Lawrence looked at the trio. "I believe we can squeeze them in."

Inside the judge's well-appointed coach Lauren found herself seated opposite His Honor and beside her fractious father-in-law-to-be.

The judge studied the pair across from him, then his gaze settled on Lauren. Her heart was beating like a caged bird against her ribs as he demanded she tell her version of the story.

"I was worried about Rafe going to the docks with so many angry men. I didn't know what he would do, but I feared he would try something heroic. And, of course, he did."

Her words shocked even her a bit. She glanced at Horace, who seemed a bit confused.

"The crowd was in no mood for reason or calm. But he stood before them and spoke from his heart as well as his head, entreating them to disperse and not make matters worse. Then one man in the crowd struck another, and it sparked fighting all around the square. It was terrifying how quickly the violence spread. Rafe stood between the mob and the harbormaster's office, trying to hold them back from assaulting the place and dragging the harbormaster out for what they called 'payback.' " She tightened her clasped hands on her lap, feeling some of the same dread and horror she had experienced that day.

"I saw the blow that felled him. All I could think was that I had to help him. I managed with the help of a young boy to get to him to the side of the building. That was where crewmen from the *Clarion* found us. At first I didn't know who they were and tried to prevent them from taking him. But when they convinced me who they were I went with them as they took him to safety aboard their ship. That Juster Morgan was first mate and not at all welcoming. But Captain Pettigrew was always known as a good and honorable man, so we were put into a small cabin and given medicine and bandages. I stayed with him to tend his injury. Rafe slowly recovered. Those men from the *Clarion* — the ones who came today — were decent and charitable to us — a godsend.

"When the cargo hold caught fire it was chaos. By then Rafe was on his feet and able to respond. We found out the captain was dead . . . Rafe and Juster Morgan exchanged blows . . . I was knocked overboard and Rafe rescued me." She stopped, realizing what she'd just said.

The magistrate studied her reaction and turned to Horace.

"You believe her testimony?"

Horace looked at her and blinked, as if seeing something in her he had previously missed. "This young woman has shown herself to be as courageous as she is compassionate. She has been dubbed an angel in the popular press, and for good reason. I would take her at her word, Your Honor, and I would put my fate in her hands."

As surprised as she was by Horace's endorsement, she was more surprised by the statements she had just made. Rafe *had* rescued her. And he had risked life and limb to stand before a small army of armed and angry dock workers, trying to persuade them to a more productive path. Put in those terms, his behavior was nothing short of heroic.

The magistrate asked nothing else and the silence between them seemed to be the result of all three thinking or rethinking important matters. It wasn't long before they arrived at the main Townsend warehouse and were ushered inside by the same harbor police and constables who had guarded the cargo only the day before.

In daylight the warehouse seemed downright cavernous and was packed with crates, barrels, and bales . . . some on shelves, some just stacked at the ends of shelf rows. When they reached the center of the warehouse, where the cargo from the *Clarion* was stored, Horace jolted forward and stood in the empty space with widened eyes.

"What happened to it?" he demanded of no one in particular. "It was here when I left last night."

He turned on Ledbetter, who was declaring furiously that the Townsends had removed the cargo — secreted it out or sold it off so there would be no evidence of their malfeasance. Horace tried to rush him but was stopped by Rafe and a pair of harbor police.

"We had nothing to do with it," Horace yelled. "Why would we remove cargo that was under legal dispute? That would be asking for punishment!"

Rafe tried to calm his father, but was also looking around the warehouse. "Where are

Jake and Willie and the others?" His father stopped shouting long enough to listen.

"Find them," Horace said. "This couldn't have happened with them on watch."

The men they had left in charge were soon found. Jake Cavender stumbled out of the shadows with blood on his shirt and a battered face. Willie Evers and another longshoreman were doubled over, clutching their bellies, and had to be helped to the center floor.

"What happened?" Rafe asked, pulling out a handkerchief to press against the wound on Jake's head. Blood had dried on the man's face and hands, but with the effort of moving the head wound had reopened. Rafe helped the fellow to a seat on a nearby crate. Clearly he had fought hard to defend Townsend property.

Lauren didn't hear the man's response, for at that moment something tugged on her skirts and she turned to find Jims Gardiner, sweaty and breathing hard, seeking her attention.

"Jims." She drew him aside. "What's happened?"

"Blokes tryin' locks on the doors," he panted out. "Have t' tell the guv."

"Did they have torches or kerosene?" she asked. He shook his head, still recovering his breath. "Were they trying to get inside?"

He took a final deep breath and shrugged. "They went aroun' to another place — we didn' see after that."

"It's probably . . ." She had no finish for that thought. It could be anything but probably wasn't. Missing cargo and now men trying to get into Townsend Imports' old warehouses. It could be a coincidence, but probably wasn't.

She looked to Rafe, who was busy trying to keep his father and the nasty little undersecretary from each other's throats while the customs inspector questioned the men who had tried to protect the cargo the magistrate was there to investigate. It was chaotic and no time to call attention to yet another impending calamity.

Making a decision, she grabbed Jims's hand and led him to the main doors and out into the street. "Which way?" she asked, and he pointed down the street.

"That way, miz. But . . . I come for the guv . . ."

"He has a lot on his plate just now."

"He's eatin'?"

She sighed. "I mean he's busy dealing with other troubles just now. I'll take a look and report back to him if something untoward is happening." Taking his hand, she waved him onward. "Let's go."

Jims led her across a few streets and down an alley that had her holding up her pretty skirts and stepping gingerly to avoid puddles and soggy piles of offal she didn't want to examine. He pulled her to a stop across from an older wooden structure with faded lettering above a pair of tall, padlocked doors.

Those Consolidated men were right, she thought. The old Townsend warehouses didn't look especially sturdy. She looked around the street and didn't see anything out of the ordinary: the occasional stray dog, an old fellow stumbling along and using the sides of buildings for support. She was thinking about checking on the old man when Jims pulled on her arm and dragged her back against the side of the nearby building with him.

He pointed across the way and she spotted two burly fellows disappearing around the warehouse beside Townsend's with wrecking bars in their hands. A moment later she heard glass breaking and looked to Jims.

"Did that come from Rafe's warehouse?" she whispered, flattening back against the wall as the men headed down the street.

"I ken slip b'tween the buildin's and see,"

Jims declared. Before she could quash the idea he darted across the street and her hushed command to "stop" and "come back" fell far behind him.

She muttered about the stubbornness of the male sex from cradle to grave and then hurried across the street after him. As thin as he was, Jims slipped down the narrow space between the warehouses with ease.

"Jims! Come back here!" she whispered as loudly as she dared.

"Jims!" But she was forced to stop at the opening between the buildings and watch Jims negotiate the narrowing way. Out of frustration she tried to fit herself in the passage, too, turning first one way, then another. Her hat, bustle, and draped skirt prevented every approach she made. She would choose today to wear one of her most feminine, frilly, and incapacitating dresses!

She squeezed her way back onto the lane and scowled at the front doors. Her gaze focused on the old-fashioned padlock and she had an idea. She pulled her hatpin and stuck it into the drape of her skirt while removing her hat. It didn't take long to find a sturdy hairpin in her upswept coiffure. It was a big lock, so to be safe she extracted another hairpin and mashed the two together. They were a surprisingly good fit in the old lock, though she had to shove hard several times to get them past the rusty levers inside. She chewed her lip as she concentrated on working the lock. She was running out of length when something inside the mechanism broke free and allowed her to turn the hairpins and open the lock.

She squealed in victory before clamping a hand over her mouth and sliding the lock out of the metal fittings on the doors, which creaked as she opened them, and slipped inside. The place seemed larger on the inside than it did from the street. It went back quite a way and the windows, set high in the walls, admitted enough light to show a dusty floor and stacks of empty crates and rusted barrels. There was little stored at the front, but she knew that the business end was always at the rear, near the warehouse dock. She moved farther in and began seeing footprints in the dust . . . a few at first, then more as the number of dust-free crates and newer barrels increased. She paused to listen and heard the creak of floorboards that seemed to be coming from behind — she whirled and gasped.

Two beefy, hard-looking dock workers stood behind her with their arms crossed. "Where did you — how did you —" she stammered.

"Thanks fer workin' that lock fer us, yer laidyship." A tall man with a flattened nose and a number of scars on his chin and eyes spoke. "It were givin' us trouble."

He and his companion were scrutinizing her face and frame with suggestive grins. She read menace in those expressions and realized she was in trouble.

"This is my fiancé's property and I was just checking on a report that it had been disturbed. I have sent for him and strongly suggest that you depart before he arrives. He is quite particular about who enters these premises and you wouldn't want him to mistake your presence for anything untoward."

The shorter, stockier fellow with a severe case of "boozer's nose" looked at his mate. "Hear that? 'is Lordship Towns-send won't be happy wi' us in his pre-miss-es." Their chuckles contained no humor.

She started around the pair, but Scarface moved to block her way with a nasty half smile. "Where you goin', Miss Too-Fine?" He dropped his gaze to her breasts. "He buy you them silks?"

A sudden crash shook the aged walls and filled the rear of the warehouse with dust, sunlight, and the smell of burning gunpowder. She whirled to find the rear doors had exploded inward and a number of men stood outside with sledgehammers, wrecking bars, and what looked like cargo nets.

"Too late, Miz Totty-Swell." They seized her and despite her furious resistance clamped her arms behind her back and tied her wrists. "Yer comin' wit' us." She tried to scream but got a slap across the face that left her dazed enough to allow them to stuff a kerchief in her mouth. They shoved her past the wrecked doors and dragged her down the dock to a ship berthed there. It was two-masted and painted black with a yellow band between the deck and the waterline.

Men were rolling barrels across a gangway, and when they reached it they hoisted her and carried her across like another bit of potential merchandise. They were met by a glowering man wearing a top hat and an old-style frock coat.

"What the hell is this?"

"Th' twitch caught us at th' warehouse. Says she's Townsend's promised wife," Scarface said with an edge of defensiveness.

"Does she indeed?" The Top Hat looked her over, recognizing the quality of her clothing and the sense of privilege present in her defiant bearing. He grabbed her face and forced it up with a punishing grip. "An unexpected problem." He looked her over with a dawning smile. "But problems sometimes turn out to be opportunities. I think we can find a use for you, Fancy." He leaned close enough that she could smell the absinthe on this breath. His voice lowered to a ragged sneer. "There's always a way to use a woman."

The pressure of his hold on her jaw remained even after he released her. If it weren't for the nasty cloth in her mouth, she would have spat in his face. Her heart pounded as he ordered her taken below and bound properly, hand and foot. As they pushed her toward the main hatch she heard a yelp of pain and managed to turn her head enough to see a sailor give Jims a smack across his face.

" 'At's the last time ye'll bite me, ye little shite!"

Her spirits sank as they prodded her down the stairs and into the captain's cabin. No matter how hard she fought, she couldn't keep them from binding her feet and throwing her onto the captain's bed. They managed to handle her body thoroughly in the process and laughed as they described in detail what Murdoch had in mind for her.

She lay on the wide bunk, shamed by what

she had just endured and horrified by what was yet to come. And Jims — they had Jims, too. No one would know where they had gone or what had happened. They'd have no idea that the vile Murdoch held her on a ship in the harbor. Murdoch . . . the man Mrs. Trimble identified as the agent for Consolidated's owners. Then it struck her that she had glimpsed sailors checking rigging and sails and calling for the longshoremen to hurry with the cargo. They were preparing to depart? If they did, what would happen to her and Jims?

For the first time in her life she had no way out, no help, no options. As she lay there, all she could think was that she had wasted so much time being stubborn and judgmental with Rafe. Would she ever see him again?

She remembered the way he had held and comforted her in the carriage, the tender way he'd kissed her, the eager way he had listened to her family's stories as a way of learning about her. Tears slid back into her hair.

If she ever saw him again, she would tell him what he meant to her, how much she cared for him. How much she had come to respect and . . . love him.

If.

Twenty-One

There was turmoil on the floor of the Townsend warehouse as accusations flew. The magistrate bellowed for silence and ordered the harbor police present to arrest the next man who spoke without permission. Tense silence fell over the group and the arbiter of justice leaned heavily on his cane as he stalked to where Jake, Willie, and the other Townsend workers sat nursing their injuries.

"You two" — he pointed to Jake and Willie — "what did these men who assaulted you look like? Did you recognize them?"

Jake shrugged. "Whoever they was, they knew how to handle 'emselves in a fight. Some wore kerchiefs over their faces. Most didn't talk. They come busting thru th' door the minute Willie opened it."

The magistrate turned to Willie, who winced as he shrank back, clearly still in pain. "Can't say fer sure, but one sounded like a bloke what used to work wi' us. A big fellow. Mean. Liked to talk big." He looked to Jake. "You remember. You got in a dustup wi' him once. The guv fired his arse for stealin'."

"Morris?" Jake said.

"That's the one. Morris — they called him Mo."

"So, we have a start at figuring out who is responsible for this theft."

"Really, Your Honor." Ledbetter stepped forward, now choleric at the turn the legal proceeding had taken. "It's clear enough what happened here. Surely you aren't gullible enough to be taken in by such a pretense. This whole debacle was engineered by Townsend to —"

"Constable, arrest this man." The magistrate pointed at Ledbetter.

The shock on Ledbetter's face was almost worth all the trouble he had caused that day. Rafe looked to his father and tried not to grin.

Held physically by harbor police, Ledbetter sputtered, "H-how dare you treat a member of Her Majesty's Government with such disregard? The secretary himself will hear of this."

"You may depend upon it." The magistrate swayed over to Ledbetter. "But right now I want to know how you knew the cargo was missing here. You knew about it early this morning. I want to know who told you and when. I warn you, I will have the truth or nothing. You already tread on thin ice."

"It is you who treads on thin ice." Ledbetter raised his chin. "I am not on trial here — I will not be questioned like some lowly civil servant. I have connections in the Inns of Court . . . all through the government. I can see you stricken from the rolls of the bar. After witnessing your inept conduct in this matter I am surprised that has not already occurred."

There was a quiet intake of breath all around as they watched the clash between the powers of the government and the judiciary. No one could have predicted that the magistrate would break out in a laugh.

"So you believe you have influence and you wish to spend it prosecuting Townsend over a few crates of God-knows-what. My old mentor once said a man should choose his enemies wisely. You clearly were not mentored as well as I." He edged closer to Ledbetter.

"You should know, Undersecretary, that as a retired high justice, I can choose what manner of hearings I wish to conduct. I chose this one because it was suggested to me by the secretary of Commerce himself. He was most curious about your valuation of cargoes, the rising tariffs, and the unrest they are causing. When you are released from custody — eventually — you may find you have more to answer for than your reprehensible performance in this matter.

"Take him to your station," the magistrate ordered the officers, who seemed uneasy in the face of such conflict. "Enter his full name and the nature of his employment into the arrest rolls. He is not to be released without my express permission."

Ledbetter looked as if he might explode as they forced him through the doors. They could hear him protesting and threatening as he was taken away.

Rafe grabbed his father's arms and glared at him to keep him from celebrating. There was more to the situation than Ledbetter's abuse of power and his puzzling vendetta against Horace. They needed a clear and impartial assessment of facts and they could only get that by showing respect for the inquiry. The magistrate was not a man to be trifled with, and he clearly intended to get to the bottom of the matter.

For the first time in over an hour Rafe looked around for Lauren and didn't see her. His attention was forced back to the matter at hand as the magistrate went over the evidence and demanded to know where the cargo might have been taken. Rafe thought for a moment and decided this was the time to mention . . .

"There have been threats against our warehouses," he said, drawing the magistrate's keen gaze. "An acquaintance brought word to us of danger posed by a competitor with murky connections. We discovered that their operations are located near our old warehouses on Cutter Lane. I am reluctant to make accusations . . . but . . . Consolidated Shipping bears looking into."

The magistrate nodded, acknowledging both the information and his reluctance to name the company on such hearsay.

"Take me there. Let's see what this competitor has to say."

The magistrate insisted on taking his coach there, and soon Horace, Rafe, and Lawrence were leading several customs men and harbor police to Cutter Lane. They pointed to the first of their old warehouses, but they stopped dead when they approached the second. The door was open and the padlock used to secure it lay on the ground.

Rafe rushed through the doors and halted halfway to the rear of the warehouse, staring at the sight of the wrecked doors on the dock side.

His father soon joined him, panting from the run, and stopped dead just behind him. "What the bloody hell?"

Behind them came customs officers and harbor police, who hurried past them to examine the damage. Rafe ran out onto the dock and looked down the way to their other warehouse and found those doors similarly damaged. Rafe watched the constables moving about, checking the damage and making notes.

When the magistrate stepped onto the dock Rafe spoke his thoughts aloud. "Why would anyone break into this warehouse and take things stored here? This is where we keep goods that moved slowly or haven't proved profitable enough to keep at hand."

The shattered rear doors of both warehouses had charred and blackened edges that smelled like burned gunpowder. Clearly they had been blown open with a small and expert explosion . . . an unheard-of tactic in the annals of burglary. An officer came from the dock with something white in his hands. As he approached, the sight of a hat trimmed with bright coral ribbons was like a punch to Rafe's gut.

"Where did you find this?" he demanded,

347

grabbing it.

"Just down the dock," the fellow said, pointing.

Rafe turned to his father and Lawrence, who looked as if he'd been impaled. "Lauren was here. Whoever broke down these doors has our goods . . . and her."

"Not so fast, Son," Horace said. "There could be another explanation."

"What other explanation?" Rafe demanded, aware of the magistrate watching them. "She was here, in this warehouse, and now she's gone. I don't know why she would come here, but she had to have been here." He held up the hat. "This is proof." When Lawrence reached for the hat he surrendered it and watched her father clutch it tightly.

"I saw 'er talkin' to that other boy . . . the one on th' ship with ye." The *Clarion* crew members clearly had been listening and Little Rob now spoke up.

"Jims? He came to get her?" Rafe didn't know whether that made her prospects better or worse. Jims and the other lads were watching out for trouble, and from the looks of things, trouble was what they'd found.

He rushed out onto the dock to look where the ship he and Barclay had watched last night had been docked. The empty berth behind Consolidated's warehouse sent a chill through him.

He ran down the quay behind the warehouses only to find the Consolidated facility locked and silent. Banging on the doors failed to raise anyone. Wasn't there supposed to be a manager overseeing the place? He went around to a window they had looked through last night and climbed up on the barrel they had placed beneath it. Inside, the storerooms seemed dark and silent, but he had to be sure no one was there.

He ran back to the dock, grabbed a loose stone, and climbed up on an old barrel. The crash of glass threatened to bring the harbor police running, but he quickly climbed inside. He heard their whistles and smiled grimly. What were the penalties for breaking and entering under a magistrate's nose?

After his eyes adjusted to the light he prowled the dimness looking for an office. There was none, just a desk in a corner and some shelves holding mismatched bits of crockery, frayed tariff tables, and yellowed bills of lading. A few papers lay in a bin on the desk, but the drawers contained only dust, a dried inkwell, and scraps of blotting paper. If this company kept regular books they weren't here, and he found no hint of where the ship might be headed.

He stood with his fists clenched. There was no trace of Lauren here, which could mean only one thing . . . she was on the ship, the *Cormorant.* If she was aboard, the ship had to have left the dock within the last hour or two. How long would it take them to reach the Thames, head for the tidal waters, and then out into the Channel?

There was forceful banging on the rear doors as he pulled over a well-worn ladder to climb out the roof hatch. From the flat, tarred roof, warehouse workers could watch for ships headed for their berth with cargoes to unload.

He shaded his eyes and scoured the cluttered harbor for movement. Most of the ships were anchored off the docks, still locked in a stalemate with the Customs House. There was precious little movement among the forest of masts until he glimpsed something a bit farther on . . . maybe in the Channel leading from the docks to the Thames. It was hard to be sure, but he could have sworn he'd spotted the tops of two masts with mains and mizzens deployed. It was close to the turning into the Thames. He felt his gut tighten and clenched his fists. When the thought came a stream of others quickly followed.

He needed a ship.

■ ■ ■ ■

Lauren was miserable, feeling the bunk sway softly beneath her but scarcely capable of feeling anything else. Her arms and legs were numb and her shoulders ached from the way her arms were bound behind her. But the worst of it was knowing the vessel was carrying her away from her home, her family, and Rafe.

How long would it take for them to realize she was gone? And how much longer after that for them to make connections to the boys watching the warehouses and finally the man Murdoch?

The whole thing was her fault. It was her idea to liberate herself and Rafe and the *Clarion*'s cargo with the same stroke. She thought she was being so clever, putting it all together, convincing Rafe to be a party to it . . . then enlisting Jims . . . Fosse, Gus, and Little Rob . . . the rest of the crew . . .

Now look at them. Rafe's family business was on the edge of legal ruin while poor Jims was stuffed in a dank hole somewhere on a ship taking them both away from home and hearth. Heaven knew what the magistrate had in mind for Fosse, Gus, and Little Rob. And she was slated for ravishment and degradation by a crew of thieves and cut-throats run by a man who stole from widows and orphans. It couldn't have turned out worse for them if she had planned it.

She looked around the cabin, searching for anything that might help free her hands and feet. There was nothing . . . a charting compass, a number of rolled charts, an inkwell and old-fashioned quills. On the table was a chessboard set up to play. Her gaze went back to the cup of quills. Writing quills had to be sharpened regularly . . . there had to be a knife hereabouts. She scooted to the edge of the bunk and tried to stand but collapsed back on the bunk.

Just as her spirits sounded the depths, the cabin door opened and in strode Obadiah Murdoch looking satisfied. He removed his top hat and set it on the chart table before turning to the bed and studying her with a glint in his eyes.

"Poor little miss." He made a moue with his mouth, crossed the cabin, and removed the rag from her mouth. "There, that's better, isn't it?"

"What are you going to do with us?" Her voice was dry and raspy.

"Us?" He paused, running his eyes over her and smiling.

"The boy Jims and me."

"We'll find some use for him. If we don't, the fish will." His eyes narrowed in speculation. "It's *yourself* you should be worried about."

"What good will I be to anyone with no hands or feet? I can hardly feel them, I'm bound so tight. Perhaps you should just make me fish bait right now and save us both the trouble."

He considered that, then secured a knife from a drawer in the chart table and came back to cut her restraints. When she struggled to push herself upright he pulled her up.

"You think you'll be trouble, do you?" he said.

"I usually am. Ask my intended, Rafe Townsend. He certainly got more than he bargained for."

"I'll wager he did." He backed away and dropped the knife on the chart table. He was smarter than he looked, Obadiah Murdoch, not turning his back on her even when he had a knife's advantage.

"Let's see just how much trouble you can be, Miss Alcott." Her eyes widened at his use of her name, and he smiled. "I know who you are, *Street Angel.* I've heard of you." He removed his coat and hung it over a chair at the large table, then started to unbutton his vest.

"Without even offering me a sip of water?" she said, emphasizing the crack in her voice.

"Rude of me." He went to the captain's table and poured her a glass from the pitcher there. "Hands behind your back and sit still. At the first sign of movement I'll send you all the way to dreamland."

He insisted on holding the glass while she drank. She was too thirsty and exhausted to try anything at the moment, so she did as she was told. The water was fresh and felt like a godsend. By the time he backed away her wits and throat were lubricated enough to function. When his hands went to his shirt buttons she sighed wearily.

"Really? Now? Not very imaginative of you."

He paused. "I've never been accused of having an imagination, Angel. I certainly don't aspire to it."

He was a man of pride, however, and she hoped appealing to it might buy her some time. "But you speak like a gentleman . . . when you're not cursing at your men." She looked him over, pretending to find him interesting. "Surely you've had enough women to know that there is nothing unique I can give you in the carnal realm. I am a 'miss,' after all."

He nodded at that information. "That might be a novelty in itself. Not sure I've ever had a virgin, though some claimed to be."

"However, I could give you an experience you may never have had."

"Yes?" He did seem curious, so she glanced at the chess set on the far end of the table.

"A trouncing in a game of chess."

He studied her. "You're just delaying the inevitable, you know."

"Perhaps." Then a truthful impulse struck her. "But perhaps I'll delay just long enough to be rescued."

"You are forthright." He crossed his arms and spread his legs. "I'll give you that. I've never matched wits with a female before."

"You might find it more pleasurable than you expect."

He grew serious for a moment. "Damn, woman. Are you like this with Townsend? Talking dogs down off of meat wagons? Too bold by half?"

She sighed, unable to hide her relief to have put off the carnal ravishment aspect of her imprisonment for a while.

"Why do you think we're still just 'intended?' "

■ ■ ■ ■

"Barr Howard!" Rafe roared as he stalked into Barclay's house leading a trio of seamen who stood in the entry hall looking around at the luxury they had heard of but had never actually seen. They halted while Rafe charged back to the study to find the master of the house.

Barclay was totally absorbed in the book he had abandoned last night to help Rafe. He sat — boots on — in a grand, tapestry-covered wing chair that had probably belonged to a spendthrift nobleman at one time. He looked up with a scowl as Rafe filled the doorway.

"Damn it, Rafe, not again. I've got just a few pages left."

"I need help, Barr. They took her." Rafe felt his throat tighten around those words.

"Miss Alcott?" Barr sat up sharply, though he refused to put down the book. "Who took her?"

"That Murdoch bastard and his Consolidated thugs. She went to our Cutter Lane warehouse and found them raiding the place — at least I think that's what happened. Their ship — the *Cormorant* — set sail this morning right after she went missing. Damn it — she should have waited for me. But no, she had to go and be heroic again."

"Are you sure they took her?" Barclay demanded, shrugging into his coat and calling for his butler. "I mean, she could be out there in the City somewhere, performing some miraculous deed."

"She was at the hearing this morning, and later we found the hat she was wearing on the dock beside the *Cormorant*'s berth. She hasn't been seen since."

"She could be shopping or at a fitting. Women can spend whole days getting fitted for a dress."

"Damn it, Barr, she's missing and Murdoch's got her!" Rafe was ready to throttle him. "Are you going to help us or not?"

"Who is 'us'?" Barclay asked, tucking *Ivanhoe* under his arm.

Rafe grabbed his arm and hauled him out of the study and to the entry hall. Fosse, Gus, and Little Rob stood gaping at the plaster ceiling embellishments and the giltframed paintings on the walls. At the sight of him and his brawny friend, they straightened and came to attention as if under military inspection. "Boatswain Fosse, Seaman Gus, and Cabin Boy Rob," Rafe introduced them. "They came from

357

the *Clarion* to testify at the hearing."

Barclay nodded to them before turning to Rafe. "Just what do you plan to do to get her back?"

"We're going to go after her . . . fight whoever we have to fight . . . and rescue her."

"Wait — we're going to sail? On what?"

"The *Clarion*. Fosse here is the boatswain, and he swears the ship is still seaworthy. The fire was put out before it ruined the masts and the paddle wheel was untouched. There's a bit of charring on the deck and hatch, but we can step around that."

"There is one hitch, sarr," Fosse spoke up. "We got no capt'n."

The three *Clarion* crewmen looked to Rafe with unabashed concern.

"Do we really need one?" Barclay looked from crew to friend and back.

Rafe joined the stares of horror turned on his best friend.

"Hell yes, we need one," Rafe declared. He thought for a moment and one name came to mind. "We need to head to the Crystal Palace."

"Aw, hell no," Barclay said, realizing Rafe's intent.

"Got another suggestion?"

"There must be fifty captains cooling their

heels in the harbor," Barclay declared, adjusting the book under his arm.

"Any of them willing to abandon a ship full of cargo to step aboard a burned-out hulk with a strange crew?"

"I thought you said she was seaworthy," Barclay protested.

"Speaking from a salt's point of view," Rafe said. "She'll float and catch the wind. That's enough for any sailing man."

He strode for the door while the *Clarion*'s crew looked on, confused.

"Hope you've all made peace with your maker," Barclay said and strode after his friend.

Captain Harlow Stringer was at his usual haunt in the Crystal Palace, the café at the intersection of the halls. He sat at a table with his cheek propped on his hand, looking glum and out of place. The afternoon crowd had thinned and there was no one to listen to his tales of daring. At the sight of Rafe and a couple of odd-looking fellows in seamen's proper dress, he lifted his head.

"Captain." Rafe stopped beside the table and gave a smart salute. The old boy rose and returned the honor.

"What're ye doin' here . . . an' in such questionable comp'ny?" Stringer asked, gesturing to the *Clarion* crewmen, whose eyes widened on the ranks of tarnished medals on the old boy's chest.

"We need a seasoned captain," Rafe said, "for a dangerous mission."

Stringer rubbed his grizzled chin. "What kind o' danger?"

"My intended — you remember Lauren Alcott — has been abducted by some sea-going bastards and we're going after her." He paused, watching the old boy's eyes alight. "It'll be hard sailing and probably vicious fighting at the end. But I'm determined to get her back and you're my best hope to captain a ship to do that."

"What kind o' ship and when are ye shovin' off?" the old boy asked with a pucker to one corner of his mouth.

"A cargo ship, iron hulled, with steam as well as sail. Short on crew, but the men we have are as loyal as they come. We leave as soon as we can get to the docks," Rafe answered, praying the old boy had one last adventure in him.

"Merchant swabbies." Stringer winced as he looked over the three from the *Clarion*. But the thought of a deck beneath his feet again was clearly tempting. He squared his shoulders.

"Ye got rum aboard?"

"With your name on it," Rafe answered with a relieved grin.

"Then wot are we standin' about 'ere for?" The old boy straightened his coat and struck off for the entrance, setting a brisk pace — even with his peg leg — that left the others scrambling after him.

Barnaby Pinkum spotted them the minute they entered the Docklands. He had gone to the Customs House, hoping for information on the hearing, only to discover the proceeding had moved to the main Townsend warehouse. It had moved again by the time he made it there . . . to some ramshackle warehouses along a little-used dock. There were still a few coppers hanging about and, being the slight and sneaky fellow he was, he managed to overhear them talking about Lauren Alcott's disappearance. They argued about whether she'd been abducted or not and what the odds were that she'd left on a ship.

Roused by the possibility of another profitable Angel story — perhaps the biggest one yet — he hung around the entrance to the Docklands until he spotted Rafe Townsend and what looked like an old sea captain and sundry seamen headed for the main quay. Whatever was happening he wanted in on it. He was willing to stow away on the ship if necessary . . . though he'd never been on a ship before . . . not any kind of boat really.

But he was nothing if not resourceful, so he ran after the carriage until it stopped to allow a string of wagons to pass on a cross street. While the passengers were occupied with the traffic, he caught a ride, unseen, on the rear of the fancy carriage. And he congratulated himself on his cunning and physical prowess.

TWENTY-TWO

Lauren had drawn out the game of chess as long as she could. Murdoch was good at it but grew increasingly annoyed at her slow play, which always seemed to match his own. Every time she caught his king in a vulnerable spot he managed to escape, ratcheting her tension higher. Beneath the table she grabbed handfuls of her skirts. When there were only four pieces on the board she checkmated him.

The moment the words were out of her mouth he swept the pieces from the table. "I believe I've been had. And shortly so will you." He stood, breathing heavily, outraged by her unexpected cleverness at the game. She'd struck his pride too much of a blow. For the second time since she was brought on board, she felt a trill of terror run down her spine.

She grasped the sides of her skirt and felt something straight and wirelike that sparked the memory of removing her hat and placing the long hatpin in one of the lace-covered drapes at the side of her skirts. A hatpin could be a proper weapon wielded correctly. But she would have to be prepared for whatever punishment might follow. She glanced at the expanse of sea outside the cabin window. If he decided to strip her naked and throw her to the crew, there wouldn't be much she could do about it.

He grabbed her arm and yanked, but she hardly moved. Her bones seemed to have turned to jelly.

"Get up!" he snarled, reaching for her other arm and pulling hard. When she slid from the chair her limp weight caused him to drop her and anger got the better of him. "Get up and take yourself to the bed or I'll take you where you lay — on the damned floor!"

"I–I will not." She swallowed hard, looking at his boot, expecting a kick. But he fell on her, literally, rolling her onto her back and using his knees to try to force her legs apart. "So this is the only way you can get women — abducting and raping them?" A cruel twist appeared on his mouth, letting her see that talking was done. No amount of cleverness or appealing to his excessive pride would help her now.

The attack was so fast and fierce that she realized she had been duped by his gentlemanly façade. He had been playing with her, savoring the thought of what was to come. She shoved against both him and the floor, trying to scuttle away. But he knelt on her skirts to trap her as he raised up on one arm to unbutton his trousers. His movements were so quick and efficient that she realized he had probably done it numerous times before. He truly was the monster Mrs. Trimble had described.

"No! You can't do this."

"You can't stop me," he bit out.

She tried to kick him, but her skirts prevented her from raising her legs far enough. In desperation she pulled the hatpin from her skirt. It wasn't much compared to his brute force, but it was all she had.

The minute his trousers started to slide she struck . . . jamming the point of the hatpin somewhere in the pale strip of his half-bared flesh.

He convulsed back with a howl, grabbing himself. The moment he recovered enough breath to curse, he lashed out with his fist but failed to reach his target. She had already scrambled away and was pulling herself up on the side of the captain's bunk.

When he lunged for her she brought the

hatpin up again, jabbing it deep into his arm. Though he was more prepared for her resistance, the stab of pain made him recoil. "What in bloody hell is that?"

He couldn't see her weapon but was determined to find it and wrest it from her. She kicked at him and twisted to avoid his fist, but she managed to keep her hand with the hidden hatpin out of reach.

"Bitch — you'll be fit for nothing but a prick in a dark alley when I finish with you." This time he threw his shoulder into her and knocked her back, halfway onto the bed.

She sensed her next strike would be her last and went for his face. In her fury she prayed for an eye, but her aim was low and she managed to ram the hatpin through his cheek.

"Aghhhhh!" He flew back off the bed, grabbing his face and howling as she ran for the door. She made it up the steps and through the hatch. On deck the crew stopped dead at the sight of her rumpled dress and frantic state. More than one sailor smirked, thinking that their boss had taken a bite of that tasty piece. But a moment later Murdoch roared out of the hatch, clutching his bleeding face and snarling a command to "Seize her!"

The crewmen rushed her from all sides.

Though she fought with every ounce of her strength, they subdued her and held her as their master stalked close with a rage that few in his crew had seen and lived to talk about. They looked anxiously at one another.

"You'll wish you'd never set eyes on me," Murdoch declared, shaking with fury.

"I already do," she responded, raising her chin a bit too high.

A blow snapped her head to the side and her legs collapsed. She barely heard him decree that she was to be taken below and thrown in the "meat locker." It was all she could do to remain half-conscious as they dragged her down ladderlike stairs that carried them into the bowels of the ship. There they opened a rickety wooden door and shoved her inside. She fell onto something soft and foul-smelling. It turned out to be straw bedding for what was likely an animal pen. A pained grunt came in the darkness and she gasped, fearing she'd been imprisoned with a pig.

"Miz?" came a voice that brought her upright. "That you?"

"Jims?" As her eyes adjusted, she saw some shelves and a large wooden box on which the boy lay. "Are you all right?" She moved cautiously forward.

"Tha' big guy got a wicked fist," he said weakly. "I reckon I'll live."

She climbed up on the wooden box and he grunted again as he struggled up to look at her. Her first response on seeing his swollen face was one of anguish. She put her arms around him and drew him against her. His eyes were swollen and his lips were split. A dark smear across his cheek was probably blood. How could anyone beat a child like this? She closed her eyes, wishing she could have taken the beating and the pain on herself. As he put his thin arms around her, her heart felt as if it was breaking. But deeper inside her, deeper than tears or sadness or disgust . . . in the part of her where the very marrow of her bones was formed, anger began to coalesce into strength.

Bastards. The filthy, soulless animals.

She didn't know how, but she was going to make them pay.

Getting underway was something of a challenge, as shorthanded as they were on the *Clarion*. The minute their coal-fired boiler began belching smoke, a boat from the harbormaster's office pulled alongside demanding the customary berth payment before they moved. Captain Stringer answered with a stream of salty rebukes, but Rafe intervened with word that they were moving the damaged ship to the shipyards for repairs. Their duty done, the harbormaster's minions withdrew and the *Clarion* was free to continue preparations for leaving.

Chief among the requirements before departure was introducing Stringer to the crew as the acting captain of the *Clarion*. The men muttered to one another and looked askance at the rum-nosed old sea dog. But when he began barking orders they quickly learned he knew how to prepare a ship for the deep blue and fell to following his right-and-proper orders.

Stringer studied the burned hold and structural timbers and the smoky char of the aft cabins. He glowered at Rafe, tested the deck planking with his own feet, and ordered the boatswain to fasten planks across the gaps and weakest areas. The next problem they encountered was stoking the fire needed to turn the paddle wheel. Their two brawny stokers had been the first to desert the ship after Captain Pettigrew's death.

Stringer — believing that nothing bound men together like adversity — decreed that every man aboard would be assigned stoking duty for as long as they needed "that damnable wheel."

There was an undercurrent of grumbling, with the worst coming from Barclay, who was assigned to the first shift of stokers. When it was pointed out to him that he knew nothing about sailing or ships, he protested that he knew nothing about shoveling coal either. When Rafe revealed that he was scheduled for the next shift himself, Barclay muttered that he had signed on for fighting and rescuing, not manual labor. Under the crew's testy glares, his face heated. Patrician attitudes clearly had no place on a ship short on crew. With a twinge of guilt he headed belowdeck to make a few blisters and earn the right to his nightly grog.

Rafe watched his friend surrender to necessity and turned to Stringer, who stood on the aft deck, considering the ship and her crew.

"What do you think?" he asked the old salt. "Will she do?"

"She's got a few cinders in her belly, but 'er hull and masts are sound. Hell yeah." He grinned. "I could sail 'er to China an' back."

He gave Rafe a whop on the shoulder and turned to bellow orders loud enough to wake all three King Georges.

Between Stringer, Rafe, and Fosse they

managed to get the crew moving and the ship underway. The paddle wheel hadn't been damaged in the fire, and when the boiler heated they cleared the docks and channel and headed into the Thames in little more than an hour.

A lookout was posted on top of the main with a spy glass and orders to look for a black-and-yellow, two-masted ship in the tidal waters. The acting captain ordered men into the rigging to release the sheets and increase their speed. They had to find out what direction Murdoch and the *Cormorant* took when they left the tidal waters of the Thames.

Though it was useless to search from that vantage point, Rafe went forward and scoured the broad, tidal regions of the river for signs of the ship they sought. His stomach was in a knot and he gripped the railing with whitened hands.

He tried not to think of what was happening to Lauren, but he kept recalling the man Murdoch and his vicious behavior with his crew. They were hardened men, he knew, and probably had to be kept in check. But the curses, blows, and threats Murdoch used revealed how much he relished using violence. Lauren was more than fine in appearance, but she was not a meek and compliant female. He could imagine what a man of such power lust would make of her, and it made him sick to think of her suffering under his hand. Or his body.

Stringer appeared at his side, surprising him. He hadn't heard the thumps of the old boy's peg leg approaching. It occurred to him that Stringer hadn't once mentioned rum since boarding the ship.

"Yer worried, lad." The old fellow leaned on the railing to give his back a rest.

"I am." There was no denying it.

"She's a purty thing, yer lass. Think they'll be askin' ransom?"

"I have no way of knowing. What I do know is, the longer she's on that ship, the worse it will be for her." He made himself focus on the task ahead. "They have a two-or three-hour head start. You think we can run them down?"

"The ol' gal's got some spunk left. The wind looks to give us ten to twelve knots. Runnin' that wheel will give us a couple or three more. Those whirligigs don't add much if th' water's choppy, and" — he scanned the sky — "it looks like we got some wind comin' outta the west."

"Sailing against the wind if we go south," Rafe said miserably.

"Yeah. It'll be a race. But we got an' edge."

"Yes? What's that?"

"Me."

Stringer scratched his chest as he turned and managed to dislodge the polished cross-and-crown badge on his rank of medals. It caught the light briefly, casting a flash toward Rafe's eye.

Rafe wondered if he'd imagined it.

He turned to watch the old sea dog thumping his way back along the deck to inspect the planking Fosse had tacked over the burned section. The old boy did seem to have Poseidon's own luck when it came to wind and sea. He had to pray it would be the edge they needed to catch the *Cormorant* before she reached the open ocean and disappeared.

How long they had been imprisoned in the locker she had no way of knowing. But the ship was rocking more, and when Jims asked why she could only say it was because the water was rougher. What rougher water meant, she had no idea. He nodded and laid his head back on her lap. And she leaned her head back against the chilled planking behind her.

She tried not to think about what happened in Murdoch's cabin, but that ugly battle was likely a foretaste of things to come. She didn't believe for a moment that he would ignore her for the rest of the voyage to . . . wherever they were bound. She'd wounded his pride and his face and lost her only weapon in that last strike. When he came at her again she'd have to be prepared to deal with him or pay a heavy price.

The darkness deepened and she surrendered to fatigue and dozed. Something startled her awake later, and she sat up straight, staring in the direction of the door. It opened, admitting light from a lantern, and a man smaller than Murdoch or any of his knuckle-dragging bruisers. She drew up her legs under her, ready to spring, but the sound of her name spoken softly made her hesitate.

"Miss Alcott." The fellow brought up the lantern to look at her and revealed a round face topped with thinning hair and a pair of smudged spectacles. "I brought you and the boy some food. Don't tell anyone — I'm in enough trouble as it is."

"Bless you, sir," she said, assessing his voice and the way he glanced over his shoulder at the door. When he held out the bowls she took them gratefully and set one down beside Jims, who was struggling to wake fully and sit up. "Who are you?"

"Merrell Hampstead. I — was — the head

of Consolidated's warehouse and shipping."

"You're the man Mrs. Trimble told me about," she said, watching Jims sit straighter and sniff the food.

Hampstead was watching Jims, too. His shoulders rounded and his face filled with pain. "The sick bastards. To do that to a small boy . . ."

Nothing he could have said would have marked him as an ally faster than that quiet judgment.

"It's all right, Jims. He's a friend." She wrapped her cold hands around the warm bowl. "Mr. Hampstead, you're the head of the warehouse. What are you doing on this ship?"

"Murdoch forced me to come. He collected my ledgers and bills of lading . . . said we were starting over. It was becoming too dangerous to keep doing business there. I refused at first, but he had his men . . . convince me." He shuddered visibly. "They boasted that Mr. Trimble's death was no accident and threatened me with the same."

"Do you know where we're going?" she asked. "Where are they taking us?"

"All I heard is" — his voice dropped to a whisper — "somewhere on the west coast. Could be Dorsett or Cornwall, maybe Devonshire. It has to be someplace the Coastguard isn't too busy." He looked pained to admit it, but "Consolidated is in the smuggling business, miss. It's a vile and brutal trade."

They heard a voice outside, approaching, growing louder. Hampstead doused the light. They held their breath until the voices began to fade. After a few moments Mr. Hampstead struck a match and relighted the lantern.

"I brought you a candle and a couple of matches. I'll check on you when I can, and bring you more food and water."

"Maybe some water and cloths so I can tend Jims's injuries?"

"I'll see what I can do." He slipped out the door and she heard the latch slide into place.

She felt for Jims's hands and found them wrapped around the bowl of soup. The last thing she wanted to do was eat just now; her stomach was too filled with tension. But she had to keep his spirits up. "Eat what you can, Jims. We have to keep up our strength."

Barnaby Pinkum lounged on some cloth-wrapped rolls containing rugs and congratulated himself on slipping aboard Townsend's ship with supplies that were being loaded. With several new faces aboard and hectic preparations for departure, no one stopped him to demand what he was doing there. He disappeared belowdeck and made himself a cozy nest in the forward cargo hold. Before long he had memorized the layout of the ship. He would snatch some food from the kitchen later . . . maybe even some ale. He stretched out on the rugs with his arms behind his head.

"Pinkum, you are one sharp tack."

An hour later the ship reached the capricious channel waters and began to rock. And Barnaby Pinkum began to groan.

TWENTY-THREE

The next morning the lookout called ship ahoy and Stringer, Rafe, and the entire topside crew rushed to the starboard railing to see it.

Stringer used his telescope for a better look and nodded with satisfaction before handing the glass to Rafe. They had run hard through the night, fighting fatigue and changeable winds, but the stoking that made their muscles ache and backs sore had paid off. They spread every inch of sail they had, and though they were tacking into a westerly, it was clear they were gaining on the *Cormorant.*

Stringer ordered the two small-bore deck guns mounted starboard. The crew stepped lively and soon had powder and iron shot stacked by them. A couple of older sailors — both naval veterans — stationed themselves possessively by the guns, polishing them. When Rafe questioned their placement on the same side, Stringer chuckled and tapped his temple.

"Strategy, boy. We'll be runnin' up on their port . . . keepin' 'em boxed in. There be rocks an' shoals in these parts. I know 'em like the back o' my hand, and I'm bettin' that Murdoch bastard don't." His face grew flinty and his eyes narrowed as he stared at the smaller ship. "We got her. Best you break out the guns an' get those landlubbers o' yours ready for a fight."

"Oh . . ." When the old boy held up a hand, it shook a bit. "And now'd be a good time t' break out that rum wi' my name on it."

Rafe and Barclay unlocked the armory and handed out rifles and ammunition to every crewman, few of whom would qualify as sharpshooters. But most of them had blade weapons tucked into their belts, some of which looked wicked indeed. Whatever reservations he had about a merchant crew fighting smugglers were soon allayed. Most of these men had been in ports where they had to stand armed watch to keep their cargoes and ship safe from predators.

As soon as they reached the deck guns' range, Stringer started them firing at the sails. Nothing dispirited seamen more than watching their sails being shredded by iron balls, he declared. The crew stationed themselves behind barrels along the forward railing, waiting for the order to fire.

Barclay, who had handed out guns and ammunition, joined Rafe on the deck with a rifle over each arm. He handed one off to Rafe.

"What's she wearing?" Barclay asked as Rafe checked the gun.

Rafe looked askance at him. "Why would you ask that?"

"I want to know what *not* to shoot at."

Rafe froze for a moment, realizing the danger to her in the coming fight. He forced a deep breath that did little to dispel his tension.

"It was a reddish dress. Though, there's no guarantee she is still" — the words stuck in his throat — "wearing that." He had to pause a moment to shake off the emotion that could impair his responses.

"I've got it." Barclay read his turmoil and put a hand on his shoulder. "No shooting at red. I'll pass the word."

As Rafe watched Barclay leave, his gaze caught on a small figure near the bow, emptying his stomach over the portside rail. He scowled, trying to recall the man and what his job was on the *Clarion*. He carried the gun with him, checking its sights as he crossed the deck. He stopped dead when the little fellow turned around and he recognized that pug nose, prominent ears, and squinty eyes. Up came the gun.

"What the hell are you doing on this ship?" Rafe demanded.

The fellow took one look at the gun and slid down the rail post behind him like a limp noodle.

"Just shoot me now," he whined. "Get it over with."

"You're that news hack, the one writing those stories about Lauren and me," Rafe charged.

"Not all of 'em. Just the best ones." He swiped a hand in an arc, as if writing a headline on the sky. "Barnaby Pinkum, newswriter extraordinaire." The man was actually green around the gills. "If you've got a drop o' mercy in you, you'll see that chiseled on my tombstone."

"Feel like you're about to expire, do you?" Rafe said, with no regret for enjoying the wretch's discomfort. Barclay came rushing across the deck to see what was happening and pushed the muzzle of the gun aside.

"Oh, him," Barclay said, staring at Barnaby Pinkum.

"He's in bad straits. Been up here at least three times, puking his guts out."

381

Rafe's smile turned wicked. "It couldn't happen to a more deserving fellow. He's the son of a bitch responsible for those 'Angel' stories."

"Ahh." Barclay gave a grim chuckle. "Then I'm surprised you're not hanging him from the yardarm."

"There's still time for that," Rafe mused with intentional menace. "Until then we'll make him pay for his passage by writing a story or two about our valiant pursuit of the Angel's abductor."

"She's been abducted?" To a reporter the scent of a juicy story was as restorative as a bottle of smelling salts. Pinkum sat up. "Who has her?"

"The fellows on the ship we're chasing." Rafe tossed a thumb over his shoulder. Pinkum craned his neck to see the ship visible behind him.

"I'll need details," Pinkum said, no longer penitent and rubbing his empty, aching belly. "And a dram of whiskey to settle my stomach."

It had been a miserable night in the smelly former pigpen for Lauren and Jims. Hampstead had slipped below to bring them some cloths and a pitcher of water. It brought relief to poor Jims, but he hurt too much to fall asleep easily. When he began to chill she lifted her skirts and removed the warmest of her petticoats to wrap him in. He asked for a story to pass the time and tears pricked Lauren's eyes. She blinked to keep them from falling and told him stories from the books she had read to the children at St Ambrose. Eventually he fell asleep, and she was able to let her brave front drop.

Focusing on the memory of Rafe's care and tenderness kept her from complete misery, but it was hard to see much hope in her present circumstances. She eventually dozed.

When the latch scraped open the next morning, she wondered if she was so exhausted that she imagined it.

She hadn't. It was one of the surly crewmen with bread and a tankard of ale for the prisoners. He mumbled that they had run out of fresh water, ducked back out the door, and slid the latch home.

Jims roused, and they chewed some of the hard bread, washing it down with the bitter ale. After a few sips she left the rest to Jims, thinking it might dull his discomfort.

Midmorning, the sounds around them changed. They could hear running on the deck above and the feel of the ship passing through water changed, sounding ominous and confused. While bracing to keep from being tossed about, Lauren heard the latch being drawn back and feared it would be someone to fetch her to Murdoch.

But it was Hampstead with a few precious words.

"Another ship is coming on fast. Murdoch is worried and preparing for a fight."

"What kind of ship?" Her heart lurched and beat faster.

"Bigger than this one. Black hull. Driving us toward shore, they say. I'll leave the latch open, but don't come out unless you hear gunfire. He'll be too busy, then, to deal with an escaped prisoner."

"Mr. Hampstead —" She stopped him as he withdrew.

"Yes, miss?"

"Take care of yourself."

He looked a bit embarrassed but nodded and ducked out.

She waited nervously, praying it was the ship she needed it to be. She went over an escape plan with Jims and made him promise to stay below, near the deck ladder, until he heard someone call him by his full name. Then and only then he would know it was safe to come out. It was a measure of how exhausted he was that he didn't protest his ability to help and simply hugged her. "Ye be careful, too, miz."

When the gunfire started it was something of a jolt. She felt a shiver of fear, but her need to see what was going on overpowered it. Screwing up her courage, she climbed onto the deck above and hid near the stairs, listening. The *Cormorant*'s crew was mostly out on the deck. She could see men on the yardarm firing at the ship that was fast approaching. She had to see what that ship was. Coastguard or yet another smuggler? She remembered Captain Stringer's story of smugglers meeting up and prayed that wouldn't be this story, too.

Steeling herself, she rushed up the last few steps and burst out of the hatch with her head down, running for the aft railing. Men stationed there spotted her but after a moment's distraction went back to firing their guns from behind barrels, positioned there for cover. She found an empty place along the rail and crouched low to peer at the pursuing ship.

It was bigger than the ship she was on . . . black . . . triple-masted . . . with a paddle wheel on the port side. A cargo ship like the *Clarion*! Her heart beat faster as she spotted char marks on the middle and forward masts. She couldn't afford to make a mistake. If it were the *Clarion,* what was it doing running down some smugglers? She squinted, shading her eyes to make out more details.

She didn't realize she had risen until the firing around her stopped and she found a number of men staring at her. The next moment she spotted what looked like a tricorn hat at the bow of the pursuing ship. There was only one old sea relic she knew of who still wore such a hat. Beside him crouched a figure with light hair who shouldered a rifle and took aim at the men stationed above. While the firing around her was stopped, the man stood up and waved his arm. Was she imagining things?

It was Rafe — it had to be Rafe! She waved back, barely able to breathe for the hope exploding inside her. And he waved again — he'd recognized her!

She knew what she had to do. She lifted her skirts to her waist to untie her remaining petticoat. The men staring at her gave one another knowing smirks as she removed it and tossed it at them. Next came her boots — unlaced and thrown aside. Then she pulled up her coral-red skirt and peeled her garters and stockings down her legs, tossing them at the men who came running to the aft position at Murdoch's furious command.

Had her captor seen her there, or was he just desperate to make them continue firing? A few of the new arrivals snarled orders at the others to keep firing and took shots themselves. But the sight of her raised skirts and bare legs was enough to distract even them for a few precious seconds. She climbed up on one of the barrels against the rail and waved both of her arms, trying to catch Rafe's attention.

Murdoch arrived, spitting curses and slinging a rifle butt at every man in sight, screaming at them to keep firing. She gave him a defiant smile and dived into the water.

Rafe's heart stopped for a moment when she appeared atop the aft railing. She must have had the same effect on Murdoch's crew, for they stopped firing for a moment. He had a feeling he knew what she intended and could only say, "No . . . no, no, no!" He could see how turbulent the water beneath her was and tried to wave her off such a dangerous move. The nearby rocks and incoming tide were helping them force the *Cormorant* aground, but diving into that churning water was pure madness. She was a strong swimmer, but she had no chance in such chaotic conditions!

She surfaced — a small dot in a swirling sea. Panic welled in him.

He froze as that long-ago day came back to him in a rush — the pounding sea, the shouting, the roar of guns overhead. He was back in the water once again, clawing to stay above the surface, gasping for air, trying to avoid being smashed to a bloody pulp against jagged rocks.

His chest heaved as he fought the impulse to breathe. His need for air overwhelmed him and his body pulled in water along with the oxygen he craved. His body convulsed and tried to cough out the water but couldn't. Surrounded on all sides by churning water, he panicked. The cold . . . the darkness . . . he couldn't see anything . . . he was losing control of his body . . . couldn't make his limbs obey. As the sea closed in, his body gave a last spasm and surrendered. . . .

The sound of rifle fire and a nearby shout broke through the memory that had paralyzed him. Barr thudded against the railing beside him and pulled him to the deck.

"The bastard is shooting at her!" Barclay shot up behind the barrel, took aim, and fired at the men on the aft of the *Cormorant,* striking one.

Lauren! Rafe dove for the edge of the ship

to look for her. It took him a minute to spot her through the foam and spray. She was fighting to stay afloat and being dragged ever closer to the dangerous rocks that surrounded the beach. She was strong and determined — she had a chance, he told himself — a very slim chance.

Then he heard the crack of a shot and saw her jerk and go under. He looked up, and with the closing distance he could see a sneer of satisfaction on Murdoch's face. He had no time to plan or reason or even curse. He ripped off his boots and coat — there wasn't time to remove more. Every second could be the margin between her life and death. He climbed over the railing, braving gunfire, and jumped.

The water closed over him and slowed his descent. Then it buoyed him up to the surface again. There was no time to acknowledge fear, only to act. His head, his heart, his every breath centered on her. He made her name a prayer . . . saying it with every stroke of his arms and kick of his legs . . . making her his strength . . . determined to make himself hers. He would not lose her — this woman he intended to share his life with. She was a light, a beacon to a better world. *His* world.

Right now she was fighting with everything

in her, and he was bloody well fighting, too, for her life, her love. He heard the whirr of bullets entering the water near him but paused to call for her. "Lauren — where are you?" He leaped as high as he could to search the breaking waves and churning surf. He spotted her head and began to swim again. Every stroke took him into more turbulent waters, but he charged on . . . calling her name so she would know he was coming . . . so she would hang on long enough for him to reach her.

She had thought ridding herself of those troublesome skirts and boots, baring her legs, would make it easier to swim. It did, but this water was so much more turbulent than she'd realized. The ship she'd escaped was being driven onto the shoals. She'd had no idea how steeply the bottom banked or how fierce the wind-driven waters could be.

She fought to keep her head above water while gathering the skirt of her dress and twisting and tucking it around her waist. Her legs were free and she was able to stretch out and kick as well as use her arms. But the blasted waves kept coming, pushing and turning her. For every stroke that moved her forward there was a push from the water that moved her back.

Then she heard the cracks of gunfire and saw the impact of bullets hitting nearby water. A frisson of fear shot through her, and she redoubled her efforts. She had to get — something slammed into her, pushing her under the water. A second later pain exploded through her shoulder, chest, and head. The impact was so great that all she could do at first was contract into a ball of pain.

A breaking wave crashed over her as she came up for a breath. Her body fought the inhaled water . . . she choked and coughed. Before she could clear her lungs another foaming wave hit, pounding her, forcing her under. Panic seized her as she searched for air and found only water. By pure grace she managed to breach the top, sucked a gurgling breath, and then emptied her lungs.

She felt raw inside and had lost track of the ships and the battle going on around her. Her eyes were stinging and the urge to cough was so forceful that it doubled her up in painful spasms. She called for help, but her cries were being swallowed up in the increased noise and fury of the water. Desperate now and drawing on the last of her energy, she tried to stroke away from the rough water around the rocks. The pitiless waves found her and the sea held her down. . . .

Rafe had lost sight of her. She was being pushed under and toward the rocks. He filled his lungs and dove under the foaming white maelstrom. Saltwater stung his eyes, but he kept them open to search for her. Just as he was forced to surface and breathe, he spotted her. She was being tossed from crest to trough, no longer moving her arms . . . drifting dangerously.

He plowed through the chaotic water toward her. She seemed to hear him calling, but had trouble locating him. When he reached her, she was gasping and alarmingly limp. Her eyes barely focused on him.

"You're here?" she choked out.

"I've got you." He pulled her against him for a moment, relieved to have her in his arms. He was treading water for both of them but realized they would never make it back to the ship with the water churning powerfully around them and the threat of gunfire from above. He looked frantically around and spotted a stretch of sand farther down the shore. The water was calmer there, and the small beach would give her a place to rest.

"Relax, Lauren. Just float." He turned her

on her back and repositioned his grip on her so he could swim. "I'll get us to the beach —"

A trickle of red flowing from her torn dress stopped him for a moment. "He hit you? The bastard *shot* you?"

The next few minutes he cut a rage-fueled course along the shoreline for that undisturbed stretch of sand. His muscles were strained to their limits, and despite his tremendous expenditure of energy, his body was growing cold. But he gritted his teeth and pushed on, watching Lauren's breathing and encouraged by her attempt to help by kicking her feet.

The water warmed as they approached the small beach and he put down his feet. It felt good to stand up . . . even if it was on shifting sand.

He picked her up as soon as they reached the shallows and carried her to a patch of dry beach. He collapsed beside her and closed his eyes while gripping her hand. Relief spread through him.

"We made it," he murmured.

His relief was short-lived. She coughed, and he quickly turned her onto her side so she could spit up water. When she finished he eased her onto her back again and let her rest while he recovered, too. Then he spotted some red on the sand beneath her and he sat her up and unbuttoned the back of her dress.

"Sorry, angel, but I have to check your wound." He inspected her injury. The sight of what Murdoch's violence had done to her made him want to put a fist through something.

Her voice sounded raw. "How bad is it?"

"It's a clean, in-and-out wound." He looked to her front, where the bullet had exited, and moved her arm back and forth. She winced and bit her lip at the pain it caused, but her arm had proper motion. "It seems to have missed bones and important sinews. We need to bind it to stop the bleeding until we can get you to a physician. I'm afraid we'll have to sacrifice your —"

...for her.

TWENTY-FOUR

The fog in Lauren's head had cleared enough for her to realize he was staring at her bare legs and tucked-up skirt.

"Where the devil are your petticoats?"

She pushed up on her good arm to untuck her skirt and roll the crumpled silk down a bit. "I took them off before I dove in. Well, one of them. Jims was using the other. And my shoes and stockings, too. I thought I'd swim better without them. But the water was so . . . so . . ."

He forced a grin to cover his anxiety. "So you managed to take off only some of your clothes this time." He removed his shirt. "We'll use mine."

He bit the cloth and tore off the bottom of the shirt, then rolled up the shoulders and outstretched sleeves and tied them around her shoulder, covering her wound. It felt and looked to her as if he was hugging her by proxy. She gave a pained smile and looked up at him as if what he had accomplished had just registered.

"You came for me."

He paused, looking into her sunrise eyes.

"I will always come for you, Lauren." He stroked her hair.

Tears spilled down her cheeks even as she smiled.

"You saved me," she said, touching his cheek, then his bare shoulder, as if testing to see that he was real.

He pulled her into his arms, careful not to touch her shoulder, and held her close. She trembled as she looked out at the water and said softly, "It was so cold and I couldn't tell which way was up. The waves swallowed me . . . I couldn't get my breath. I thought I was going to —"

She stopped, unable to say it, so he said it for her.

"Die."

She nodded and buried her face in his chest. "I've never been overpowered like that . . . by water."

"I have." He took a deep breath and confessed, "I drowned once."

She pushed back in his arms to look at his face. His expression was oddly calm to accompany such a harrowing statement.

"It was some years ago, while I was at the

Academy. There were naval exercises just off the coast and bad weather came up — fierce winds — water roaring from every direction — the sea heaving and half swallowing our ships. I was knocked overboard, and even though some of my fellow cadets saw me fall, conditions were so bad they couldn't rescue me right away. By the time they did, I . . . wasn't breathing.

"One of the officers pounded on my chest and my heart started to beat again. It was something of a miracle, I suppose. But my fellow cadets looked at me strangely after that. Sailors are superstitious. Drowned men who come back to life are often considered 'Jonahs.' I left the Academy and came back to London. And from that day to this, I have not been in any body of water larger than a bathing tub."

"It must have taken something powerful to make you plunge into a turbulent sea again."

He looked out to sea for a moment and then down at her.

"It did. I couldn't let what happened to me, happen to you. You mean a lot to me." He shook his head at that small deceit and corrected it. "No . . . you mean *everything* to me. The thought of you abducted and being abused by that bastard nearly drove me crazy. I harangued Barclay into helping, hijacked Harlow Stringer's pride, and pushed everyone aboard the *Clarion* within an inch of their sanity. But it was worth it. You're here with me, safe and" — he nodded at her wounded shoulder — "mostly sound."

She leaned into him, content to revel in the strength and solid feel of him. He kissed the top of her head and a rumble came from his chest, letting her know he felt the same about her.

For a few minutes the restless sea, the raging surf, and the battle between the two ships seemed far away. But as they sat together savoring those precious moments, the world intruded in the form of strange sounds . . . rasping, then groaning and shuddering came from the *Cormorant.*

Rafe stood and helped her to her feet. He put an arm around her to steady her while they watched the smaller ship begin to list to starboard.

"He's done it. Old Stringer said he'd run her aground and he did. She's stuck on a shoal and keeling over a few degrees."

As they watched the ship surrender to the elements, they spotted boats being lowered from the *Clarion.* They identified Barclay and Fosse and realized they were carrying guns, intent on seizing the injured ship and her crew. They had almost reached the wreck when a handful of dark figures on the lower side of the *Cormorant*'s deck dropped from the edge into the shallow water that covered the shoal.

"What are they doing?" she asked. Murdoch's men waded through waist-deep water to a stretch of sand, then spotted the men from the *Clarion* and began to run for the rocky banks that led inland.

"Escaping," he said irritably. "The bastards. We can't let them."

"Jims," she said, looking up at him. "Jims is on the ship. He was with me when I was taken. Would they just abandon him along with the ship?"

"They're cutthroats and thieves. They'd abandon their own mothers if it meant getting away free and clear." He looked down the beach, searching for a sandy path he could take to reach the ship. He took her hand and looked into her eyes. "Stay here, Angel, where you're safe."

She looked down the shore, then back at him.

"But Barclay and the others will be there soon."

He was already in motion.

■ ■ ■ ■

Rafe ran with his gaze fixed on those fleeing cowards — one in particular. He was able to identify Murdoch by the frock coat he wore. The wretch carried a large satchel that made it difficult to scale the stretch of bank with only his other hand. Bullets striking the rocks around him caused the bastard to flinch and throw himself against the rocks. There was no cover to be had, and each time he tried to move, bullets rained around him. He must have realized they weren't trying to hit him and took the chance to scramble toward the top of the bank, dragging his precious satchel.

Bullets flew again, gouging chips from the stone in front of Murdoch. Rafe grinned. There was one man in England who could shoot with such accuracy . . . besides himself. He reached the bottom of the bank and started to climb, heedless of the sharp rocks digging into his bare feet. When he grabbed Murdoch's ankle he pulled with all the fury he possessed and brought Lauren's abductor crashing down on him.

They slid and fell together onto the sand at the bottom. Rafe recovered quickly enough to pounce on the bastard and deliver several punches. They were forceful blows, but not enough to stop Murdoch from finding his knife. The blade raked Rafe's side as Murdoch brought it up, and Rafe just managed to seize his wrist and hold the blade at bay.

"Damned coward . . . running away," Rafe uttered as they struggled over the knife. "Kidnapping . . . stealing . . . shooting women . . . you deserve to be keelhauled . . . until you die."

He wanted those to be the last words Murdoch would ever hear, but the sick bastard had fight left in him. He bucked unexpectedly and threw Rafe off. By the time he scrambled to his feet Rafe was up and rushing him again . . . dodging the knife . . . getting blows in where he could.

Rafe was vaguely aware that the shooting had stopped and the fighting going on around the beach was now more scuffling than deadly combat. When they broke apart he shook his head to clear it and plowed into Murdoch again. He glimpsed men lying on the sand with others standing over them. He prayed his side were the ones who were upright.

But that was the last coherent thought he had. Instinct took over as Murdoch slashed at him with the knife, and he twisted and spun out of range. Then, as Murdoch hesitated, saying something, Rafe saw his chance and charged with his shoulder lowered. But it was his legs that did the work, sweeping Murdoch's feet from under him, sending him sprawling in one direction, his knife in another.

Rafe fell on him with fists and arms hardened by years of rowing. No amount of shifting or trying to block his blows was successful. Soon Murdoch lay slack, still being hammered by Rafe's fury.

Barclay finally pulled him off. "Townsend, stop! He's out. He's finished. You don't want to kill him . . . yet."

Rafe fell backward on the sand, panting, bleeding from his mouth and a cut on his side. A quick inspection said it was more painful than serious. And suddenly Lauren was there, cradling his head on her lap and stroking his hair . . . telling him what an idiot he was and how he'd better never abandon her again to go fight and nearly get himself killed.

Then she kissed him, fully and resoundingly, in front of God and everyone.

Barclay and Fosse took charge of Murdoch, trussing him up like a Christmas goose and stowing him, along with his battered henchmen, beside some dry rocks.

When Rafe made it to his feet, he looked at the men who'd caused Lauren and him such trouble and said, "We ought to bury them up to their necks in the sand . . . so they can watch the tide come in from a new angle."

Barclay chuckled darkly. "No. Digging holes is too much work. And lining them up and shooting them doesn't seem quite sporting. I say we take 'em back to London and hand them over to Scotland Yard."

Rafe gave a grudging nod of agreement. "But I have a few questions to put to one of them first."

Captain Stringer had stayed on the *Clarion,* so the shore party was led by newly promoted Second Mate Ben Fosse in company with Barclay Howard. A second boat arrived from the *Clarion* to help ferry the prisoners to the ship. Barclay climbed aboard with a gun at the ready and cautioned his charges to make no suspicious moves. From their behavior they seemed to believe he would shoot them on the spot. Before long, they were hauling the men aboard the venerable merchantman and introducing them to their new accommodations in the belly of the ship.

■ ■ ■ ■

The *Cormorant* was strangely quiet as they climbed aboard. Effects of the battle were everywhere. There were holes in boards, bullet casings collected in the seams of the deck flooring, and ripped sails that hung limply, as if offering surrender. Crossing the tilted deck was hard enough, but when they tried to climb down the forward hatch, Lauren's injured shoulder made it impossible to negotiate the canted ladder.

She had to settle for sitting at the top of the hatch and calling to her little cellmate. "Jims Gardiner, come out. We're here to take you home!"

Rafe managed to climb around the canted interior deck avoiding objects that had slid and collected at the damaged starboard side of the hull or were caught by structural timbers. He called several times to Jims before he caught a sound and asked Lauren to help him listen. Jims's voice sounded more weak than timid. Rafe made his way to the lower deck ladder and climbed down. Lauren worried until Rafe came out of the lowest deck with Jims hanging on his back. When they reached the ladder near Lauren the boy climbed the last few feet on his own and fell into her open arms with a sob.

"I waited, miz, like ye said to."

"You certainly did, Jims Gardiner." She hugged him tightly with her good arm, before setting him back to inspect him. "You're the bravest, strongest boy I've ever known." She tousled his hair and gave him a kiss on the cheek before looking at Rafe, who had climbed out beside them and now watched their reunion with a warmth that made Lauren's heart glow.

"I think Master Gardiner here deserves a reward for all his help," Rafe said. "Something really special."

Jims looked at Rafe through still blackened eyes and smiled.

As they searched the vessel they found not only the *Clarion*'s old cargo, they found one more survivor.

Merrell Hampstead came staggering out of the aft hatch without his spectacles but with a huge bump on his head. He was overjoyed to find Lauren and the boy Jims safe. He directed them to the ship's medicinal box, and before long Lauren's shoulder was bandaged properly and she was given something that dulled the pain and made her more comfortable.

Jims's injuries were inspected and salved, then he was given some medicine that he swore tasted like horse piss. No one asked how he knew that, but he was soon given a piece of sugary peppermint from Murdoch's personal stock to rid him of the taste.

There were a few other tasks to complete before they returned to the ship. Rafe collected the satchel Murdoch had been so set on carrying with him. In it were records of transactions, sales, bank accounts . . . it would take days to comb through such records and make sense of what Consolidated's agent was so determined to hide. Merrell Hampstead located the ledgers and documents Murdoch had stashed in his cabin and they inspected the cargo in the hold, finding crates from a variety of storehouses and vessels besides their own.

They decided to build a fire and dry off before returning to the ship. Hampstead found some brandy to ward off the chill. Lauren was reunited with the petticoat she had loaned Jims and found her lady boots in the captain's cabin. She wore those items and a blanket while her dress was drying. Rafe commandeered a shirt that must have belonged to Murdoch and decided it was clean enough to wear.

Finding food and staying warm was enough to occupy them for a while. Once again in her own dress, Lauren spread the blanket on the sand and lay down for a much-needed nap. Young Jims curled up beside her, and Rafe found just enough room on the blanket to lie down beside her, too. They woke up to find Barclay standing nearby with his arms crossed, watching them.

"Time to go, slug-a-beds. A coastal cutter came by and hailed Stringer. He told them who he was and they seemed downright thrilled to make his acquaintance. Apparently he's every bit the legend you said he is. Anyway, he explained that the bark run aground is full of stolen cargo, and they're dispatching some riders to watch the wreck and keep looters at bay. We're heading back to London at first light."

Lauren looked at Rafe, who seemed to read her thoughts.

"And go back to sleep on a cold deck or in a cabin that smells like wet dog and smoke?" Rafe shook his head. "We'll stay here, thank you. You can pick us up in the morning."

Barclay's laugh was downright insinuating. He looked to Hampstead, who picked up one of several pasteboard boxes, clearly eager to be on his way. Barclay helped him load Murdoch's satchel and a dozen other boxes of books and papers. He came back to pick up the last box and beckoned to Jims.

"Let's go, boy."

Jims looked uneasy and Lauren put an arm around him.

"He'll stay with us tonight."

"That so?" Barclay said, looking to Rafe.

Rafe just sighed and nodded.

Barclay laughed all the way to the boat.

The next morning they brought Murdoch up to the deck for questioning, and according to him, he was duped into carrying untaxed, illegal cargo from various ports to London and from London to sundry west coast locations. They realized that — short of torture — they couldn't make him incriminate himself. Fingering others, however, was totally within his criminal ethic and might prove even more valuable to them . . . starting with the names of Consolidated's secretive owners.

After some negotiating but few promises given, he spoke the name that was his ace card. All he had.

"Creighton. Leddy Creighton. He's the main man and the only one I ever saw or took orders from. He wasn't around much. He left it up to me to run the place . . . just provided dates and locations . . . made sure the local coppers were lookin' the other way wherever we anchored."

Rafe was stunned at first. It couldn't be a coincidence that Creighton was Ledbetter's given name and that "Leddy" was half of Ledbetter. The man was too arrogant to even use a true alias? He looked at Barclay and at Lauren, who stood behind Murdoch, watching. He couldn't let Murdoch see that he was making an important connection.

"And what about those books and papers in your satchel? What is contained in that bag that is so important you took it with you when you ran?"

"Things. Stuff Creighton wouldn't want seen." He gave Rafe a dark look. "Especially by you. He's not a great admirer of things Townsend."

That cinched Ledbetter's identity as the owner behind Consolidated.

"What kind of things?"

"I'm through talking. Figure it out for yourself. And if you do . . . watch your back, Pretty Boy. My guess is there are people higher than Creighton that would like it all to stay hidden."

"One more thing," Lauren said, coming around him and standing for a moment under his arrogant sneer. Then she reached up with her good arm and slapped his injured face so hard it sent him stumbling. When he regained his footing and looked up with fire in his eyes, his cheek was bleeding again where she had stabbed it.

"I'll see you rot in prison, Murdoch," she bit out. "And I'll make certain Creighton Ledbetter knows that it was you who gave him up."

Murdoch was dragged away cursing and calling her the foulest names imaginable — not one of which caused her to blink. She had a look on her face that would have chilled a pack of ravening wolves.

Barclay hooted a laugh and turned to Rafe. "That is one woman not to be trifled with. Are you sure you're up to marrying her?"

There was a twitch of a smile at the corner of Rafe's mouth. "It does bear thinking about."

Lauren heard them and decided to show them how Alcott women got things done.

"There is one more thing we should get straight. Now seems as good a time as any," she said, swaying to Rafe with a wicked gleam in her eye.

Barclay's grin disappeared and he took a step back, abandoning Rafe to his fate.

Lauren lifted her chin and met his gaze.

"There's been a lot of loose talk about

marriage of late. We've had contracts negotiated and announcements made and expectations raised, but as yet no one has proposed to anyone. I think you should know . . . there will be no marriage without a proposal that is duly witnessed and freely given. With all the standard verbiage and customary promises." She broadened her stance and tucked her good arm across the injured one in her sling.

"So you think I should propose," he said, looking a bit blindsided by her demand.

"One of us should," she said emphatically.

"You are determined, I see. Perhaps you should show me how it's done." He folded his arms and broadened his stance to mirror hers with a look of amusement.

"A lesson in proposing?" She looked skyward, knowing he was calling her bluff, but enjoying the surprise on his face. "Very well. It should go something like this:

"You kneel."

She knelt.

"You take my hand."

She untucked his hand and held it gently.

"Then you tell me what's in your heart."

She watched the change come over his countenance and knew this was the time to reveal: "I am mad about you, Rafe Townsend. You amaze me and perplex me, thrill me when we're together and make me yearn for you when we're apart. I respect you and am proud of the man you are. You are my *hero*. I want to spend my life with you, have my babies with you, do great and noble things with you, and do little, tender things with you that only we will ever see."

This was no longer a tease or a contest of pride. This was about hearts and minds and the future they could make together.

"I love you with all my heart, my soul, and my body. I want you to know that I will gladly, happily, eagerly marry you. And I'm asking you to marry me the same way. If you can."

There wasn't a breath taken or let out as half the ship watched her propose to him. The silence afterward seemed interminable. But she gazed into his beautiful eyes and handsome face, knowing the goodness in his heart and how much he was willing to dare for her. She trusted him to do the right thing.

And he did.

He reached down and lifted her to her feet.

"Let me know if I leave anything out," he said softly.

He knelt.

He untucked her hand and took it between

his big, warm ones.

And he spoke.

"I love you, Lauren Alcott. You astound me and confound me, you excite me when you're near and leave me aching for you when you're far away. I've never met a woman like you — a woman I could respect and enjoy and desire all the way to my bones. You match me thought for thought, kiss for kiss. I had no idea that a marriage could be more than just a contract and a duty until I met you. You've shown me things, made me feel things I never thought possible. I want you to be my partner, my lover, my confidante. I want to have children with you and grandchildren. I want to help fulfill your dreams . . . because . . . you've fulfilled mine.

"You want me to marry you joyfully, eagerly. Sweetheart, I will. Anytime and anyplace you say." He took her face between his hands. "I adore your courage and your faith in me. I pray I am worthy of both."

She sank to her knees before him and kissed him tenderly.

"Are your conditions met?" he whispered.

"More than met," she whispered back. "I think we just proposed to each other. Which, I have on good authority, is the best way to start a marriage."

There was a gruff rumble that resembled clearing a throat.

When they looked up Stringer was looking down at them with tears in his eyes. Fighting tears was contorting Barclay's face such that he looked like a happy gargoyle. Beside him, Fosse, Gus, Little Rob, and Jims were all dabbing their eyes. And there was another fellow — small, pug nose, large ears — sniffing and wiping his nose on his sleeve.

"Ye know," Stringer said, wiping his cheeks, "out here on open sea . . . bein' a retired capt'n an' all . . . I got marryin' rights." The offer seemed tentative, as if it might be improper or they might turn him down.

"Really?" Lauren looked at Rafe, who shrugged and nodded, and she turned to Captain Stringer with happy tears streaming.

"Yes, Captain, if you please. Marry us. Here and now."

"Well, now," he puffed out his chest, brushed his sleeves, and donned his tri-cornered hat. "Considerin' yer already on yer knees . . . this is as good a time as any. Join yer hands, you two." He looked around, and when they indicated they were ready intoned solemnly, "Dear belovers . . . we be

414

here on this sad excuse for a deck to join this brave feller and his sweet lady in th' holdin' state o' matri-money . . ."

Lauren grinned and Rafe chuckled as they looked at each other and listened to the words that would bind them together just as they had just been bound together in spirit by their own words. It was lovely and funny and perhaps not entirely legal. But from that day on, it would indeed be their true wedding.

She even managed to slip a last-minute bit of negotiation into the ceremony. She wanted to call the new company being formed Alcott-Townsend Shipping instead of Townsend-Alcott Imports. Her second point was that a trust be set up for each of their children on their christening day.

Rafe threw back his head and laughed, affirming her wishes. Stringer paused, seeming confused, and asked, "She always like this?"

Rafe responded, "Yes. And I wouldn't have her any other way."

Afterward Stringer had them break out extra rations of grog for the whole crew and one of the seamen brought out a concertina and played some lively tunes that set their toes tapping. With another round of grog they were soon dancing up and down the deck and asking permission to take the bride for a whirl. Lauren graciously agreed and managed to dance with at least half the crew before the sun started down.

"Well, Mrs. Townsend," Rafe said as he held her in his arms to watch the sun set, "how does it feel to be a married woman?"

"Splendid," she answered. "I'm the luckiest girl in England . . . married to the handsomest, bravest, richest man I know."

He lowered his lips to her ear. "You'll feel even luckier if you don't mind sleeping in a room that smells like somebody smoked a pig in it."

"As romantic as that sounds," she answered, "I think I'd rather wait until we have a mattress and some clean sheets. And just possibly a marriage license and an entry in a ledger."

"We do have a license, sweetheart." He kissed her temple. "Our fathers got the bishop to issue one the day they signed the merger contracts. All we need to do is sign the papers and have it recorded."

TWENTY-FIVE

It wasn't until they docked that she realized who the little fellow with the pug nose and big ears was. She saw him writing on a pad as the ship was made fast and customs officials arrived. Then he put on his bowler hat and she recognized him as the reporter who'd written those awful stories about her. She hurried to Rafe, who welcomed her into his arms and listened to her outrage at the fact that the little blighter had sneaked aboard and been on the *Clarion* the whole time.

"I knew he was there," Rafe said, bracing for her reaction.

"And you didn't tell me?" She was shocked he could be so calm about being followed and scrutinized.

"When I saw him he was puking his guts out over the rail. Turns out he's not much of a sailor. It was throw him over the side or let him come along as we rescued you. He

417

was at our wedding, too, you know."

"Oh, dear." She looked stricken.

"I insisted on reading his version of things, and I have to say he did a smashing job of it. Made it sound exciting and heroic and romantic." He pulled her into his arms. "We'll be the envy of intendeds everywhere." A wicked little smile curled his lips. "And if he writes about us or the Angel ever again, I'll break both his legs."

"Oh. Well. In that case . . ." She nestled against him. "I suppose we can weather one last blast of fame." His nearness was causing her knees to go weak. "I just wanted to ask . . . where are we going to sleep tonight? Our wedding night was spent on that 'poor excuse for a deck' with twenty tipsy sailors. I'm not complaining, but I'd really like to have some time alone with you."

"Would you really?" He laughed. "You brazen woman, you. How about Claridge's?"

"Oooh, that sound's lovely. Champagne and flowers and breakfast in bed. And I want a bath with bubbles . . . you could join me . . ." Her tongue started tracing the edge of her teeth as her mind tried to ward off more enticing images.

He laughed and hugged her tightly. "Anything you say. Just put away that delicious little tongue or I won't be held responsible."

In a romantic fog they crossed the gangway and ran into three semi-irate parents and one anxious aunt.

"Where in blazes have you been?" Lawrence demanded.

"You might have told me you were charging off to rescue your bride," Horace declared irritably.

"This is going to be a horrendous scandal." Caroline looked as if she hadn't slept in days.

"Never mind that," Auntie A said, opening her arms to Lauren, who gladly filled them. "How are you, dear? We've been worried sick."

She hugged her father next, then Caroline, and last of all Horace.

She was beaming and Rafe looked ready to burst his shirt buttons.

"What's happened to you?" Lawrence held her out at arm's length, looking her over. "You both look like you're . . . you're . . ."

"Happy?" Lauren supplied. "We are. We are also newlyweds."

"You're married?" Caroline said, torn between shock and delight.

"I was kidnapped, I nearly drowned, Rafe rescued me, we captured a wicked gang of smugglers and thieves, and the captain — who is a friend of Rafe's — agreed to marry us yesterday. Ask Barclay Howard if you don't believe us. He was there." She looked around at the drooping mouths and smiled. "So . . . there won't be any scandal and I'm reliably informed that after our marriage is announced in the papers, there will be no further Angel articles."

She looked up at Rafe. "Have I left anything out?"

"A few things. We can tell them later about Ledbetter owning Consolidated and the tons of incriminating evidence we discovered."

"What?" Horace practically yelped. "Details, boy, details! The magistrate dismissed the charges against us, but it turns out Ledbetter's friends in high places got him out of jail. He's crowing now about how he's in line for the secretary's post and claiming I've bribed the magistrate and other such nonsense."

Rafe sighed and looked at Lauren, who shared his sense of "if only."

"This is all very interesting," he said. "But see that gentleman over there?" He pointed to a balding, older fellow who was squinting at them. "His name is Merrell Hampstead and he's got a ton of luggage and boxes. He needs a place to stay and work. It's important work. Who wants him?"

Aunt Amanda gave him a looking over and nodded firmly. "We'll take him. But he'd better not be a spitter. I can't abide a man who spits."

Lauren smiled and gave her aunt another hug. "He's yours. He needs new spectacles right away and he's very fond of plum pudding. As Rafe said, he's doing vital work, so treat him well."

"Right now," Rafe declared, "we intend to start on our honeymoon and we've hardly slept a wink in two days. We're headed for Claridge's and don't want to be disturbed for at least a week. Just send us some clothes and wish us well. We'll take care of the rest."

He waved over the cab that had just returned from taking Jims home and helped Lauren in. Once settled, he stretched out an arm, inviting her to snuggle against him. She quickly accepted.

"That went better than I expected," he said.

"It's always best to give parents just a little information at a time," she said, lifting her mouth for a kiss. "Don't want to overwhelm the poor dears." One good kiss deserved another. "Imagine the fuss they'd make if they learned I'd been shot."

■ ■ ■

Claridge's was regal and comfortable and probably more expensive than they wanted to know. But it was the best place to be paradoxically both pampered and ignored. There were flowers and champagne in the sitting room and fluffy French linens and perfumed soaps in the attached bathing room. A maid came to draw them a bath in a huge tub. Lauren went first, eagerly shedding her clothes and sliding past rafts of bubbles into the warm, scented water. She couldn't dip her injured shoulder into the water, but otherwise it was heavenly.

Rafe peeked in and saw her luxuriating in a grand tub that practically shouted it was meant for two. He removed his shirt, trousers, and smalls and climbed in beside her. He didn't miss the eager way her eyes roamed him and chuckled privately.

"You are one tasty little morsel," he said, giving his hands free rein and surprised to feel her exploring him as well.

"I'm not a morsel. I'm a woman. And a wife. I don't think I've ever been happier." He kissed the tip of her nose and the curve of her neck, then braved the bubbles to kiss the tips of her breasts. "You know what I want?" she said with a doelike sweetness in her eyes.

"Name it. It's yours," he murmured against her ear.

"Kiss me. And don't stop until I ask you to."

The rumble deep in his throat was agreement.

He obliged until they were forced to move to the bed to continue their wedding night festivities. They explored and laughed and played and cuddled. By morning it was time for more baths, these taken separately.

When Lauren exited the bathing room wrapped in one towel and drying her hair with another she caught sight of him, naked against the sheets. He was not just handsome, he was splendid in every respect. Someday she would have to allay Aunt Amanda's fears about his performance as a lover. But not today. He was everything she could have hoped for . . . and so much more.

As she swayed toward him, he glanced up only briefly before returning to his book. She was surprised and dipped her head to look at the title on the spine.

"You're finally reading it?" She wagged her head in disbelief.

"I thought I'd better bone up on this 'hero' business. Besides, Barclay read it and said it was wonderful."

"You don't need this," she said, her voice husky. She tried to tug the book from his hands. He didn't let it go, but his attention did shift to the way the towel drooped, baring a good bit of skin.

"But I thought you wanted a hero," he said, finally letting the book slide from his fingers.

"I have a hero." She tossed the book aside. "A strong, brave, thoughtful, insightful, brilliant . . . *passionate* . . . hero."

She was crawling up the bed toward him, leaving no doubt of what she intended.

"But you said you wanted an Ivanhoe," he said, watching her make her way up his legs as her gaze locked with his.

She gave a throaty laugh.

"Why would I want an Ivanhoe when I have you?"

EPILOGUE

Eighteen months later

It was a wonderful late March day. Daffodils were blooming all over London and people were out on the streets everywhere, enjoying the uncharacteristically fine weather. Florist shops and stalls were doing a fine pre-Easter business, and new shoes and bonnets were in high demand. So, when Rafe came home from his office, midday, and insisted Lauren get her hat and gloves and come with him, she naturally assumed it would be one of those pick-out-a-new-hat sorts of outings. He was so good about remembering holidays and treating her to small gifts and little little treasures.

He had their driver put the top down on the Alcott carriage and they enjoyed the ride through Kensington and into the City. The City was hardly a place for shopping, she thought, but she was even more surprised to find them driving out of the City and

425

into a much less prosperous neighborhood.

Traffic was a snarl on the narrow streets, but they finally reached their destination . . . a large building with several recently installed windows. A painting crew was busy finishing the front of the place, as evidenced by the canvas draped over the main doors and spread on the pavement in front of the building. He led her inside what looked like a new entrance, and it was clear the interior was freshly painted as well.

"What is this place?" she asked, pausing in the center hallway. There were gaslights and new tile on the floors. Several doors led off the main hallway, but they were closed. If this was a new store, it was the strangest one she had ever seen. At the far end of the hallway they stopped just outside two large double doors, where he took her hand and looked into her eyes.

"This is your birthday present, sweetheart. I hope you like it."

She frowned, totally confused, as he opened the doors to a huge, high-ceilinged room with a crowd of people inside. There were tables and chairs and a huge banner stretched across the room above a table containing a stepped layer cake with two serving ladies standing by to cut it. Jims Gardiner came running, grinning, and threw his arms around her.

"Ain't it grand, miz? My ma is 'ere. Come meet 'er."

She did meet Mrs. Gardiner and greeted Jims's sisters, who were dressed in their Sunday best. There were a lot of children present and parents — mostly mothers. Then she spotted her father near the cake table, chatting with Caroline and Horace Townsend. Not far away, her aunt and Merrell Hampstead were showing the children bins of balls and piles of new jump ropes.

That was when it hit her, and she turned to Rafe with rising hope.

"What is going on?"

"Did you read the sign, sweetheart?" He pointed to the banner, and the words brought tears to her eyes. It read: "Welcome to Alcott School."

"A school with my family's name on it?" she said, wondering how that could be.

"With your name on it. Lauren *Alcott* Townsend."

"But how . . . ?" She still wasn't seeing it. He smiled.

"I built you a school, sweetheart. For you and the children you worry about . . . who wouldn't otherwise learn to read."

Tears flooded her eyes, making it hard to see anything but his wonderful face. She was especially emotional recently, since she found she was expecting. For a moment she couldn't see, couldn't speak . . . could only hold on to his arm and let joy have its unpredictable way with her.

"You extraordinary man. What did I ever do to deserve someone as wonderful as you?" She reached up to stroke his cheek, and a couple of children chasing balls around the room bumped into them, jarring the tears loose. He handed her two handkerchiefs. He often carried extras just for her these days.

Her father whistled for attention and had everyone sing a happy birthday song to her as she sniffed and wiped tears.

The mothers present were beaming, some dabbing happy tears from their eyes, too. They came to her one or two at a time, sharing how they feared their children might never learn to read and cipher — might never have a chance for a better life. They thanked her and blessed her. Some even called her an angel for giving their children a chance to learn and grow and make the world a better place.

"But it's not me," she said, looking to Rafe. "You're the one who did this. You're the one who planned it and brought it to life."

"Oh, Angel, you don't understand. I did this for you because you are the light of my life. Because of you I see the world differently and I value different things . . . like reading and feeding children and giving them a chance to grow into capable young adults. It is your school. Yours and these children's." He leaned closer to whisper. "I love you, Lauren Alcott Townsend. Happy birthday."

She was suddenly so full of happiness that she wanted to hug everyone she saw. She very nearly did as she made her way around the room. Then she came to a man she thought looked familiar. When he turned, holding two young children's hands, she was struck speechless for a moment. When she recovered her voice she had only one word.

"Rector."

He gave her a wince of a smile. "Miss — Mrs. Townsend. It's plain vicar now. I'm at St Martha's, just a block over." He held up the little ones' hands. "These are some of my parishioners. Their mothers were working and couldn't come, so I said I would . . . um . . ."

"I'm glad you brought them. They're very welcome here."

A peaceful feeling settled inside her as she turned away and sought Rafe's company.

"Are you all right?" he asked. "Do you want to sit down for a few minutes?"

She was about to protest that she was fine when her mother-in-law arrived at her side and took her husband to task.

"You can't keep her standing like this in her condition. Goodness, Rafe, have a thought for her."

Lauren laughed and looked at Rafe as Caroline ushered her to a nearby chair and put a big piece of cake in her hands. She pulled over a chair beside Lauren's and leaned closer.

"I know you're mad about him, but sometimes men need to be reminded of the important things, you know?" Caroline said.

"Oh, I think he's rather good with the important things." She took a bite of cake and sighed as she spotted him smiling at her across her new school's gymnasium. "In fact, your son is my hero."

AFTERWORD

I hope you've enjoyed Rafe and Lauren's story. Rarely have I laughed this much when writing a book. I adore these characters and I so enjoyed bringing them together and helping them see the good in each other.

This story started with an incident based on real life. My beloved niece literally jumped out of a canoe and saved two women whose boat had overturned in a fast-moving stream . . . while her date sat in their canoe watching. I thought it was a fascinating story and might be a dynamite beginning for a book. Little did I know how hard I would have to work (after such a start) to get this pair together!

One thing that struck me while writing this book was how history repeats itself. The Panic of 1873, in the UK, was just such an occurrence. It has eerie parallels to our current situation, starting with fear, panic buying, runs on banks, and the imposition of tariffs that dominoed across Europe and resulted in high prices and a sluggish economy in many countries. Protectionism, it was called then. It's still called that today. And it's still creating almost as many problems as it solves.

The choice of trading companies as a focus for family businesses was a natural once I learned of the "panic." And I learned that ships did "stand off" in the harbor, sometimes for weeks, to protest tariffs. It seemed a great place to insert danger, heroic action, and a bit of fun . . . while Lauren and Rafe learn about each other and begin to fall in love.

As to the actual operation of the harbor and the historical Customs House (which is still there, by the way) . . . a lot of research went into the few details of docking fees, customs regulations, and the kinds of intrigue that some officials and shipping companies engaged in.

Another aspect of the story that followed historical accounts was Lauren's experience with a church-run school. At the time of this story, 1880, mandatory education was relatively new. Most primary schools had been begun and were maintained by churches. During this time church schools demanded strict codes of conduct, and teachers' activities were closely monitored. Yes, women teachers were fired for reading inappropriate materials (like novels!) or attending theaters or music halls. Teaching contracts from the period on both sides of the Atlantic were draconian by modern standards.

The details of commercial vessels of the period are a bewildering mix of technologies and designs. But most commercial vessels of that date had sails and depended primarily on wind power. The addition of paddle wheels was necessary because of the failure of wind power in specific locations, like the Suez Canal. The fathers in the book bemoaned the fact that sailing ships could not "sail" it and had to be towed through the canal at a prohibitive cost.

Another historical tidbit I used in the story was the use of hatpins as weapons. There was a period in Victorian London (later in the United States) when women were accosted on the street by "mashers" who "flirted" too vigorously. Not only were there catcalls, there were bustle gropes and other touches that made women afraid to walk in some areas. Enterprising ladies took to carrying their longer hatpins for self-protection. Men actually complained in some newspapers that women would stab them if they got too fresh!

One last thing: The penny papers were as addicting to Victorians as Facebook, Twitter, and YouTube are to people today. And yes, there was only advertising on the front page, where advertisers could get their money's worth. Reporting was often full of half-truths. Once again history repeats itself.

I hope you've enjoyed Rafe and Lauren's story and you'll join me for another Hero adventure starring Barclay Howard, whose tough appearance and wolfish grin terrify proper Victorian ladies.

I would love to have you visit me at BetinaKrahn.com and leave a comment or a photo of you reading . . .

ABOUT THE AUTHOR

Betina Krahn is a *New York Times* bestselling author of more than 30 historical and contemporary romances. Her works have won numerous industry awards, including the Romantic Times Lifetime Achievement Award for Love and Laughter. Visit her on the web at BetinaKrahn.com.